ATTENTION READER

This is not a finished book.

This galley proof has not been corrected by the author, publisher, or printer.

The design, artwork, page length, and format are subject to change, and typographical errors will be corrected during the course of production.

If you quote from this galley, please refer to the final printed book.

Thank you.

The Extraordinary Secrets of April, May & June

Robin Benway

Publication date: August 2010

U.S. $16.99 (Canada $21.99)

Ages 12 and up * Grades 7 and up

288 pages

ISBN 978-1-59514-286-3

Razorbill

An Imprint of Penguin Group (USA) Inc.

345 Hudson Street

New York, NY 10014

www.razorbillbooks.com

www.penguin.com/teens

the extraordinary secrets of april, may & june

robin benway

An Imprint of Penguin Group (USA) Inc.

The Extraordinary Secrets of April, May & June

RAZORBILL

Published by the Penguin Group
Penguin Young Readers Group
345 Hudson Street, New York, New York 10014, U.S.A.
Penguin Group (USA) Inc., 375 Hudson Street, New York, New York 10014, U.S.A.
Penguin Group (Canada), 90 Eglinton Avenue East, Suite 700, Toronto, Ontario,
Canada M4P 2Y3 (a division of Pearson Penguin Canada Inc.)
Penguin Books Ltd, 80 Strand, London WC2R 0RL, England
Penguin Ireland, 25 St Stephen's Green, Dublin 2, Ireland (a division of Penguin Books Ltd)
Penguin Group (Australia), 250 Camberwell Road, Camberwell, Victoria 3124, Australia
(a division of Pearson Australia Group Pty Ltd)
Penguin Books India Pvt Ltd, 11 Community Centre, Panchsheel Park,
New Delhi – 110 017, India
Penguin Group (NZ), 67 Apollo Drive, Mairangi Bay, Auckland 1311, New Zealand
(a division of Pearson New Zealand Ltd)
Penguin Books (South Africa) (Pty) Ltd, 24 Sturdee Avenue, Rosebank, Johannesburg 2196,
South Africa

Penguin Books Ltd, Registered Offices: 80 Strand, London WC2R 0RL, England

10 9 8 7 6 5 4 3 2 1

Library of Congress Cataloging-in-Publication Data is available

Printed in the United States of America

"We are an impossibility in an impossible universe."

—RAY BRADBURY

"There is a crack in everything / That's how the light gets in . . ."

—LEONARD COHEN, *"Anthem"*

chapter 1

"I know too much already."

I hate being the oldest.

I hate it because I'm the one who has to experience everything first. And even if I haven't, my sisters still think I know everything. Which I sort of do, but that's not the point. At least, not right now.

It's just like when my youngest sister June, on the night before the first day at our new school, sat me down on the edge of my bed (which made me wrinkle the comforter) and quizzed me about high school like it was a category on *Jeopardy!*

"Where do the cool kids eat?" she asked me, blowing her bangs out of her eyes so that they just resettled messily across her forehead. "Is it okay if I can't drive yet? Are they going to haze me just because I'm a freshman?"

"June," I had to tell her. "I don't know, I don't know, and I don't know. I've never been to this school either, remember?"

"But what if I'm wearing the wrong outfit? Or it's foggy and my hair frizzes? Do you think they'll be all judge-y?"

Our middle sister, May, stuck her head into my room from the hallway. Her hair was piled up on top of her head in what June would call "a complete mess." I didn't blame May, though. It was too hot outside to worry about things like hair. "Yes," she said to June. "Forget ever having a date for the next four years. We'll call you Loser for short."

"Just because *you've* never had a date," June glared at her. "Loser squared."

May rolled her eyes and waved her black iPod at me. "I need my headphones back so I can drown out the whining."

"On my desk," I told her. "And June, seriously? Unless a pack of wild dogs are released into the halls tomorrow—"

"We hope, we pray," May muttered as she dug around on my desk, searching for her headphones and knocking over a pile of hardcover books in the process.

"—then you'll be fine. And do you *mind*, May?" I restraightened my books and glared at her. "A little respect for the written word, please."

"Only you," May said with a sigh, "would actually read the books on the summer reading list."

"Are there wild dogs out here?" June asked. "I know there're coyotes."

"There might be a spider," I told her.

"Or seven," May added.

I sighed. "Can you both get out of my room so I can pretend I'm an only child?"

I missed them after they left, though. It was weird the way I wanted them there, and when they were there, I wanted them to leave. We had only moved into our new house two weeks earlier, coming from Orange County out to the Valley because our parents divorced and our mom got a job here and because our dad took a new job in Houston and was moving there in a few weeks. At least, that's why my mom said we were moving. I, on the other hand, was pretty sure that it had something to do with the fact that May got trashed the night our parents announced they were splitting up. No one's really talking about it, least of all May, and even if we *did* talk about it, I'm not sure what I would say. "Way to be a cliché?" "So what's it like starring in your own afterschool special?" June, being the youngest at fourteen, didn't have a clue about May's night of debauchery. All she knew was that a lot of Disney Channel stars lived in the Valley, so she was excited about the move. All *I* knew was that no one asked me or my sisters what we wanted, so we went along with it. I'll tell you this, though. If I had known we were going to end up here, I would've spoken up a long time ago. The Valley at the beginning of September is ridiculously hot.

So we had this new home now, with this jacaranda tree, whose purple flowers permanently stained the sidewalk outside, and eucalyptus trees in the backyard. It was pretty, but it didn't feel like home. It was just a house that we were living in, and if I listened really hard at night, I could hear traffic on Ventura Boulevard. "It'll be like an adventure," my mom had said when we moved in, and she had smiled so hard that my sisters and I just smiled back, like we hadn't already spent the past three months on an adventure, watching our family reshape itself. I might have been the only one who was shaking on the inside; I don't know. I don't even want to know. I know too much already.

But things calmed down, and it was okay as it would ever be. We started school, and on the first day, I got lost four times because the campus was way bigger than our old school, with giant cement poles every ten feet or so and winding paths that made me trip twice. I knew that pretty soon, life would be normal and I would forget what it used to be like, but that didn't make me feel any better when I wound up in the freshman-year geography class instead of junior-year anatomy by accident.

I tell myself that a lot now. *You'll forget what it used to be like.*

June, like 99.9 percent of the freshman class, made absolutely no impression on anyone. May kept to her normal sophomore routine of shuffling around in her black Converse and ignoring people, while I just kept going along with the junior crowd. After all, why swim upstream? All that happens is that you get tired and die faster. Go with the flow, I say.

Or I *used* to say.

That was before I woke up seeing red.

* * *

It happened on the second Monday of the school year. I wish I could say that's all I remember, but I remember everything about that day. It was the day our dad was officially moving to Houston—he had already sort of moved there, but he was coming over after school to officially say goodbye. He had shown us pictures of his new condo—it looked like every other condo in America—and May, June, and I had just looked at the pictures and said, "Cool," because really, what could we say?

I remember that it was foggy that Monday morning and that it smelled like mint tea downstairs. I can even tell you that I was wearing a pair of May's socks because all of mine were in the wash, but that's not really a useful detail. And please don't tell May. She has this thing about sharing socks. I don't know—she's weird like that.

I woke up early, even before June's alarm went off in the room next to mine. At first I thought I was still dreaming because all I saw was bright red swimming past my eyes. And then I thought that it was just the sun behind my eyelids, reminding me to wake up.

You know, as if I could have somehow forgotten to do that.

But when I finally opened my eyes, the room was still dark. There was no sunlight anywhere, just the quiet pink sky and gray fog coasting past my bedroom window, and I felt this weird surge of fear and adrenaline, like when you're going up the rollercoaster and suddenly realize that it was very bad judgment to strap yourself into a rickety car and plummet down a track without asking about safety inspection records or at least wearing a helmet.

I thought it was nothing at the time, though. "You're just nervous," I said out loud to myself, watching the fog start to burn off. "That's all. You're just nervous." I said it until I believed it, even though there was nothing to be nervous about, and then June's alarm rang. I heard May sleepily yell at her to turn it off, and the day began, like nothing and everything had already happened.

* * *

"I'm going to be popular," June announced on the way to school that morning. She was in the backseat of our mom's old minivan, also known as my new car. June refused to ride in the front seat of the "mom-mobile" whenever we went to school, and May said she didn't care where she sat because we were going to school, so it's not like anything was going to make that better. (She's not an optimist, my sister May.)

May and I didn't even turn around at June's announcement. "How wonderful," I said, watching in my rearview for cops. I am very proud of my no-ticket record, and I didn't want it ruined.

"April, it's the pedal on the right," May grumbled from the passenger seat. She was slumped down with her black hoodie pulled over her dirty blonde hair. "Maybe you could press that pedal and we could go faster."

"Excuse me, but I have a no-ticket reco—"

"I *said*," June interrupted from the backseat, "that I'm going to be popular. That's my goal for this year. New school year, new school life."

"You're, like, the freshman girl cliché crossed with Oprah," May sneered, and I didn't have to see her face to know that she was wrinkling her nose. It's so annoying when she does that. "Why don't you try being unique for a change?"

"Oh, yeah," June said, "because being unique has worked *so* well for you. And what's wrong with being popular? Gandhi was popular."

"Gandhi starved himself for world peace and was eventually assassinated by his archrival," I informed her. "Is that who you want to emulate?" I watched the traffic go past the mini-mall as we sat at the red light, watched as people lined up at the Starbucks across the street. If I went a block in any direction, the view would still be the same. May calls our new neighborhood "the land that diversity forgot."

"Do you even know who Gandhi *was*?" May asked June now, finally turning around to look at her as the light turned green. I could see June in the rearview mirror, looking frustrated as she smoothed her hands over her dark hair, trying to keep the frizz at bay. She has this long brown hair and a perfect fringe of bangs across her forehead that she spends forever straightening. She also has big brown eyes, but please don't tell her that because then she'll go all doe-eyed and start batting her eyelashes and it's just embarrassing to witness. But yeah, my youngest sister's really cute.

It sucks.

"Yep, that's what I thought," May said, turning back around. "April, I swear to God, you're going so slow that I think we're going *backwards*."

May, on the other hand, isn't what I would call cute. Woodland animals are cute. June is cute. May is something else entirely. She's so thin that everything is exaggerated on her. Even her elbows look like they're about to tear through the thin skin on her arms. When she's not glowering at you, you can tell that she's actually pretty. She might even be beautiful, if her cheekbones didn't look like they were made of knifeblades.

Overall, May has that sort of appearance that says, "Don't make me have to cut a bitch." That might explain why her friend count is up to zero.

"You think you could do a better job driving?" I said to her, turning my signal on even though we were still a block and a half away from the next intersection.

"Look," June finally huffed, not paying any attention to my and May's conversation. "I know *this*. In the animal kingdom, if you don't adapt, you *die*. It's called Darwinism, look it up."

May just snorted. "This science lesson has been brought to you by the phrase 'no shit.' "

I slowed down a little as we approached the intersection, even though the light was green. "What are you doing?" May screeched. "The light is green! How is that confusing to you?"

"There's this girl in my English class," June continued. When she has a thought, nothing stops her from talking. If she had been onboard the *Titanic*, she would have babbled about how the orange lifevest was not really flattering to her skin tone while everyone else clung to icebergs.

"I'm slowing down because it is the *safe* thing to do when approaching an intersection," I snapped at May. "And what do you know? You have a learner's permit, not a license."

May slowly banged her head against the headrest.

June didn't even take a breath. "Anyway, she's in my English class? And her name is Mariah? She's a sophomore so she's in your grade, May? And she's really cool and—?"

"And why?" May interrupted her. "Does everything? Sound like a question? When you're talking?"

"*Anyway*," June ignored her, but I could see her getting flushed in the backseat. "Her name's Mariah and—"

"Mariah," May said, "is just one letter away from 'pariah.' Think about it."

"Well, you would know about pari—!" June started to yell, but as we went through the intersection, her face suddenly scrunched up like she had tasted something bad. I saw her glance out the window at the homeless guy on the corner and shudder.

"That is *so* not cool, June," I told her. "Just because he's homeless doesn't mean he's not a human being."

"Aaaaaand here comes the soapbox," May muttered.

"I didn't *say* anything," June mumbled, but her voice was quieter and she didn't mention Mariah anymore.

"Well, you didn't have to," I said. "I saw it on your face and really, I think—hey, wait a minute. Are you seriously not wearing your seatbelt?"

"Oops." June tugged the belt around her. "My bad."

"More like my *dead*," I said to her. "Don't you know that accidents happen closest to home? That we could—"

And suddenly I knew I had to change lanes. There was an image of brake lights just behind my eyes, like a memory of something that hadn't happened yet, and I clutched the wheel and jerked the car over to the left lane, making my sisters scream and hang onto their (thankfully fastened) seatbelts. Two seconds later, the brake lights flashed, and we drove past the accident just as it happened, just like I had seen it.

June was the first to recover. "If I have to wear a neck brace, I'll kill you," she muttered from the backseat.

May was just staring at me with huge eyes. "What the hell was *that*?" she gasped.

"I—I don't know," I admitted. If I hadn't been gripping the wheel so tightly, my hands would have been shaking. "I just changed lanes. That's all."

"Well, whatever it was, I liked it," May grinned and settled back in her seat. "*Finally*. A little excitement around here."

chapter 2

"I've spent my whole life getting ready for this."

may

April always makes the whole thing sound so *dramatic* in the beginning. "Oooh, I saw red and I knew it was a *sign,* and the heavens opened up and the fog rolled in. . . ." Etc., etc.

The day wasn't that dramatic.

Not until I got involved, at least.

As soon as my sisters and I got through the front door of the school, we went into our weekday routine, which basically meant that we refused to acknowledge each other's existence for the next six hours and thirty-seven minutes. Maybe, like if it's someone's birthday or something, we'll raise an eyebrow in recognition, but otherwise, I don't know them and they don't know me.

Not that they know me *after* school, either.

I guess that's the thing about being in the middle. When we were younger, my mom used to use the old sandwich metaphor to explain why being a middle child was so important. "You're the bologna in the sandwich!" she would say, and I would have to remind her that no, June was the one that liked bologna, not me, which sort of blew her metaphor out of the water.

I'm not trying to be all "Marsha, Marsha, Marsha!" about it. I mean, I love my sisters, I guess. I think I'm biologically obligated to love them. I just wish they weren't so . . . *them*. Especially at school, with June having her social-butterfly metamorphosis and April gearing up for a life of book collecting and brilliance and Ph.Ds, it's pretty easy to just slip through the cracks.

And now that my parents are divorced, I feel like I'm more mediocre than ever. Not that my self-esteem is all affected, but before, it was like the one thing different about me was that my parents were still married. But now? We're just like everyone else. Nothing to see here.

I guess in a way, I've spent my whole life getting ready for this.

It would almost be funny if it hadn't actually happened.

That Monday morning, when it all started, April drove us to school in the Lame-Mobile. I used my compass in first-period geometry to make a snowman family. Second period was P.E., and I immediately busted out the cramps excuse, wincing every minute or so while everyone else ran laps and got all sweaty and gross. I honestly feel that having to wear gym shorts should be considered a crime against humanity. (I told that to April once, and all she did was roll her eyes and say, "There are people who have actually suffered crimes against humanity, May. It's not a joke." She has the sense of humor of a flea. An unfunny flea.)

Third period was European history. I hate history. I know that old quote about how those who fail to learn history are doomed to repeat it, but really? People have been studying history for hundreds of years now, and there're still wars and famines and dictators and diseases. History's gonna repeat itself whether or not I have to spend fifty-six minutes a day learning about it.

And I especially hate European history. I like Europe just fine, and one day I'm going to live in Paris and have a view of the Eiffel

Tower and live with an artist. So I'm down with the Europeans. But their history is ridiculous. Would it have killed them to name a king something other than James, Edward, or George? What about Hector? Or Archibald? Once you're on James the Fifth or whatever, it's time to exercise some other options.

And don't even get me started on Prussia.

But the thing I hate most about European history is that they're making me get a tutor. Apparently when you fail the first two quizzes of the school year, it does not reflect well on your school record. I tried to point out that the lack of creative royal names wasn't helping, but instead of agreeing, I got an appointment with the assistant principal to discuss student tutoring options. I'm assuming, though, that it won't be much of a discussion.

So now I have to keep this on the down low from my dad. I'm sure April told you (because, you know, she's told everyone) that our dad's in Houston now. And not that my dad really cares about my European history grade, but he's promised that I can fly out and he'll take me to Austin. He promised special trips to me and my sisters, just one-on-one time with him, but all I want to do is see Austin. I mean, their city motto is "Keep Austin Weird," and I'm pretty weird. So I feel like this town and I are gonna be BFFFs. (I'm pretty sure you know what that extra F stands for, too.)

And yeah, I guess it'll be cool to see my dad. I spend a lot of time trying not to think about him. I spend a lot of time trying not to think about a lot of things.

The rest of that day continued its usual pattern of suckage. Lunch was always a low point in the day, especially since I didn't know anyone and I didn't like sitting by myself. I knew that April was probably in the school library, learning about the mating habits of larvae or something equally useless, and June was always somewhere else.

Not that I ever looked for them, though.

I spent lunch like I did every other day, ghosting through the halls and trying to look like I was going somewhere. I tried to tell myself that no one would ever even notice me, but sometimes that just makes me feel worse. I don't know. Like I said, I'm weird.

After the final bell, I trudged out into the blindingly sunny parking lot, where April was leaning against the car, jingling the keys in her hand, her normally flushed cheeks looking paler than normal. Even her blonde hair, which was already pretty light, looked a few shades lighter. "Whoa," I said. "You look like you're gonna hurl."

"Here," she said, handing me the keys. "You can drive home."

I just looked at her. "Why?"

"Just 'cause."

"I'll ask again: Why?"

"I just don't feel like driving. I . . . I have a headache."

"You look like you're gonna hurl," I said again, taking the keys as I spoke. "Please don't toss your cookies on me, okay?"

June came walking up to us before April could respond. "Yo," she said. "Let's go home."

"Now, now," I said, "is that an appropriate attitude for Little Miss Popular?"

She just looked at me. "You're driving?"

I shook the keys in her face.

"Great," she muttered, climbing into the backseat. "Well, at least I'll be young and beautiful when I die."

After we all got into the car, April checked her seatbelt three times.

"Oh, thanks for the vote of confidence, April," I muttered, but I noticed that even June was doing the same thing. "Wow, thanks, family."

"Just go slow," April replied. She kept running her hand through her hair like she was looking for something hidden there. "And don't crash into anyone or anything."

The first five minutes were fine, mostly because we were in a residential area. "You know, if you think about it," June said after a brief and blissful silence, "this is actually the most dangerous area for you, May. All the little kids and pets that could just run out into the street at any minute. . . ."

"June," I snapped. "Not helping."

"I'm just making a hypothesis," she grinned. "It's part of the scientific process, you know."

As soon as we got to the main intersection, I hit the gas pedal a bit harder, and April nearly fell out of her cardigan sweater. "May, I swear to God . . ." she muttered.

I just laughed. "Let me show you how it's done, Big Sister."

April suddenly tensed up and she said, "No, not her! Not her, no, May!"

"What are you—?" I started to say, but when I looked down, I couldn't see my hands on the steering wheel.

That was not cool.

It happened so fast that at first I thought I just blinked for too long or had, like, this mental blip or something. I started to feel lightheaded. "Whoa," I whispered before I could stop myself. And suddenly the car was swerving towards the curb, and April was screaming, "Not her! Not this girl!"

"Not *who*?" I screamed back, but just as I said that, I saw a girl on the corner with this crazy black hair, and April was acting like she couldn't even hear me.

April grabbed the wheel then, jerking the car back into the lane just as the girl gasped and froze on the sidewalk. June was screaming in the back, "I knew it! I knew it!" and I had no idea what the hell she was talking about, nor did I care. I barely even noted the fact that we'd come THIS close to ramming into some innocent bystander.

I was too busy trying to figure out where my hands had gone.

When I blinked again, my hands were back on the wheel, just like I had never let go. April was still clinging to the wheel, too, her eyes huge in her face.

"What the . . . ?" she whispered.

"What?" I said shakily.

"What?" she repeated. "Did you . . . did you just . . . ?"

"Did I what?"

June piped up from the backseat, her voice sort of shaky. "Um, guys?"

We ignored her like always.

"May," April whispered, "you were here and then you weren't."

"You guys?"

"Seriously, June, shut up for a minute," I said over my shoulder, but I could hear my own trembling voice. And it sounded sort of hollow, like it wasn't really there at all.

Like it was invisible.

"That's not possible," I said to April. "Look at me! I'm operating heavy machinery! I couldn't have just disappeared!"

"Oh, my God, you're *driving*!" April suddenly gasped. "Pull over, pull over! You can't drive right now!"

"I'm fine!" I yelled back at her. "And I can't just pull over; we're in the middle of the road!"

"You GUYS!" Now June was yelling along with us. "I think I—"

"June, SHUT UP!" we both shouted over our shoulders.

"Look, you're hallucinating or something," I said to April. "You're mentally exhausted, and you're hallucinating. You need more sleep. It's not healthy—"

"*You're* rambling," she interrupted me. "And you saw it, too. Your eyes are super-dilated right now."

There was a brief silence before June leaned over the front seats. "I think I know why—"

"Well, maybe you guys hallucinated together," I said. If ignoring June was an Olympic sport, I'd be Michael Phelps.

"We hallucinated *together*?" April scoffed. "Yeah, that sounds real logical."

"Oh, I'm sorry, what's more logical for you? The theory that I *disappeared*?" I was clutching the steering wheel so tightly that it looked like my knuckles would burst right through my hands. I pushed each finger against the wheel one at a time, counting them over and over in my head, getting to ten and going back to one.

"Would you pull over already?" April screeched. "You can't drive like this!"

"And yet I am!" I retorted.

"WOULD YOU GUYS JUST LISTEN TO ME FOR A MINUTE!" June has this way of yelling that makes you wish you were deaf.

"NO!" We both yelled back.

"FINE!" she yelled, then threw herself against the backseat and crossed her arms. "Be stupid, see if I care!"

Silence reigned for about fifteen seconds as I turned onto our street. Every single home looked like the one before it and the one after it. The first week we lived here, our mom had to open the garage to tell which one was ours. But I barely noticed the houses now. I was too busy making silent promises to talk to April anymore. *I swear, I'll never ditch school again*, I thought to myself. *I'll be nicer to my sisters. I'll stop hating European history and actually study. I'll even do volunteer work with cancer patients to make up for the one time I smoked that cigarette at—*

June's voice came loud and clear from the backseat. "You smoked?"

I almost drove right into the trash cans in front of our house, but managed to slow down and park before turning around to look at her. April was doing the same thing. "What?" she said to June. "What are you talking about?"

There is no way she could know that, I thought. *No. Possible. Way.*

June sat back in her seat. "Wanna make a bet?"

April covered her mouth with her hand. "Did you just read her . . . ?"

"Yep." Now June sounded smug. "*That's* what I've been trying to tell you. And don't worry, May," she added, "it's not like I'm gonna tell Mom about the cigarette. Yet."

"You better pray that my hands disappear again before I wrap them around your neck!" I cried, already starting to dive over the seat for her.

"Wait, wait, stop!" April yelled, pulling me back as June cowered in the backseat. "May, stop it! Mom and Dad, they're right there; they're gonna—"

We all froze just in time to see my parents come out the front door together. Dad was wearing his sunglasses and Mom still had her work clothes on. Both of their mouths were set in straight, thin lines. They were talking, discussing something that we couldn't hear. It didn't look good, but then again, for the past eighteen months, none of their conversations had looked good. I won't even tell you how they've sounded.

We sat there and watched them for almost a full minute. I couldn't tell if they were arguing or if—

"No, they're arguing," June said.

"Stop reading my mind," I said numbly just as April told her, "Stop reading their minds." I just sat in the front seat, my legs sticky against the leather upholstery. It hurt when I tried to unstick them, which was a strange relief. Pain was good. Pain meant I was still *there*.

"Hey, dolls!" my dad suddenly yelled from the porch, noticing us for the first time and stopping the discussion mid-sentence. "C'mon, come say goodbye to your old dad before he turns into a cowboy!"

I almost had to throw up when he said that. Just thinking about throwing up made my throat burn with tequila memories, which made me want to throw up all over again. "Weird," June said softly from the backseat, but I barely heard her. I just wondered about the next time I would see my dad, if it would be strange to have to fly on a plane whenever I wanted to see him. I wondered if he could even see me now, if I was crazy, if there was something so strange about me that even my body didn't want to stay around to say goodbye to my own father.

I set my face and waved at him. In the side mirror, I could see June's lip quivering a little before she bit it and blinked really fast. She does that normally when she's trying to look flirtatious, even though it just looks like she's got a misplaced contact lens, but I knew she wasn't trying to be cute now.

As soon as June's face smoothed out, I opened the car door and gingerly put my foot on the pavement. When I saw it hit the ground, I wasn't sure if I was relieved or not.

chapter 3

"I remembered. Oh boy, did I remember."

I KNEW IT—OH MY GOD I KNEW IT.

I knew it when we drove past the homeless guy that morning. April thought I was being all insensitive, but I'll tell you what was really happening.

When we passed him? I wasn't being mean.

I could read his mind.

HOW CRAZY IS THAT?

Well, it's not as crazy as his mind was, I'll tell you that.

April likes to tell the story like everything was one big amazing *surprise*, and May always says that it didn't get *exciting* until she got on the scene and risked all of our lives in the middle of afternoon traffic.

Whatever.

I've been telling my sisters for *years* about how it really started, but no one ever believed me. Everyone thought it was a cute story that I invented.

Not anymore. Now they were listening to me.

See, when you're the youngest, everything gets explained by the fact that you're the baby. Let's say you're afraid of spiders and maybe—JUST MAYBE—you once saw a black widow in the corner of your new bedroom and MAYBE you were already tired and maybe you cried JUST A LITTLE BIT and so your stupid sisters decide you're only afraid of spiders because you're the baby of the family.

Way to stereotype, I know.

But I also have a memory of playing outside with my sisters. I was four years old, May was five, and April was six. It was summertime, and my older sisters were being mean and not letting me play with them, so I cried *not* because I was the baby but because May had already pulled the heads off two of my Barbies, and also because I happen to be quite sensitive to rejection.

I heard April's voice so clearly. "What a baby."

"I'm not a baby!" I yelled.

"I didn't say you were!" she shouted back.

"Yes, you did; I *heard* you!"

"I didn't say *anything*!"

I took a breath, wiped my eyes, and used my ultimate no-fail weapon. "I'm telling Mom!"

And then May stepped in between us. Her hair was lighter back then—as blonde as April's—and I remember it looked almost transparent in the sunlight. "Hey," she said with a grin, "watch this."

April and I just looked at her. April frowned and said, "Where are you going?" just before May disappeared.

The leaves rustled over our heads as if May had risen right through them, and I saw my face in the reflection of the patio doors. I had totally stopped crying, that was for sure. Next to me, April looked the same.

When I finally blinked, May was back, looking proud of herself. "Awesome," she said. It was a word she had picked up from our neighbor who surfed three mornings a week up at the Wedge in Newport

Beach. "Awesome," she said again, like she had caught the biggest wave of the morning.

She's not playing fair. I wanna disappear, too.

"You can't disappear like May," I told April. "You *can't*." And then I turned back to May, who was my new favorite sister. "Again!" I demanded. "Do it again!"

"Don't!" April said quickly. "Mom's coming!"

"No, she's not!" May protested. "She's upstairs!"

"Do it *again*!" I cried. "Again!"

"Do what again?" my mom suddenly asked, opening the back door and gazing at us. "What are you girls doing out here?"

I clasped her hands in front of my sundress and looked up at my mom with glee. She was gonna be so excited to find this out, I just knew it!

"May *disappeareded*," I announced, then gave her my best smile. "Can I have a Popsicle?"

My mom still tells that story once in awhile, laughing sometimes when she gets to the end. "June has such an imagination," she always says. Like I made it up! Like it never happened at all! Even now, my sisters don't remember. They don't believe me. They think that just because I'm the baby, they don't have to listen to me. They think I don't remember things well enough.

But I remembered. Oh boy, did I remember.

They were the ones who forgot.

* * *

Ten years later on that Monday afternoon, we said goodbye to my dad and waved as his rental car drove towards the airport. After we reassured our mom that no, we weren't permanently damaged and no, I was just blinking because my eyes were dry from the Santa Ana winds, and yes, pizza was totally cool for dinner and yes, school was as fine/ridiculous/awesome as it always had been, my sisters and I booked it for our rooms. We went to April's, since she had the biggest one. (Can we talk about the unfairness factor of that? She has like, two pairs of jeans and three shirts. What does she need all that space for? Her books? C'mon.)

April shut the door, and the three of us stood there for almost thirty seconds of silence. Well, I mean it was silent for *them*. Meanwhile, my brain was being verbally assaulted by their thoughts, April's especially. She was taking very deep breaths, like she was hyperventilating, and I could hear her voice somewhere inside her head, a jumble of thoughts and words that I couldn't sort out. "April, slow your roll," I said. "You're making me all schizo."

That was a mistake.

April slowly turned to looked at me, her eyes starting to bug out of her head. "Can you seriously read my mind?" she whispered.

I put my hands on my hips and squared off with her. I have to admit, it was nice to be the one in the know for a change. "How many times do I have to tell you?" I glared, sounding just like our mom whenever we wouldn't put our socks in the dirty laundry. "We were *little*. I could hear your thoughts, remember? You saw what Mom was going to do before she even did it, May disappeared not once but *twice*, and I kept reading your mind and saying your thoughts out loud."

April opened her mouth, shut it, then opened it again. "I thought you were just being silly," she said. "I thought you were just doing that weird little sister thing."

"You still think that now? After this afternoon? You really want to tell me that you think I'm making it up?"

"Whoa, whoa, wait a minute," May said, waving her hands in front of her like she was trying to erase something. "April, you can see the future?"

"I—I guess so," she said. "But it just happened! I didn't do anything!"

May whirled to look at me. "And June, you're *seriously* a mind-reader? What number am I think—?"

"332,941." It was so clear that she might as well have said it out loud.

May looked at April. "She can read minds. You and I are totally screwed."

"I heard Avery's mind when you almost hit her today with the car!" I huffed. "Way to go, May, by the way. Thanks for almost killing us and a total stranger."

"What did she say?" April asked. She might as well have been wearing a tweed cap and carrying a magnifying glass, she looked so detective-y. "You could hear her?"

"Of course I could hear her!" I snapped. "May almost hit her with the car! Her name's Avery! And I don't know, she was just . . . she freaked out! She was thinking everything and nothing. She thought about her mom and some guy! What would you think if you thought you were going to die on the hood of a minivan?"

But April was too busy turning around and looking pissed at May. "And you *smoked*?" she demanded.

May just rubbed her forehead and sighed. "*Shiiiiiiit.*"

April put her hands on her hips. "Do you know the damage that *one cigarette* can do to your molecular structure? Do you?"

"April," May said. "In case you haven't noticed, my molecular structure is already a bit *damaged*. Let me refresh your memory. I disappeared in the middle of the *intersection*! While I was *driving*! I almost *hit* someone! Let's focus on the bigger picture here, like the fact that you can see the *future* and June—*June*!—can read our *minds*!"

"Hey!" I snapped. "At least I'm not Casper the Friendly Ghost and going all disappear-y while I'm driving a *car*! By the way, you totally freaked out the guy next to us! He thought he was having an acid flashback!"

"I would advise not reading my mind right now," May said through clenched teeth. "It may be emotionally damaging to you."

"All right, stop!" April suddenly shouted. "Stop! We don't have time to argue about . . . about whatever's happening right now. We have to . . . we have to do something."

May started to laugh. She was so upset that I couldn't even focus on a coherent thought in her mind. Great, now both of my sisters would have to be committed to insane asylums, and I'd be forced to roam the earth alone, isolated by the very thing that makes me special.

And then I wondered if they'd make a movie about my life. That would sort of be awesome, I had to admit.

Meanwhile, though, May was still losing it.

"Do *what*, April?" May gasped in between giggles. "What are we supposed to *do*? Start working on our costumes? Find a city that's actually named Gotham and move there? What exactly is your plan, Miss Fortune-Teller?"

April put her hands on her hips. "Oh, I'm sorry!" she sneered. "I must have misplaced my 'What to Do When You Get Crazy Superpowers' manual! Maybe it's under the 'How to Kill Your Sisters and Dispose of the Bodies' pamphlet! I'll go double-check."

"Oh, whatever, you're freaking out, too," I said as I flopped down on her bed. "And you can't kill us. I'd know your plan and be able to hide, and May could just disappear."

"God, June, how are you so *calm*?" April demanded. "You're, like, all Zen about this!"

"Hey," I shrugged, "maybe if someone had actually listened to me for the past ten years, this wouldn't be such a surprise."

I would tell you what May thought after I said that, but I'm not comfortable repeating those kinds of words.

"So let me get this straight," April said after a few seconds. "They're . . . they're back?"

I nodded.

April swallowed hard, gripped the back of my desk chair, and didn't say anything.

"You know," I finally said, shoving my bangs out of my face, "you'd think that one of us would have been able to *fly*."

chapter 4

"I heard the crack and saw the spark."

april

I woke up the next morning after not sleeping at all the night before. I kept having weird dreams, but then I would realize that they weren't dreams; they were snapshots of things that were going to happen, which was pretty much the scariest thing ever, aside from when May disappeared from behind the wheel of a moving car. (And by the way, she still has not apologized for that. Rude much? God.)

I didn't see anything that seemed too significant. I knew that our neighbor's cat was going to become a late-night coyote snack in two weeks, and that June would get all upset and want to give the cat a funeral, even though it wasn't hers. Just things like that, nothing terrible. At least, assuming you're not the cat.

But then I wondered if I should be scanning my brain for any catastrophic events that may be occurring. Was that my new responsibility? Did the fate of planet earth lie with me?

It couldn't hurt to be sure.

Mushroom clouds? No. Nuclear apocalypse? Not yet. Armed robbers raiding our house in twenty minutes? Not likely. It was like the anti-news in my head: "Things that are most likely *not* happening today! Story at eleven!"

By seven thirtyI had managed to get into the bathroom because I knew that June wouldn't need it until seven thirty-two when she would coming knocking and demanding to be let in. And sure enough, she was right on time.

That sort of freaked me out, not gonna lie.

"APRIIIIILLLLLL!" she yelled. "I need to talk to you!"

I was dragging a toothbrush through my mouth as I opened the door. "Wha?"

"Okay!" she announced, her round eyes taking up nearly all of her face as she put one hand on the door and shoved her way in. "I need you!"

I spat, rinsed, and turned to her. "What? What'd you see?!"

"What?"

"You look all flappy and panicky! Did something happen? Did you see a tumor in Mom's brain or something? Is May still smoking? Or is she—?"

June just looked at me. "Whoa. Captain Morbid much?"

"What do you expect?! I'm a little on edge here. I didn't get a lot of sleep."

"Yeah, join the club. Anyway. I need to know something." She cleared her throat and held up a short pink skirt that looked like it was made out of clouds. "Are people going to laugh at me if I wear this skirt today?"

I blinked twice. "You can't be serious."

"I'm totally serious."

I sighed. "Of course you are."

"Look, I realize that you and May are on a campaign to be Most Unpopular," June huffed, "and hey, that's great. Go you. But some of us would like to be appreciated by our peers." She held up the skirt again. "Yes or no? Are people gonna make fun of me?"

"I honestly doubt that I got the ability to predict the future just to make you more popular." I paused. "And I cannot *believe* that that sentence just came out of my mouth."

June shook the skirt. "Yes. Or. No."

"June, would you please just go—?"

"April!" she protested.

May drifted out of her room and past us just then, still wearing her flannel pajama pants. She stopped when she saw June's fluffy skirt. "You're wearing that today?" she asked.

"Maybe. Why?"

May snorted with laughter.

"And there you have it," I announced. "Yes, June, people will laugh at you if you wear that skirt. You're welcome. Now will you please leave me alone?" I headed to my room and started to shut the door.

"Some help you are!" she yelled. "It doesn't count if it's *May* who laughs!"

"What does that mean?" May demanded. "What, I can disappear so I don't even count anymore?"

"Mom is downstairs!" I hissed at them. "Can you *please* pretend to be normal for once in your lives?"

May quivered with anger and then she was gone, literally, in the blink of an eye. I had seen her do it yesterday, but that had only been for a second or two. This time, though, it took my breath away. I think she could disappear every twenty minutes for the rest of her life, and I'll never get used to seeing her leave.

Next to me, June gasped. She even took a step towards where May had been, which I thought was sort of sweet. "Whoa," she whispered.

And in the next blink May was back, looking a bit tousled and aggravated. "Dammit, I got pissed off," she said. "I was trying to stop it, but that didn't work."

"So . . . so where do you go when you . . . go?" June asked.

"I don't *go* anywhere," May said. "I need to get dressed." She went towards her room again, but this time June and I trailed behind her down the hall. "Breathing room, please. The great Houdini still needs oxygen."

"What do you mean, you don't go anywhere?" I pressed. "You weren't there."

"I was standing right there the whole time," May said. "Same thing yesterday. I was there, but nobody could see me. I could yell and scream, and it wouldn't matter."

"So it's not that you disappear," I said slowly, "it's that people don't see you. You can make people not see you."

"Oh, no." May yanked her bedroom door back open to glare at me. "I don't make people *do* anything. This isn't my fault, and June, why are you staring at me like that?"

June was still watching her, wide-eyed. "It was like magic," she said. "You were here and then *vamoose*!"

"Vamoose?" May repeated, but there was a smile playing at the edge of her mouth.

"You're missing the point," I interrupted them. "May, you can control people with your brain. You control what they see."

"Cool. I wonder if I can make them all into zombies next. Big flesh-eating zombies."

"Ew." June wrinkled her nose. "You're so masochistic."

"Big word, Junie," May said. "Is that gonna be your next mental feat? Getting a polysyllabic vocabulary?"

"No, it's going to be taking over the world," June said. May just grinned, only because I think she secretly likes seeing June stick up for herself.

I decided to take advantage of their brief truce for a few more minutes. "Okay, so our brains are working overtime now," I started to say, but June interrupted.

"No, they're not," she insisted. "It's like that guy Einstein said. Most people only use 10 percent of their brains, right? Maybe we're just using more."

"I don't think Einstein said that," I interrupted.

June shrugged. "Insert famous science guy here, then."

"Maybe one of Mr. Dwyer's chem labs went awry," May said, "and our brains got exposed."

"Then why isn't this happening to the whole school?" I pointed out.

"Maybe it is!" June cried. "Maybe we should make, like, a secret Facebook group or something."

May rolled her eyes. One day they'll be permanently stuck in the back of her head, I swear to God. "Get a real plan and report back to us, June," she muttered.

June opened her mouth to snap back, but I heard our mom's feet clomping up the stairs before she could say anything. "Crap," I whispered.

"Nice future predicting, April," May muttered at me. "Way to give us the heads up on Mom."

"Shut up, it's not an exact science. Good luck not disappearing in front of Mom, by the way."

May flipped me the bird.

"Oh, did your other four fingers already disappear?" I sneered, but June cut me off with a cheery, "Hi, Mom!" while nudging both of us into good behavior.

My mom was carrying her mug of peppermint tea, just like she has every single morning of my life. It's nice to know that some things don't change. I'm pretty sure that's why Batman kept his butler Alfred around. Sometimes you just want to hang out with someone that's normal. "April, honey?" she said to me.

"Yeah?"

"If you want, you can take my car and drive to school today. I'm working from home, so I don't need it today."

I paused and leaned against the door. I knew what the car was: another pity offering, something to make my mom feel better about all the upheaval in our lives, but it just made me feel weirder. When things were changing so fast all around me, I wanted everything to stay the same. I didn't want the car. I wanted our old house and our old neighbors and our old school and our old friends.

"Word," June sighed under her breath.

I shoved her so that it looked accidental. I've had years of practicing that move.

"Okay," I said to my mom as June frowned at me and rubbed her arm. "Thanks!"

"Of course. And girls, you have fifteen minutes before—" she started to add, but she stopped when she saw us. "What happened?"

I saw June's hand tighten on the doorknob. "What?" she said. "We're fine, nothing happened, nothing weird at all happened."

Good grief. Someone's gotta teach her how to be an effective liar, *fast*.

Luckily, if there's one person who knows how to be blasé, it's

May. "We're fine, Mom," she said, drumming her fingers (all of them still present and accounted for) on the doorframe. "Junie's just still shaken up because she saw a spider. You know how she gets about the creepy-crawlies."

Our mom looked unconvinced, though. "All of your eyes are *ver-rrry* big," she said, narrowing her eyes at us. "Have you been doing drugs in your bedroom?"

"*Moooom*. We go to other people's houses to do drugs," May dead-panned, then grinned when our mom laughed a little. It's a lucky thing for May that our parents still appreciate her sense of humor. She and my dad are really similar that way. When the two of them get going, they can go a whole day without making one sincere comment.

"Chillax, Mamacita," May told our mom. "We're fine."

June looked like she was about to hurl, though, and I realized she was probably trying her hardest to stop reading our mom's mind. "Yeah, we're fine," she echoed May and tilted her head up when our mom kissed her forehead en route to her bedroom.

* * *

"Oh, goodie," May said wearily as we climbed into the car thirty minutes later. "Another car ride with my sisters. What joy will it bring this time?"

"That's funny coming from *you*," June said as she slammed her passenger side door shut.

I glanced over at her outfit. "So you're wearing that skirt?"

"Yep. It's important to not care what other people think, after all."

"So says the mindreader," May sneered.

"It's a bold decision in a new direction, June," I told her.

She beamed at me. "Thanks!"

In the rearview mirror, May raised her eyebrows and said nothing. I could see her hands were white-knuckling the strap on her backpack, the same one she'd had for three years. "So," she said in her casual-but-not-really voice, "what do you think the chances are that I'll disappear in the middle of class today?"

"Signs point to yes," June mumbled. "Big time yes."

"Seatbelt," I told her.

"Yes, boss," she intoned.

"And you just have to control it," I said to May as we backed out of the driveway. "Pay attention, don't lose focus, keep your eye on the ball, all that sports advice stuff."

"Well, that'd be great if I actually played sports," she muttered. "What if I get called on when I'm not even raising my hand?"

"Oh, that," June said dismissively. "Just answer a lot when you actually *know* the answers. Then they don't call on you when you *don't* know the answers." She settled into the seat. "Easy peasy."

But I knew the real problem: May always knows the answers. She just doesn't like to say them out loud. When we were three, four, and five years old, May practically had an emotional breakdown when she had to be an angel in the holiday pageant at our preschool. (June, on the other hand, would have worn every single halo in that room if she could have, and I was just eager for the whole shebang to be over because I had heard there would be cookies afterwards.)

Once we were in the parking lot, we climbed out of the car along with the rest of the bleary-eyed kids straggling towards school. We looked like zombies, none of us wanting to be there, all of us in various stages of caffeine deprivation. (Well, everyone except for June, who I'm pretty sure was riding an emotional high off her pink skirt.) Whoever has to teach first period at our school must have drawn the short straw because we aren't a pleasant group to be around.

"So true," June muttered next to me. "We're bitchy."

I sighed. "June. C'mon. You gotta stop doing that."

"I'm trying," she protested. "I swear, April, I really am. But sometimes it's like I can open a door to your *mind*."

May tossed her hair over her shoulder. "June, if you open my door, so to speak, I'll maim you and enjoy it."

"Ha. No, you wouldn't. That's illegal and besides, Mom and Dad would ground you for, like, a bazillion years."

I couldn't handle listening to them argue again, so I turned it off. I was too busy trying to keep track of what was happening now and what was going to happen. The scenes interchanged too fast, and I almost fell over a parking block in my hurry to get towards school.

"April?"

Both my sisters were looking at me quizzically. "Earth to you," May said. "What's wrong?"

"Oh, you mean besides the fact that I can predict the future of millions of strangers?"

May shook her head. "Oh, no no no no. *No*. You do not get to play the Martyr Card. We're all going through shit right now."

I sighed. "My brain is already tired."

"Let's ditch!" June's eyes lit up. Ever since she saw *Ferris Bueller's Day Off* when she was eight years old, she longs for the day she can ditch school. I guess she thinks it involves downtown parades while singing Beatles songs, but from what May's told me, it's mostly just hanging out at Denny's and watching crappy horror movies at other people's houses. Not that I'd tell her that, though. Everyone has their dreams.

"May, can I ditch with you?" she asked.

"JUNE," May snapped. "Enough with the brain intrusions!"

"Sorry!" Her eyes were glassy, though. "But you ditched last year! I saw it! Can I come next time? I won't even talk or read your mind or *anything*, I swear."

I glanced at May, who studiously looked away, and I could tell by the worry wrinkle between her eyes that she was doing everything in her power to keep June from reading her mind. The truth is, May used to ditch more than all of us, including half the student body. Let's just say she's had a lot of day-long orthodontist appointments for someone who doesn't even wear braces.

"Ditching is wrong," I tried to tell June.

"Whatever."

"Look," I said. "Let's all try to get through today without attracting national media attention or becoming lab experiments, all right?"

"Yeah, like the biology frogs," June said. "Or the anatomy cats."

"Should we synchronize our watches, too?" May rolled her eyes. "Code names? Set up a secret meeting place in case the world ends?"

"Don't joke about that."

"I want my code name to be something awesome," June replied. "Like a celebrity baby name."

I pressed my fingers to my temples, willing my headache away. "Our parents couldn't stop at one," I sighed. "They had to have two more." But really, I was nervous. My sisters and I were pretty much loose cannons, and I kept searching to see if May would disappear to get out of a history quiz or June would read the mind of our assistant principal and cause everyone over the age of thirty to have a meltdown.

"Buck up," June said to me as May started trudging towards school. "And stop freaking out. Some day you'll be glad you have us."

"I don't see that vision coming for a long time," I scowled at her, but I fell in line and followed my sisters toward school. Halfway to the front door, I grabbed May by the elbow while June pranced ahead of us. "Hey," I whispered. "Don't leave today."

"Yeah, I know," she whispered back, and when she looked at me, I felt it, whatever that thing is where you can talk to your sister without saying a word.

I guess it's always special when you can do that. No matter how special you are.

* * *

To my immense glee, my day wasn't disastrous. I kept my head down, didn't look at anyone, and tried hard not to see anything. And it worked.

At least until lunch.

I was standing at my locker, pulling out books and putting books away as this guy stood over me, trying to get into his locker. "Uh, excuse me," I muttered as he knocked me in the head with his elbow. It didn't help that I'm kind of short, and he's the human equivalent of a redwood tree. You could probably hollow him out and drive a car through him, just like those Sequoias in the national forest.

But he never said "Sorry" or "Excuse me" or "Forgive me for being the rudest person alive." He never said anything. I don't even know what his name is.

Not that I care what his name is. I've just seen him at his locker before.

Anyway.

So there we were, doing our daily locker do-si-do, when I saw something. At first I thought it was a memory, but when I realized what was happening, I sucked my breath in and grabbed my locker door, as if my power could pull me right off the gorund.

I couldn't see anything in front of me, not even Sequoia Boy's stupid elbow inches away from my face. It was like someone lowered a movie screen in front of me and hit play.

I saw people running, ducking themselves into every doorway. Some people even ran outside, the morons. I saw the ground roll right underneath my feet, coming towards me like a wave. I saw a light fixture falling, the fluorescent one that was right over my head, and I saw it coming right towards Julian and me.

How did I know his name all of a sudden?

"—my way."

I shook my head and glanced up. "What?"

"In my way," the guy—Julian—was saying, motioning to where my hand was gripping the bottom of his locker. He couldn't shut the door without slamming my fingers.

"Oh," I started to say, but for some reason I knew to keep hanging on, and it's a good thing I did, since the initial jolt made the building feel like someone had driven a Mack truck into the side of the school.

There was a flurry of tiny screams, and then someone yelled, "Earthquake!" And I saw it again, people going into doorways or streaming outside. Just like in my . . .

In my *what*? My vision? My daydream? What the hell was I supposed to call these things?

The linoleum floor seemed to rise up like a tiny wave, curling itself up and down as the earthquake shook us. I was still standing by my locker, still hanging on to its metal frame while everyone around us ran for cover.

That's when I heard the crack and saw the spark.

I shoved Julian so hard that he staggered backwards. "What the hell?" he yelled at me, but I was too busy ducking out of the way of the crashing light. And then I heard him yell, "Oh, shit!" as the glass flew everywhere and the hallway went dark.

The earthquake, I knew, only lasted for ten seconds or so: 5.2 on the Richter scale, which wasn't too crazy by Southern Californian standards. The light only fell because it hadn't been bolted in correctly. I saw press conferences on the news and school officials looking at the damage, even though none of it had happened yet. I knew that the chem teacher would need three stitches in his hand because he got cut by a broken glass test tube.

The visions came so fast that it felt like the earthquake was still happening, and when I could finally see normally again, I saw my fingers still gripping the edge of Julian's locker.

I can still feel that locker in my hand sometimes—that's how hard I was holding on.

"Whoa," someone said to me. "You're kinda pale."

"Yeah," I replied, even though I had no idea what I looked like. Across the hall, Julian was staring at me, but I didn't have time to stare back because we were all getting herded around by the vice principal, who finally had the opportunity to use the whistle that always hung around his neck. "PHWEET! PHWEET!" The sound was worse than the earthquake. Everyone looked either dazed or freaked out or excited, and I caught a glimpse of Avery, the girl with the black hair May had almost run over with the car the day before. She definitely looked freaked out, and I couldn't blame her. Almost getting hit by a minivan one day, and dealing with an earthquake the next? I could almost hear May's voice in my ear saying, "Sucks to be her."

"Hey," Julian said to me, but when I turned to look at him, I couldn't see him anymore. I was getting something else now. Something a hundred times worse than an earthquake premonition.

I could see myself kissing Julian. He was holding my face, and his eyes were really brown, like deep-set marbles. And his skin was softer up close than it looked from far away. He smelled really good, too, like laundry even though his shirt looked a few days' worth of dirty. And his lips were—and his hands were—and—

Whoa, Nelly.

I closed my eyes hard, then opened them again, but it was the same thing. We were making out, I was seeing it like it was HDTV, and I couldn't stop it.

What?

WHAT?

HOLY HELL HOW WAS THIS EVEN POSSIBLE?

"Hey," Julian said again, and this time I managed to look up at him. "Hey, what—" But I slipped past him and out the door with everyone else, trying to find a way to turn off my brain. The images were pummeling me, flashes and glimpses of everyone's lives. I didn't know if I was seeing the past or future or what, but I suddenly remembered being six years old again, standing on the hot concrete with my sisters.

I remembered watching May disappear.

My sisters.

"Oh my God," I whispered.

It was like I could see everything behind me and in front of me, and yet I had no idea where I was. All I knew was that it felt like something bad was on its way . . . and I was the only one who could see it coming.

chapter 5

"You have no idea how fast things can change."

may

I got hauled into the office that afternoon after the earthquake. Not because I caused it or anything, obviously (although that would be one awesome power, I have to admit), but so I could get set up for tutoring.

Honestly, I'd take the earthquake again.

Luckily, I was outside when it happened, getting ready to sit under a tree and eat lunch by myself like the loser I am. When the first shock hit the ground, I disappeared without even thinking about it, but after it was over, I didn't bother coming back.

I mean, why would I? I was sitting by myself. Under a tree. Who cared if I was there or not?

I have to say, disappearing without anyone noticing was pretty fantastic.

But you know what's not fantastic?

Tutoring in European history.

It would have been helpful if my psychic big sister had mentioned this plot development. But she never said a word and I got summoned out of geometry and sent to the assistant principal's office to discuss my "course of action."

I can't say I was too disappointed about missing geometry, but sitting in that office wasn't my idea of a fun time, either.

"Maaaaaaaay," Mr. Corday said in his best I-may-be-in-a-position-of-not-entirely-deserved-authority-but-let's-be-friends-anyway voice. "Let's talk. I heard that you might need some extra help in one of your classes."

"Do you have a reliable source?" I asked him. "Signed affidavits? Eyewitness accounts?"

"Your initial two test scores." He raised his big bushy eyebrows. It's gross how old dudes' eyebrows get all gray and long.

"Oh," I said. "Those test scores. Maybe I'm being framed?"

"Let's focus on the issue at hand," Mr. Corday replied, adjusting his glasses as he pulled out my transcript from my last school. "Your grades in your freshman history class at your old school are excellent. As and Bs." He set the paper down and folded his hands over it. "What's different this year?"

I started to laugh. I couldn't help myself. "What's *different*?" I said through my giggles. *Well, for starters,* I imagined saying, *my parents divorced, we moved here, my mom's stressed, my dad's becoming some sort of hippie/cowboy hybrid, I had a tequila-filled night that still makes my liver cringe, and oh yeah, I almost forgot! I can control your mind and make you think I'm disappearing! Other than that, though, not much is new.*

I bit my tongue, though, and tried to stop laughing. "Sorry," I said. "Look, here's the thing. My history teacher at my old school? She was old and half-blind. We all cheated like we were counting cards in Vegas. *Everyone* was making As. I only got a B on my final 'cause I was too lazy to even cheat." This was only semi-true, but unless this guy was a mindreader like June, I didn't care.

Mr. Corday's eyebrows drew together like angry centipedes. "You know we have a zero-tolerance cheating policy at this school, Miss Stephenson."

I tried to make my eyes wide and innocent, like Bambi. "Well, as you probably can tell from my test scores, Mr. Corday, I'm *not* cheating."

He couldn't argue that point, that was for sure.

"I've amended my ways," I continued. "Consider my Shawshank redeemed."

"Yes, okay, May, the point has been made." He sat back in his chair and pushed his glasses up high on his forehead. Not a great look for him. "You know," he said, "I happen to think you're a very smart girl."

"You're not alone in that," I replied.

"But you might just be too smart for your own good."

I just blinked. "With all due respect, Mr. Corday," I said, "I think more people should be too smart for their own good."

We had a little stare-off for a few seconds, and I thought I might have pushed it too far and would now have to deal with a month of detention or something. But instead he just put his glasses back on and said, "It's currently two fifty-three. At three o'clock, you'll be meeting Henry in the library."

"Who?"

"Your tutor."

I could only blink. "My European history tutor is named Henry?" I said. "You don't find that ironic? Which of the many Henrys is he? Henry the Ninth? Henry the Benevolent?"

"Pick one. Either way, you will be meeting him in the library at three."

You kind of have to respect a guy who uses the Jedi mind trick.

"No problem," I told him. "Are we done now? I have to go explore other options for my teenage angst, now that I can't fail European history anymore."

"May—"

"Kidding, kidding," I said quickly. My toes were starting to tingle, and I had learned that wasn't a good sign. All the witty banter was starting to take its toll. I was pretty sure that if I got too tired, too angry, too much of anything, I would suddenly become nothing at all. "Catch you later, gator," I said to Mr. Corday before scooting out of the office and into the hallway.

Henry the Tutor was waiting for me in the library when I got there at 3:03. I hate the school library. It always smells like old yellow paper and pencil shavings and nerds. April always says, "That's just the smell of history and knowledge." She's ridiculous sometimes.

Henry the Tutor's head was buried in a book that looked neither interesting nor frivolous. The amazing thing about Henry, though, was that nearly every item of clothing except for his jeans was from Stanford—the shirt, the sweatshirt, the pin on his backpack, the actual backpack. And I was willing to bet money that he was one of those douchebags that had a lame license-plate frame, too, like "FUTURE STANFORD ALUMNI" or something.

In short, Henry was a brochure with legs.

Fantabulous. These types were always my favorite.

"What's up, buttercup?" I said as soon as I was close enough. "Apparently you, you lucky guy, are going to be the savior of my European history education. Good luck with that."

He just looked up, startled. His eyes were wide and blue, and he had a perma-frown across his brow, like he was waiting for something to disappoint him. "You're May?" he asked.

"Are you expecting someone else? Or do you just hang out in libraries for kicks?"

I wouldn't say he glared at me, but it wasn't exactly his happy face, either. "Okay," he said slowly. "Let's start."

I slunk into my chair next to him. "So you don't find it ironic?" I asked him.

"Find what ironic?" He was already pulling out a pen and pencil that both had—wait for it—Stanford written all over them.

"That you're named Henry and tutoring me in European history," I told him. "Like there's not enough Henrys running around already in this subject?"

Henry just sighed. "You're one of *those* girls, I guess."

I bristled. "Well, if by 'those girls,' you mean one of those awesome and amazing girls that are light years beyond their peers but unfortunately stuck in high school due to circumstances beyond their control, then yes. Yes, I am one of 'those girls.' Wanna join?"

He just started flipping through his textbook, and when I didn't follow suit, he looked at me. "Did you bring your book?"

"Excellent question." I opened my bag and shook out a geometry textbook, some silver gum wrappers, four watermelon-flavored Jolly Ranchers, some crumpled-up papers, six pens, one broken pencil, and then surveyed the pile. "What do you think? Do you see it anywhere?"

Henry sighed again. "Yeah, that's what I thought. Here, use mine."

"Goodie," I said.

"What about homework?" he sighed. "Did you even bring that?"

I thought for a minute. "You know, it's entirely possible."

Two and a half minutes later, I managed to produce the crumpled worksheet from the bottom of my bag. "They should invent a paper iron," I muttered as I tried to smooth it out on the edge of the desk.

"They did," Henry replied. "It's called a folder."

"I've heard about those," I shot back. "I just don't believe in all that newfangled technology." But I made a note to order some folders online. From the UC Berkeley store.

"So," Henry said with a sigh. "Prussia."

Henry talked for awhile, but to be honest, I didn't hear a word he was saying. It just seemed impossible to focus on anything that had happened in the past when there was so much happening in the present. I was pretty sure that what had happened to me and my sisters hadn't happened to anyone else before. And if it had, well then, these history books were definitely not covering the important stuff.

Henry, though, was way into this old-school history. He actually got a little flushed talking about it. That's the kind of thing that April would find charming, some guy getting all passionate about school and college and life plans, but it doesn't do a thing for me. *Plan all you want, dude*, I thought to myself. *You have no idea how fast things can change.*

"Can we take a break?" I said after about fifteen minutes or so. "All this historical excitement is starting to tax my delicate sensibilities."

"Hey, let me guess," Henry said. "You're being sarcastic. Wow, how original."

"Well, just don't go telling everyone or my secret will really be out," I shot back. So Henry and I were not going to be wearing "Best Friends" necklace charms, I think it's pretty obvious to say.

"Like I said. One of *those* girls."

It was like waving red in front of an angry bull, and I suddenly found myself wishing for the kind of power where I could shoot fire-balls out of my eyes and obliterate this guy. "What is your *problem*?" I finally demanded. "God, if you don't want to tutor me, then don't. It's no skin off my back, trust me. You've probably had your head so far up your ass that you haven't heard about this yet, but there's a series about another jerk named Henry on Showtime. I'll just watch that instead."

Henry just rolled his eyes and waved his hand over the mess I had made on the table by emptying my bag. "Do you mind cleaning this up?"

"Wow, Mister type A, is it making you uncomfortable? Do you need meds to cope with daily life?"

"Look, I'm only doing this because volunteering looks good on my transcript," Henry snapped. "Believe me, I don't want to be here, either, but Stanford—"

"Who's Stanford?" Yeah, I was messing with him. I had to. It was too easy.

"WH—WHO'S Stanf—?" he started to gasp.

"You might want to take some deep breaths, pal," I said, crossing my arms over my chest. "I was kidding. And what the hell do you mean, 'one of those girls'? What sort of psychological damage is that supposed to do?"

"I *mean*," Henry spluttered, "that you're one of those girls who doesn't even study because you think you're so *cool* and *above* everything. You just think your life's so hard all the time when you probably have this like, picture-perfect life. Seriously, do you even have any, like, future plans? Or goals?"

"Sure I do," I snapped. "Like not causing you any bodily harm, for examp—"

Just then, I felt my foot tingle. As much as I wanted to verbally bitchslap him, I couldn't. Not when it meant that I could disappear at any minute.

"I have to go," I said, scrambling to my, uh, foot. The bathroom was less than a hundred feet outside the library door, and I had no idea if I could make it there in time. "I, I . . . I'll see you later."

Henry just stood back as I jumped out of my chair, grabbed my bag, and hoofed it towards the back door of the library. "May, wait . . ."

"It's been swell!" I hissed over my shoulder, then slammed the door and dashed down the hall, looking for somewhere to go, where I could be nowhere at all.

chapter 6

"It turns out that being a mindreader does have its upsides."

june

I have to admit, I was not at my perky best Tuesday morning. I was awake from two forty-seven to four thirty-three the night before, listening to whoever was awake with me. I figured out that the quieter it is, the more I can hear. Like, in the school hallway or whatever, it just sounds like a bunch of people shouting at me. But at night, when it seems like no one in the entire world is up, I can hear the awake ones like they're whispering into my ear.

Some of it is stupid stuff—our next-door neighbors worrying about their mortgage and whether or not they should refinance—but other voices are terrible. There's that homeless guy on the corner a few blocks away, and all I get from him at night is yelling—crazy nonsense that's so angry that I have to put a pillow over my head. It doesn't stop the noise, but at least I feel safer.

The only thing good about that Tuesday morning when I woke up was the idea of my pink skirt.

Okay, so here's the deal with the pink skirt. I didn't wear it because it was like my favorite skirt of all-time or anything. I mean, it's cute, I can't lie, but I wore it because because I wanted to impress Mariah and Daphne and Jessica. And now that I could read minds? I'd be able to get an honest opinion about my entire wardrobe.

It turns out that being a mindreader does have its upsides.

April hates Mariah and those girls. She calls them the Angelas because I guess there was some snotty girl named Angela in fourth grade that used to tease April about being smart. I tried to talk to her about it before all this craziness happened. I tried to tell her that *these* girls aren't like *that* girl and please do not put your childhood issues on me, but she doesn't listen. "They're nice!" I finally told April. "They do *volunteer work*."

"They have to," she replied. "It's a *graduation requirement*."

I don't even bother talking to May about it. It doesn't take a mindreading skill to know what she thinks about it. She's sort of transparent that way.

But whatevs. April and May are too old to remember what it's like being a freshman. They don't remember what it's like to go from eighth grade to ninth, which feels like moving from the minor to the major leagues. And after these four years, I have to go to college. And if I don't learn how to be popular now, I might as well just join a convent and learn how to make soup for orphans, or whatever it is that nuns do, because I am *doomed*.

(Also, I don't ever tell anyone this, but every time I think about going to college, I get nervous. Flock-of-butterflies nervous. I have to leave my house? My room? My friends? My mom? I have to pay thousands of dollars to live at *school*?)

April and May also don't know that on the first day of school, I ate lunch by myself. I would seriously die if they ever found out, or if *anyone* ever found out. It was really far away, way out by the softball field and behind a tree. But a tree isn't a friend, and sitting in the dirt watching everyone talk to everyone else wasn't how I wanted to spend the next four years' worth of lunch periods. No thank you very much.

Of course, this was all before I could read minds. It was a new ballgame now, as far as I was concerned, and I was team captain of everyone.

Batter up.

There was just one thing that stood in the way between me and intense popularity: my pink skirt.

A funny thing happens when you walk through the front doors of high school. Maybe it happens to you, too.I don't know what your life is like, but whatever looks good in the mirror at home or in the parking lot suddenly seems like the worst idea you've ever had. I know all the magazines tell you to be an individual, but when you're not the air-brushed model in the photo spread, it's really hard to be an individual. I'd rather be a follower any day of the week than wear legwarmers to school again. (That was just a bad idea, but I was in eighth grade then and didn't know any better.)

But judging from what people were thinking as I walked down the hall in my new pink skirt on Tuesday, this was gonna be right up there with the legwarmer incident. I was so excited to read people's thoughts that I forgot I could actually *read people's thoughts*.

That skirt should be shorter so you can see her ass.

Who wears pink anymore?

Did she tie cotton candy around her waist?

You get the idea. I certainly did.

I needed to remember to start bringing a back-up outfit to school. Something normal, like jeans and a hoodie. Sometimes May makes me so jealous because she just blends in with everyone else. I can't do that, and once in a while, I wish I could.

By the time fourth-period English rolled around, I was half-ready to chase down April and beg her to change clothes with me. Maybe she would see all this happening and come to rescue me. Maybe she'd at least take me home to get a new skirt. Something from the safe denim family, perhaps.

No luck. My sister's stupid future-seeing brain wasn't seeing anything *important*, obviously.

I spent the rest of Tuesday working overtime trying not to hear anyone else's thoughts. It takes so much effort, though. My sisters always get mad at me for reading their minds, but they have no idea. Imagine person after person coming up to you and telling you their secrets, one right after the other, and some of the secrets are the most juicy things you've ever heard in your life. And some of the secrets will keep you awake for the next three nights. Try doing this for a day and then tell me how you're doing. Tell me if you still have friends, if you love your parents, if you even know anyone the way you thought you did. Tell me that.

I certainly wouldn't blame you for wearing a potentially tacky pink skirt if this was your lot in life, let me tell you.

And then of course, there was the earthquake. Again, thanks so much, April. What good was it to be able to see the future when you can't even predict a freaking earthquake? I was pretty sure she was gonna be the weak link in our chain.

I hate earthquakes. I hate the ground shaking, and I hate the way buildings make all those cracky, screamy noises during the whole thing. It wasn't even a bad one, but then I had to listen to everyone's thoughts afterwards.

So cool.

My dog is totally gonna be freaking out.

She's so not wearing a bra. I love earthquakes.

(That last one was Jeremy Steston's. He's a disgusting perv.)

But I could hear everyone in my brain for minutes on hand, and I shook my head like it was filled with water, trying to shake them out.

I hope my dad's okay—what if my mom—I wonder if we still have to go to school on Mond—shit, what the hell was—

I couldn't make it stop, no matter how hard I tried. I even started singing "Supercalafragilisticexpealadocious" in my head, but that only added to all the noise and I couldn't remember the second verse.

I was starting to feel a little crazy. I won't lie.

I was so upset, in fact, that when the last bell rang, I didn't even care that my face was oily in the T-zone area, or that my bangs were flipping up all weird, the way it always does no matter how many times I flatiron it. I managed to get my books together and went outside to wait for April because she was my ride home. If there's anything else I hate more than spiders and earthquakes, it's sitting outside and waiting for my sister to give me a ride home. All the cool kids get rides home from their friends, and all of us freshman peeps are left behind, looking like losers. April's always late, too, talking with some teacher or handing in her nerdy extra-credit assignments, so I have to sit there by myself and wait for her and start developing a complex about the fact that I have no friends.

When twenty minutes went by and April didn't show, I put my little antennae up and started listening for my sisters. (Just between you and me, I kind of like the image of me with antennae. I'd be a really adorable bumblebee.)

I walked around the outside of the building a couple of times, trying to pick them up, but no luck. No one was really around so I couldn't even read people's minds to pass the time. It's kind of nice to do that, listening to people when they're just thinking their rambly thoughts.

It's like floating on your back in the ocean, bobbing up and down on the words. No effort required whatsoever.

I was just circling back for the third time when I saw someone come out of the front office, carrying just one textbook in her bone-china arm. *Whatever*, she was thinking, *whatever. It's not like I'm going to Mexico anytime soon..*

It was Mariah. I'd know that voice—I mean, those thoughts—anywhere. I quickly hustled over to her and tried to get closer without seeming like one of those sweaty, overeager type of people. I'm not like that, of course, but last week I wasn't a mindreader, either. You never know what could happen.

"Oh," I said as soon as I got close to Mariah. She was the only girl I'd ever met who could wear that much eyeliner and not look like a sad panda. Her brown hair had a raspberry-red tint to it, and it was so straight, too, like frizz didn't exist in Mariah's world. I took a deep breath and prayed to not sound like a dork. "Um, hi."

Mariah glanced at me, judging me from head to toe in a thought that came so fast I couldn't grab it. "Oh hey," she said. "What's up?"

"Nothing much," I said. I hoped my pink skirt was still fluffy and didn't look as deflated as I had felt all day. Behind Mariah, Jessica and Daphne, two girls I'd seen surrounding her before, sidled up alongside her out of nowhere, like the Queen's guards or something. Judging from their thoughts, they weren't big fans of mine. Jessica was sneering at me down her little skislope-shaped nose, and Daphne's freckles seemed to get darker the more she stared at me.

Yeah, definitely not the friendliest group.

What does she want? Mariah thought as she inspected me, and I moved fast before the opportunity passed.

"I-I just wanted to say that I really like your hair," I told her.

Oh, God, Jessica thought, even though she just smiled a bit, but Mariah's thoughts jolted like a TV had suddenly turned on. "Oh," she said. "Thanks."

There was sort of an awkward pause, which was just enough time for Daphne to think *Can we please go now?* before I added, "Do you flatiron? Because it's always really nice and straight."

Abort! I thought. *Abort! Danger! You're trying too hard!*

But Mariah didn't even think about it. "Yeah. Thanks. I can never get it this straight with just a blowdryer." She shook her hair over her shoulder and looked so cool doing it that it made me feel like a balloon filled with margarine to stand next to her.

It didn't make Jessica and Daphne feel that great, either. They had a low murmur of jealousy around them, and it had nothing to do with me. They just hated me, but they were jealous of Mariah.

Very iiiiiiiinteresting.

"So," Mariah said to me. "Who are you?"

"I'm June," I said. "I'm just waiting for my sister April."

She smirked. "April and June?"

"I've got a middle sister named May, too," I offered.

She just laughed. "Let me guess. Hippie parents?"

I started to answer, but then she went on before I could say anything. "Yeah," she said, "I just had to fix this thing in my schedule. Otherwise I'd have been outta here."

She was lying. She was there because she was failing Spanish and had to talk to the vice principal. It was supposed to be a parent-teacher conference meeting, but her mom hadn't shown up. *Bitch*, Mariah had thought about her, and the word sounded icy in her head.

In a weird way, her lying sort of empowered me. (My mom Tivo's *Oprah*, so I know all about being empowered.) Mariah was lying to *me*, some stupid freshman girl. She was trying to make herself look better in front of *me*.

I was pretty sure that this was what the Pearly Gates looked like.

"That's cool," was all I said, though. "Yeah, I know, I'm having the worst time trying to get out of my Spanish class. It's like—" I remembered what she had thought to herself earlier "—I'm not going to Mexico anytime soon, you know? Why does it even matter?"

Mariah smiled then, a real smile. "Yeah," she said. "And you know everyone in Europe speaks English, anyway, so we don't even need Spanish to go to Morocco or whatever."

Morocco is actually in North Africa, but that wasn't important. It could have been an Ohio suburb for all I cared. "I know!" I said. "And who cares where it is once you get there, anyway?"

Mariah laughed, and I saw a flurry of images go through her brain. She was thinking about parties, parties she had attended before. *The small house packed with people, red plastic cups everywhere, music so loud it made my chest feel tight, a real high school party. People laughing. Girls dancing. A guy was there with Mariah, his arm slung across her shoulders.*

I wanted to go to a party like that. I wanted it more than I have ever wanted anything in my life. Well, except for the golden retriever puppy when I was four. Or those red Mary Janes when I was eight. Or tickets to see—okay, fine. I've wanted a lot of things in my life, but this was suddenly *the* most important one. For so long now I had been just waiting for my *real* life to begin. And now it seemed like maybe that was going to happen. Yeah, it had sucked that we had to leave our old friends and old neighborhood, but maybe that was the point. Maybe I had to shake off the sad stuff and embrace my new life, the life I was *supposed* to be living. No more lonely lunches. No more awkwardness in the halls. My heart raced, and I grinned all of a sudden, surprising even myself.

Mariah gestured over her shoulder. "So. You wanna ride? My boyfriend Blake is picking me up in a few minutes. It's cool."

I was about to open my mouth to say "YES!" but just then I heard a voice in my head.

Stupid fricking disappearing act European history Henry ASSHOLE MORE LIKE IT . . .

Guess who.

"Um, thanks, but I can't," I sighed. "I have to go, um, meet up with my sister." I silently cursed May in my head.

"Okay, cool." Mariah nodded towards Jessica and Daphne. "What about you guys?"

"No, we're gonna go study," Jessica said. "We have to or we're gonna fail chem."

But they weren't going to study. They were going to hang out at Daphne's house and watch crappy DVDs and drink Red Bull. I could see the plan in both of their minds, and I knew that they were lying.

And somewhere in the back of my brain, *my* plan started to form.

"Fine, whatever," Mariah said to her friends, then looked over to me as she started down the hill. "See ya later."

"Bye!" I said, sounding as nerdy as I didn't want to sound, but her last thought caught me cold.

That's a cute skirt.

I grinned and fingered the hem of my now-wonderful skirt. My God, April and May would never even belie—

May.

Crap.

The clock in the hallway said three twenty-two as I went inside and towards the girls' bathroom, where May's thoughts were cutting in and out like a flickering lightbulb. I wondered who Henry was, though, and I have to admit that I was impressed at my sister's ability to work so many curse words into one sentence.

I went into the bathroom and flipped the master door lock behind me. May was nowhere to be seen, and I started searching the stalls for her. "C'mon, May," I muttered. "I really don't like public restrooms. This is gross."

"June?" It was May's voice. Her real voice, not her brain voice, and I went down the corridor and carefully opened the last stall.

She was slumped against the wall, her hands over her face, and she peeked at me from between her long fingers. "Oh, fantastic," she muttered, then covered her face again. "What the hell are you doing here?"

"Oh, you know, I just love staying after school." I rolled my eyes at her. "Seriously, what's wrong with you? Is Henry your history tutor?"

May moved her hands and shoved herself off the wall, glaring at me. "Do *not* say his name around me. Actually, better yet, do *not* read my mind. What are you doing here?"

I watched as she went over to the sink and started to wash her hands. Not the worst idea, that was for sure. "I heard you," I said. "You were, like, all yell-y in your brain, so I came to save you. Too bad my cape's at the drycleaner's; I would have gotten here faster."

Superhero humor: It never gets old.

"Oh yeah?" May splashed cold water on her face. She wasn't even listening to me, I could tell, and she looked a little bit like this deer we once saw in our backyard, all knobby knees, shaky limbs, and big eyes.

"Yeah," I replied. "So who's Henry?"

"One of the many kings of England, don't you know?"

"No, I mean modern-day Henry. Who is he? What'd he say?"

May jerked some paper towels out of the dispenser with more force than necessary before turning to look at me. "You look happy," she muttered. "Why are you so happy-looking?"

I sighed and examined my manicure. I was way overdue for a new one. Maybe I'd get french tips like Mariah. "Oh, nothing." I pretended to act all casual. "It's just that I think Mariah and I are really gonna be friends, and she's awesome and her friends hate her."

May laughed. "Three reasons to be ecstatic, for sure."

"Whatever." I had no time for May's glass-half-empty routine. "So tomorrow? Do you think that I should talk to Mariah again or should I just—?"

"Jesus, June, I don't know! I'm too busy dealing with that fact that I got pissed at Henry and we started arguing and then *my foot disappeared* and I had to flee like a goddamn library refugee!"

"Yeah, because we weren't talking about me just now or anything." I fumed. No one ever listens to me, and it seriously gets old. May's brain was a jumble of curse words and adrenaline and Henry's face. I couldn't get a coherent thought out of the mess, and a new wave of realization hit me. "Oh my God," I suddenly said, trying not to laugh. "Do you *like* Henry?"

May whirled around so fast that her hair almost slapped me in the face. "Okay, June, now you're delusional."

"No, I'm a truth-teller," I replied, then ducked when she threw her wadded-up paper towel at me.

"You're a psychopath."

"Revealer of light."

"A representation of deranged lunacy."

I tried to think of something more clever than that, but I couldn't. "Takes one to know one," I finally said.

"Ha, I win." May pushed her hair behind her ears and added, "The only reason that I would ever like Henry is if they used him as a tackling dummy at football practice." Then she added, "This is gonna be way harder than I thought."

"What is?"

Duh, she thought, clearly for my benefit.

"Oh," I said. "*This*. Got it."

"I mean, aren't you tired of reading people's minds?"

I shrugged. "Not really. It's just like having a bunch of radio stations on at the same time. But I got to read Mariah's brain today. That was pretty cool."

May just looked at me. "That's it?"

"It's a lot!" I protested. "She liked my skirt!"

May just shook her head and started to gather up her bag again. "It's good to know that some things haven't changed," she muttered. "You're still all about shiny pretty things. Can't worry your lovely little head about anything."

"Oh, give me a *break*," I said, pushing my bangs out of my eyes. "Look at you! You could eavesdrop just as easily as I can, and what do you do? You're still avoiding everyone! What a crock."

"Well, excuse me if I don't want to cause mass hysteria by disappearing into thin air in front of the entire student body!"

"Well, *excuse me* if I'm actually putting these things to good use!" I shot back. "I'm sorry if I'm trying to win friends and influence people like any other normal person would!"

"You think we're *normal*?" May yelled back. We were squared off now, and obviously April hadn't seen this happening or she would have hauled her ass in here a long time—

There was a sudden knock on the door.

Oh. Maybe she had seen it after all.

"You guys, I know you're in there!" April called, and then in a softer voice, "Will you just open the door already? I feel ridiculous standing out here."

I walked over and yanked the door open. "Nice timing."

"Thanks." She looked past me. "Where's May?"

I looked over my shoulder and saw that May had disappeared again. "This is getting old," I muttered. "And I know you can hear me, May!"

She came back so fast that I barely saw it happen. One second she was gone, and in the next second, she was back. "Yo," she said. "'Sup?"

April rolled her eyes. "How much did I miss?"

"You tell us," May retorted. "You're the one who knew we were in here. And thanks for the warning on that earthquake, by the way. That was great."

"Yeah," I agreed. "I could have *died*, you never know."

"Actually, I *did* know. And you are not dead. So can we go, please? God, of all the places you two pick to argue, a public restroom? Really?"

I grabbed my bag, and May hitched her backpack up further on her shoulders as we followed April out of the bathroom. "You know," May was starting to say, but just then I got a thought from April that was so intense that I couldn't ignore it.

I'm gonna lose my virginity to him?! her brain was shrieking. *With him? Julian??? That can't be right! Something must be wrong! I don't even like him, how can I—!*

"Oh, my God!" I cried, and both April and May turned around to look at me. "Oh my Goooood," I said again, then clamped my hand over my mouth.

"What?" April said, trying to look all innocent.

"You know *what*!" I slapped her arm. "I saw you! With *him*! In your thoughts!"

"You saw that?" she said in a sort of whispery scream that was scarier than if she had actually screamed.

"With who?" May said, looking confused. "Who's 'him'? What just happened?"

"June, I swear to God that it's not—"

"His name's Julian," I told April, just to prove what I had seen. "You know you can't lie to me; I can read your mind! Oh my God, oh my God, oh my God!"

"Just because you *can* do something doesn't mean you *should*!" April was turning a nice shade of purple now.

"What?" May said. "Seriously, what's going on?"

I just grinned at April. "I didn't know you like the rebels!" I said gleefully.

April sighed and hugged her book tighter to her chest. "I am totally, completely, *metaphorically* screwed."

chapter 7

"That's, like, Superhero 101!"

Driving home with my sisters was not the way I wanted to spend the next ten minutes. June kept babbling on about her skirt and Mariah and God knows what else, and then she'd look at me in the rearview mirror and giggle. Meanwhile, May was pissed that we wouldn't tell her anything, and when we got home, she stomped upstairs to her room. "Stupid mind-game-playing sisters," I heard her mutter.

"I heard that!" June called after her.

"I *wanted* you to hear it!" May yelled back.

I didn't care if they were arguing, though. I had bigger problems on my plate, like the fact that apparently I was going to to sleep with Julian.

It brought new meaning to the word "mindfuck," that was for sure.

I was already coming up with my plan, though, the How to Avoid Julian Forever & Ever Plan. I'd get to school early so I wouldn't have to see him at our lockers, carry all of my books with me so that I wouldn't have to see him during class, and then hang around late so that he'd be gone by the time I went to put my books away.

Plans are good. I like having a plan.

"So what do you think?"

I glanced up and realized that June was standing in the kitchen with her hands on her hips, waiting for my response to something. "What?"

"Oh, like you even heard anything I said," she scoffed. "Please. It's okay, though. You're probably too occupied with thoughts of Julian. I get it."

"I'm not—!" I started to shriek, but thought better of it. "I am going to be very calm," I told her. "Extremely calm. I'm radiating the calmness of a yogi right now."

"Whatevs, Dalai Lama."

"Can't you even *talk* like a normal person?"

June just laughed. "Why? News at eleven, April. We're not normal."

"Well, *you've* never been normal," I retorted.

She made her way towards the kitchen, and I went upstairs, eager to get to my own room and away from my mindreading little sister. "I give that a three out of ten on the comeback scale," she yelled after me, but I was too far away to retort.

May was lying on her bed as I walked past her room, listening to her iPod and working on her online photo album. I had seen it a few times, but all it had were pictures of Paris in the rain and French singers and things like that. "Oh, hey, it's one half of the paranormal peeps," she said as she glanced up at me. "Go away."

I opened my mouth to speak, but June started screaming downstairs. "WE'VE BEEN ROBBED!!! OH MY GOD CALL THE POLICE!!! CHECK AND SEE IF THEY TOOK ANYTHING OUT OF MY ROOM!!!"

I immediately whirled and looked into my bedroom to make sure no one had stolen my *Harry Potter* books. My dad and I read that whole series together, and I couldn't imagine something happening to them. They were still there, though, arranged sequentially on my bookshelf, even while June continued screaming downstairs.

May and I both raced towards her, my heart in my throat. I hadn't seen anything about a robbery! It couldn't be true! Next to me, May was gone but still there. I could almost feel her pulse at one point, and I guessed that I had run straight through her in my hurry to get to the living room.

June was standing there, the television remote control in one hand and an accusing finger pointing at the blank space where our television once had been. It was gone, making the whole room look like a six-year-old with a missing tooth. "LOOK!" June gasped. "They took it!"

May was suddenly there, staring along with the rest of us, and then she turned to me and crossed her arms. "Congratulations, April," she drawled. "Since you've become a future-predictor, we've almost hit that Avery girl with a car—"

"There's no 'we' in that sentence!" I protested.

"—had an earthquake, and been robbed. Can you even *see* the future, or are you just making this up?"

"Oh, she can see it, all right," June defended me. I would have felt better about her statement if I knew she wasn't thinking about Julian and me. She was still pointing at the gaping hole in our entertainment center, and I reached over and tugged her arm down.

"You shouldn't point," I said automatically.

"Yes, I should, because OUR TV IS MISSING!"

"Okay, wait a minute—" I started to say, but May interrupted yet again.

"Why, April? Why should we wait? Is the roof about to come

crashing in?" she glared. "Not that you could predict it happening, of course."

"*No*," I fumed. "I just think that we should call Mom before we get all crazy."

Ten minutes later, things had calmed down considerably. "Oh, *that*," my mom had sighed when June frantically explained about our missing television via speakerphone. "Yeah, your dad wanted the TV back."

"Dad?" May said. "They don't sell TVs in Houston? He had to have ours?"

"Well, your dad says it's his," my mom replied. There it was again, that "*your*" word, the same way people say "*your* bunion" or "*your* stomach flu." "He said he was gonna have some people pick it up today to have it shipped back. I'm sorry, girls, I thought I mentioned it."

May was still glaring at the phone, but June had bigger concerns. "But *Survivor* is on tonight!" she wailed. It fascinated me that she sounded as traumatized about missing *Survivor* as she did when she thought we'd been robbed. I love her, but wow, June has a narrow emotional capacity.

"Oh, shut it," she glared at me.

"I didn't say anything!" I shot back. "And stop read—!"

"Mom, seriously, we need a TV," May said while giving both June and me a shove. "We're not Luddites."

"Ew, no, what's that?" June wrinkled her nose. "I'm not that."

My mom laughed over the phone, and I got a vision of her climbing into her car after work and rolling the windows down, looking neither happy nor unhappy. Just looking like herself.

"Relax," she said now. "I'm a mother of three teenagers; you think

I want you in my house without a TV? We'd all go crazy. April, honey, do you still have that credit card?"

"Yeah, it's in my wallet," I said. My mom had given it to me when I started driving, "for emergencies only," she had emphasized. She probably hadn't realized that the word "emergency" had taken on new meaning over the past several days.

"Okay, then you officially have my permission to go over to that shopping center on Topanga and buy us a new TV."

June elbowed her way in front of me. "Can we get surround sound, too?"

"Don't push it, sweetheart."

* * *

An hour later, my sisters and I were standing in Best Buy, surrounded by a bunch of electrical equipment and people wearing blue polo shirts. "Why do stores always make their employees wear khakis?" June grimaced. "That's just not right. It doesn't make me want to shop here *more*."

"Can I please wait in the car?" May sighed.

"No way, we're suffering together. Besides we need to talk about what we're going to do. We need a plan, a—"

"I don't even watch TV!" May protested, ignoring me completely. "And besides, I'm going to Houston to see Dad next month. I can bond with our old TV then. I'll tell it you both said, 'Hello.'"

"Do you think you'll come back wearing a cowboy hat and saying, 'Howdy'?" I asked her. Teasing May will never not be fun.

She wrenched her hand away and shook her head. "You're so strange."

"Yeah," June scoffed as she pushed past us. "No freaking kidding."

We found ourselves in front of what seemed like hundreds of TVs, all of them showing the same episode of *Oprah*. "Whoa," June said as two hundred Oprahs of different sizes and hues laughed at the same time. "Anyone else getting dizzy?"

May sighed and went over to a television that threatened to dwarf her. "What about this? Subtle enough?"

June's eyes grew huge, but I shook my head. "We are getting the exact same thing that we had in our old house," I declared. "Nothing crazy, nothing that's bigger than the living room or—"

"Jesus, April," May said. "I don't give a rat's butt about our TV. Relax."

June glanced over at us. "She said this afternoon she's radiating calmness like Yogi Bear, May. Give her a break."

May looked up at me. "Can you please interpret our darling sister for me? I don't speak June."

"Calm like a *yogi*!" I cried. "Not Yogi Bear! I said this afternoon that I was radiating calmness like a *yogi*!"

May just snickered and turned back to the TV. "Yeah," she snorted. "It's obvious. You're cool as ice."

"Ice cold," June added.

"I *was* before I started talking to you two," I glared. "Look, can we just get the TV and go, please? We need to figure some things out before this gets really out of control. And I have homework to do, too. Unlike you guys, I can't disappear to get out of a test or read minds to know the right answers."

May hesitated before smiling to herself. "Thanks for the idea, April."

"Oh my God, I might not have to ever study again," June said dreamily.

I pressed my hands against my head and began counting to ten. I didn't get past "three" before I saw that May was starting to wander a little too close to the stereo equipment, and I reined her back.

"April," she said, "unclench."

"Gross," June frowned. "And April can't help it. She's really stressed about . . . that thing."

May tilted her head to look at me. Two hundred Oprahs were also looking at me, too, making me feel like the most judged person alive. "Stressed about what?" May demanded. "Or is this gonna be a special little secret between you two? Do I just get to be metaphorically invisible this time?"

I took a deep breath. "It's nothing."

"Oh, it's *so* something." May smiled. "What is it? Twenty Questions? I'll go first. Is it a guy?"

"Yep!" June cried.

"June!"

"Good job, little sister," May said. "Okay, second question—"

"Um, excuse me," I interrupted her. "You can't play Twenty Questions with someone who's not playing." I began looking at TVs that looked like our old set, that one that was about to become an official Texan, but I realized that I couldn't quite remember what it looked like. For the briefest second, I wondered if it would ever be like that with *Dad*. Forgetting little things here and there about what it was like to live with him. . . . But I really couldn't think about that now, not when June could be listening.

"Fine." May sighed. "I was just trying to be all sisterly and understanding, but if you can't accept my love, I get it, Yogi Bear."

"Okay, fine, fine, fine!" I cried. "But you can't tell anyone, okay?"

May looked over to June. "You already know the big secret, don't you?"

June pretended to look confused. "I'm sorry, which one of your sisters is a mindreader? Tell me again?"

May kicked at her calf, and June scooted out of the way. "Child abuse," she said. "I'm telling Mom."

"Well, I guess you're not interested in what I have to say," I told them, going towards a set that looked vaguely familiar, but May pulled me back and kicked at June a few more times. "Spill," May said to me. "Or the mindreader gets it."

I sighed and looked at the ceiling. It looked so far away. "So today, I had this vision about me and Julian."

"Who's Julian?"

"Ssshh!" I hissed, looking around to make sure that no one was listening. "He's just Julian. He's the guy that has the locker above mine? You know . . . ?" How to describe someone I didn't even know?

June didn't seem to have that problem. "Tall greasemonkey," she said in what she probably thought was a helpful manner. "Lurks around school. You know, that guy."

May still looked confused. "Do I know him?"

"Do you know *anybody* at school?" I asked her.

"Well, no, but that's because I made a conscious decision to avoid people."

"Ugh, this is taking way too long," June said. "April got a vision of her and Julian doing the nasty. There, you're welcome."

I covered my face with my hands. "Thank you, June," I said into my palms. "Thank you for announcing that with the dignity and grace that it so deserved. In *Best Buy*."

"Okey-dokey, artichokey," she said.

May started to snicker, then giggle, then finally laugh uproariously. "That . . . is . . . mother—"

"Language," I snapped at her.

"—effing . . . hilarious!" she wheezed. "Oh my God, that is amazing! April, you win the award for Worst Heightened Sense ever."

I groaned and kept my face covered. "It's obviously not possible to die of embarrassment because if it were, I'd be dead."

May shoved my shoulder. "Oh, come on," she said. "At least you're not me. I mean, think about it. Some guy might one day kiss me and POOF!" She clapped her hands together. "Guess who disappears into thin air? Imagine what'll happen when I have sex with someone!"

"I'm trying not to," I said.

"I'm gonna be lying there, and the next thing you know, POOF!" She laughed again. "That's gonna be an interesting story for all involved."

"I'm jealous," June said. "I wish my superpower had a sound effect like May's."

"Stop calling them that," I told her. "They're not super."

"They're anti-super," May agreed.

"Well, you know what *else* is not super?" June said. "Being able to read a guy's mind when he's kissing you or doing . . . other things."

"Like the nasty?" I asked her. "To use your delicate terminology?"

"Well, *yeah*. What if he thinks I'm a bad kisser? What if . . . what if he thinks I'm fat?" June shuddered. "I hate him already, and I don't even know him."

May rolled her eyes and turned back to me. "So is your future boyfriend hot?"

"I don't know?" I replied. "Maybe? Kind of? In a certain light?"

"And by that, do you mean 'utter darkness'?"

"He's one of those guys that you don't think is hot until you find out that another girl likes him," June announced (with, I have to say, a startling amount of authority). "Then he's hot."

I looked at May. "He has dirt under his fingernails."

She thought for a second. "That's kinda hot. Was he a good kisser?"

"I don't know; I haven't even kissed him yet!"

"But in the vision?"

"It doesn't work like that," I said. "It's like watching two people in a movie kiss. I can't tell you if it's good, only what it looks like."

"Bummer." May whirled around on her heel. "June, do your stellar mindreading skills tell you that he'll be a good kisser?"

"Oh my God!" I cried before June could respond. "I don't knooooow! I know nothing other than the three of us are genetic freaks and at some point in the future—could be next week, could be fifteen years from now—I'm hooking up with Julian. That's all I know."

"You're on the honor roll," June said. "You know a lot more than just those two things."

"June, having you around is like having the Greek chorus from *Oedipus Rex* following me all the time."

She just shrugged. "I don't know what that means, but I'm pretty sure it's not a compliment."

"You got it."

A salesperson came wandering over to us, looking like they'd rather be shot than spend their evening selling electronics. But as they got closer, my sisters and I froze.

It was Avery, her black hair pinned back in a somewhat professional-looking manner.

"Do you need help with anything?" she asked us.

May, June, and I all froze. "Um," June started to say.

"Well—" I said, then cleared my throat. Avery just stared at us, like we hadn't almost mowed her down with our car the other day.

May, of course, answered for us. "Do we need help?" she repeated. "Oh, honey, where do I even begin?"

I nudged her hard in the arm. "Um, no, we're fine, we just . . . you go to our school, right?"

Avery nodded. "Um, yeah, I guess so. I think I've seen you."

"We drive to school," June added helpfully.

"Okay, yeah," she said. "That's cool. I think I've seen you hang out with Mariah before, right?"

June beamed like a star. "We're friends."

May muttered something I couldn't quite hear, but June shot her an angry look and then turned back to Avery. "Those are really nice khakis," she offered.

"Okay!" I said, stepping in. "I think we're gonna need a few minutes, but thanks."

"Cool," Avery said, then walked away from us.

"Is it just me," May asked as soon as she was out of earshot, "or is that girl on some sort of animal tranquilizer?"

"She thinks Mariah and I are friends!" June said gleefully. "She totally knows who Mariah is, oh my God this is so great!" She hopped up and down, making her hair bounce.

May just looked at June. "June, the girl's a moron! She doesn't even know we almost hit her with a car! She didn't even recognize us!"

"Maybe she was in shock," June offered. "Don't judge."

"I'm pretty sure that if someone almost hit me with a car," I said, "I'd remember what they looked like."

"So get this," May said, apropos of nothing while June wandered over to a television that looked almost right. "Guess what we're reading in my English class now?"

"A book," June said. "I win."

"Oh, not just any book," May told her. "Guess which one?"

I thought back to my sophomore-year reading list and started to laugh. "Oh, no!" I giggled. "Oh, that's terrible."

"Right?" May sighed. "Thank you."

"What book? What book?" June came back over and swatted at both of us. "Tell me, I want to—oh!" Her eyes lit up, and I could tell she was reading our minds simultaneously. "*Invisible Man*?" she gasped. "Are you serious?"

May just nodded her head. "I've read the first ten pages and none of it rings true. It's very poorly researched. The dude's clothes don't even disappear so he's both invisible and naked." May shuddered. "Seriously, I could write a remake."

"It's a good book," I told her.

May glanced up at me. "Don't Pollyanna your way through this one. I'm an invisible girl reading about an invisible man. There's no way to sugarcoat that."

She had a point.

"I have an ironic twist, too!" June announced to me. "So get this. Everybody at school today hated my skirt—"

"Shock me," I said.

"But Mariah liked it!"

I was shocked. (If you could see this skirt, you'd be shocked, too.) "Really?"

June nodded. "Really. No one else did, but *she* did."

"*Really*?" I wasn't trying very hard to keep the surprise out of my voice.

"Yeah," June gloated. "Bet you couldn't predict that."

"I don't think anyone could have." I glanced down at her skirt. "Seriously, no one could have seen this coming."

May wrinkled her nose and leaned against a stack of speaker boxes. "Is this even a good thing?"

"Oh my God, how have you two survived in the pirahna fishtank that is high school?" June looked so perplexed that it was almost cute. "She's the most popular sophomore girl. If you're friends with her, it's like having an E-Z pass to the golden gates of popularity."

"How long have you been dying to say that sentence?" I asked her.

"About a week."

"Mariah?" May asked. "Is she the blonde one?"

"No!" June said. "The dark-hair one with the cool highlights. *And* the one with the amazing fashion sense, obviously." She fluffed her pink skirt as though it were peacock feathers. "She likes my skirt, so I'm in."

"Mariah?" May said again. "Isn't she the one that always looks like she's trapped in someone's headlights?"

June either didn't get or ignored the headlights comment. "That's her!"

May let out a short laugh and leaned against a stack of boxes. I scanned furiously to see if they would topple on her, but nothing seemed perilous. "Dude, are you kidding?" May grinned. "I know that girl. She looks like a walking pharmacy. Every time she opens her mouth, I think an Adderall's going to come out. She's a Pez dispenser."

"She's not a walking pharmacy," June huffed. "You just heard some stupid rumor probably, and you're all jealous because she's not *your* friend."

"She's not yours, either."

"Not *yet*. But she's gonna be. Right, April?"

"Hey, sorry to interrupt this verbal tug-of-war," I told them, "but can we get back to the issue at hand?"

"To be honest," May said, "I'd rather not discuss your future sexual partners. I'm sure you understand." She put her hand up and pretended to high-five me. "Godspeed, big sister."

I ignored her. "You guys, we really need to talk. This is gonna get out of hand if we don't do something. We need a plan."

"A plan?" May asked. "How can you make a plan for this . . . this insanity?"

June just beamed. "You're in luck! I have a plan! I wrote it out in fifth period because we were watching a film about earthworms, ew."

"No wormy minds to read?" I asked her, but she just stuck her tongue out and rooted in her purse until she found a piece of scratch paper covered in pink ink.

"Our plan is written in pink ink," May grinned with what I've learned to recognize as false sincerity. "Great. What could possibly go wrong now?"

I took the paper from June and smoothed it out in my hands. "Let me see it," I said. "Maybe this will be the great thing that saves us from eternal damn—" I read the first item and stopped. "Oh, you've gotta be kidding me, June."

"What? What?" May tugged at my arm. "I can't read it; the pink ink is burning into my corneas. Tell me what it says."

"There're a lot of DVDs," I said after a minute. "And something about dressing up as witches for Halloween."

May looked down at June. "Are you for real?"

June pouted. "I'm filing you both under 'Lame.'"

"Put it on the list," I told her.

"We could go buy all those movies now!" June protested. "They're probably right over there!" She pointed towards the DVD section, where more khaki-wearing employees lurked.

"This 'plan' of yours," May told her, "is really an Amazon Wishlist."

This was getting way out of control. I already knew this conversation was going to end in an argument, though, so I just plowed ahead. "Okay," I said. "We need to use these things for good, not evil."

May and June just blinked at me.

"I'm serious," I said. "Like, today, during the earthquake? Right before it happened, I saw Julian almost getting hit by a falling light, so when it happened, I shoved him out of the way."

"Of *course* you did," May muttered. "He's your sexy man—you gotta preserve that so you can tap that."

"That's not the point!" I protested. "I just mean that we should maybe be on the lookout for bad things and maybe we can actually do some good."

May was the first to start laughing. "Okay," she giggled. "Sure, April. What sort of evil, do you think? Godzilla? King Kong? The Joker? What? I'm curious."

"I mean the kind of evil where you read people's minds to become their friend." I looked at June this time, raising my eyebrow at her.

"You saw that?" she squeaked.

I nodded. I had seen a few more things, but I wasn't ready to get into it with her. The day had already been long enough.

"You can't tell me what to do!" June said. "And besides, it *worked*! You heard what Avery said!"

"I don't even think Avery heard what she said," May told her. "But yeah, April. Who made you the leader? Just 'cause you can see the future doesn't mean you get to tell us how to act. You're not Mom."

"I'm not telling you what to do. I'm just—"

"Telling us what to do," June interrupted. "And I'm not gonna be sorry if I'm using my special talents to make friends."

I snorted. I couldn't help it. "So you think *Mariah* needs a good friend? Someone like you?"

"Exactly! I'm honest, I'm—"

"—trying to be her friend by reading her mind," I finished.

"Well . . . yeah, but I'm not *lying*."

"You're wearing clothes you don't even like, just to curry favor with her."

"But I'm not *lying*."

"You're lying to *yourself*. That's almost worse."

May looked miffed. "Well, thanks, April, for wanting to send your sisters out into the dangerous world so we can fix it," she huffed. "God, high school's evil enough without looking for more of it."

"That's what I'm saying!" I cried. "Let's not add to it, okay? Don't start using these things all over the place and don't use them to do bad things! That's, like, Superhero 101!"

There was a pause before June said, "So I guess you don't want to know that I read Mom's mind and found out she has a date on Thursday night."

"WHAT?" I cried before I could stop myself. Next to June, May's eyes got wide, and her mouth opened. And she was gone an instant later.

"Oh, great," June said. "This is gonna be fricking annoying as heck. And I know you can hear me, May! You're lucky we're the only customers back here."

I covered my face with my hands. "This should not be happening. Mom has a *date*."

June nodded. "Yep. Unless her brain is lying."

"—only been four months!" May arrived back in mid-shriek, but I didn't bother to look at her.

"Welcome to our program, already in progress," June told her. "Nice of you to stop by."

"Like this was my idea to suddenly become a crazy freakazoid!" May shot back. "And you must be reading her brain wrong or something because . . ."

June just looked at her. "Because *what*? Because you don't like it? So you're saying I'm doing it wrong?"

"*We* don't like it," May clarified. "Well, all I can say is that I'm glad I'm the one who can disappear because I don't wanna be around to see whoever this guy is."

"June, you can't read Mom's mind!" I told her. "I just told you, we can't use these things for evil!"

"Would you stop referring to me like I'm some crazy psychopath?" June cried. "I can't help it. It's not like I'm a mindreading expert! This didn't exactly come with a user's guide!"

"Well, so far our plan blows," May said. "I blame the pink ink."

Avery circled back to us again, this time looking even more apprehensive. "Soooo . . ." he said, eyeing May warily, "did you have any questions?"

"Nope," June interrupted him, then pointed at a television. *Our* television. "We'll take that one."

"How did you know which one it was?" I asked as we went to the cash register, May leading the way.

June looked at me. "*Duh*," she said. "I saw it in your mind."

Oh. How about that.

chapter 8

"Even when you can disappear, the hurt doesn't go away."

may

After the longest trip ever to an electronics store, I got wedged into the backseat with our brand-new TV. I tried to argue, but June just said, "I called shotgun first!" And if you have a sibling, then you know that's an ironclad rule. The box dug into my shoulder, and I glared at April when she glanced at me in the rearview mirror.

"Oh, come on, May," she said. "Turn that frown upside down."

"You can put your pithy statements where the sun don't shine."

That shut her up.

By the time we got home, our mom's car was in the driveway. "Good news!" June cried as she and April climbed out of the front seat and I stayed in the back, struggling with my seatbelt and a TV that was the same size of New Hampshire. "We got a TV! It's just like our other one! It's like an evil twin!"

"Great!" my mom said as she came out of the garage. "Well done!"

"Little help," I muttered. "I'm being consumed by an electronic device."

My mom came around to my side of the car to help me. "Hi," she grinned. "Did you have fun?"

"Oh, absolutely," I said as she helped me out of the car. "Maybe next time we can go shopping for pirahnas. I hear that's even more fun."

"Haha you," she said, pulling at my arm. I stumbled onto the driveway, then glared at the TV. Really, though, I wanted to glare at my mom. A date? I mean, seriously? She's not sixteen! Aren't adults supposed to be, like, over dating by the time they're thirty?

June cleared her throat and muttered something about me being an ageist.

"Can I go upstairs, please?" I asked my mom. "I have a headache and kind of want to die."

I thought she'd say no, that I had to help carry in the TV, but instead she just leaned forward and kissed my forehead. "Sure," she said. "Go call your dad. He called to talk to you while you were out."

April suddenly looked up, stricken. "What?" I said as I walked past her, but she just bit her lip and shook her head, like her not saying anything made it *better* for some reason. "Fine, be like that," I told her, then went upstairs into the office so I could use the phone.

The funny thing is that I have a cell phone. I guess that's not the funny part of that story. The funny part is that no one ever calls it, not like they used to when we were back in our old house. Now it just sort of sits there in my bag or my pocket, which is a real bummer because I like my ringtone.

I'm not trying to get a bunch of sympathy or anything, but having a cell phone that no one calls is pretty depressing. It's a high-tech reminder that I have zero friends.

I wondered why my dad hadn't called it, though, why he called our home number instead. We text every so often, so it's not like he didn't have the number. (The only thing worse than not having anyone to text with is only texting with your parents.)

"Yo," I said when he picked up on the second ring. "It's your favorite kid calling."

"Hi, June!" he said, and I smiled even though the joke was about a million years old between us. Sometimes the oldest jokes are the best, though.

"Try again," I said.

"April!"

I had to laugh this time. "Strike two."

"Ah, a sports metaphor. It must be May."

I giggled a little (don't tell anyone) and sank down into the big chair at the desk where my mom does all her paperwork. "Good guess," I said. "You're lucky there's not four of us."

"Well, after three you lose count, anyway. There could be eight of you for all I know." My dad laughed and suddenly he was so close that I could practically smell his cologne.

"Hi, Dad," I said, wrapping the phone cord around my fingers. "Are you done being ridiculous now?"

"Maybe. We'll see how it goes. How are you, kiddo? How's school?"

"About as awesome as you can imagine high school being."

"That bad?"

"Why do parents always think that school's so great?" I asked him. "Or that something amazing happens every day?"

"Because we enjoy reminsicing about our misspent youth," my dad said.

"Whatever."

"You got me. It's a stupid parent question that we're required to ask." My dad cleared his throat then. That's never a good sign. "Hey, kiddo. I gotta talk to you for a sec."

"One second?" I said, even as my heartbeat quickened a bit. "Or do you want to go a full minute? I can do either."

"Seriously, kiddo."

"Okay, adulto."

"Look, Mayday, you know there's nothing I want more than for you to come out here."

I froze, the phone cord suddenly too tight around my hand. "But?" I said, and I didn't like how strained my voice sounded, like the phone cord was wrapped around my throat instead. "There's a 'but' coming, isn't there?"

My dad took a deep breath. "But unfortunately with this new job, I have to—"

"I can come on the weekend," I said. "That's okay. I can leave Friday after school and go home on Sunday."

"No, honey, it's the weekends. I need to travel for most of next month. And the condo, it's not set up. It's—"

"I don't care," I said. I hated the way my voice sounded, all weak and eager like the smart girls who play dumb. "I can sleep on the couch. It's cool, it's fine."

"Honey." My dad took a deep breath. "I'm so sorry, but I'm new at this job, and I need to pay some dues. They've got me traveling twenty-six out of the next thirty days. There's nothing more I'd rather do than have you come out here, you know that—"

"I'm not the one who knows those things," I said, even though he'd never understand what I was talking about.

"What?"

"What what?"

My dad sighed again. "November, okay? We can do it in November. You can even come out over Thanksgiving, and we can go to Austin."

I was biting my tongue so hard that I could feel my jaw start to ache. "Sure," I said. "Just like how in August, you said I could come out in October."

"Sweetie, it's not—"

"That's cool," I said. "Whatever. It's fine. I mean, I totally understand why you would need our television sent to you if you're going to be traveling all the live-long day, but why it's a bad idea for your kid to visit for three days. That's so logical."

There was silence then, and now my eyes burned with saltwater. I blinked hard, just like I had seen June do before. "So," I said. "Anything else?"

"May, sweetie, please understand—"

"Okay, cool," I said. "I'll talk to you later."

He started to say something, but I hung up before I could hear his voice anymore. Only it wasn't because I didn't want to hear his voice; it was because I didn't want to cry. I never cry. It's like the stupidest thing a girl can do, but sometimes holding it back takes more effort than I have.

I could hear April and June and my mom downstairs laughing about something and unloading the television. That damn television. My mom probably already knew that my dad had called to cancel (maybe they even argued about it), and now I knew why April had given me that look when I had come inside. The future predictor missed the earthquake and saw this instead. June was probably even in on it, considering that she could read April's mind as easily as one of her stupid gossip rags.

Once again, the invisible girl was the last to know.

When I finally got myself under control, I went into my room and lay down on the bed. I was so tired all of a sudden, tired of change and new things and old things and everythings, and I stared at the window as the sun set from yellow to pink to purple, just like a bruise in reverse.

When it was almost dark, April knocked on my door. "Hey," she said quietly. "It's me." When I didn't respond, she just came in, which totally defeats the purpose of even having a bedroom door. "Hi," she said. "Are you in here?"

I looked down at my hand and realized that I had disappeared. I wondered how long I had been gone. "Here," I said, snapping my body back into my skin. It's like putting on tight pants for a second, like I have to reshape my body to fit itself.

"The door's shut for a reason," I said, but I didn't even care that much. April knew that because she came in and lay down on the bed next to me, stretching out so that we were toe to toe. She's older, but I'm taller.

"I'm sorry about Dad being a lameass," she said after a few minutes. "That sucks."

"It's Texas," I replied. "It's not going anywhere. Haven't you seen those bumper stickers, 'Don't Mess with Texas'? I'm pretty sure they're serious."

"May." April reached down and covered my hand with hers. "It's okay to be disappointed."

Sometimes she sounds so much like my mom that it trips me out. "Whatever," I said, but then it was too hard to talk and I just gave up. I even tried disappearing again, but April just stayed there next to me, which was sort of nice because it turns out that even when you can disappear, the hurt doesn't go away.

chapter 9

"I'd take excitement over easy any day."

june

April tried to talk to me the next morning. I say "tried" because I met her in the kitchen and cut her off before she could say one word.

I had practiced this speech in the mirror for ten minutes that morning. I was ready.

"Look," I said. "I do not appreciate you telling me what to do or insinuating that I'm somehow doing evil because there is true evil in this world and I am not a part of it."

(I was particularly proud of that line, I have to admit.)

"And," I continued, "I just want to remind you that I am, in fact, a mind*reader*, and I know what you're thinking. So don't—"

"Wanna bagel?" April interrupted me. "Mom brought some home before she went to her early morning meeting today." She gestured towards the brown paper bag that was sitting on the counter. "Chow down."

"Do you know how many empty calories are in a bagel?" I told her. My stupid bangs were in my eyes again, and I shoved them behind my ears. I'm trying to grow them out, and it's making me insane.

"No, but I know how many *delicious* calories there are." April took a huge bite of her bagel (which, okay, looked pretty good) and raised an eyebrow. "Mmm, bagel-y goodness."

"Stop distracting me!" I said. "Like I was saying, I'm a mind-reader, in case you've had some sort of brain—"

Great big globs of greasy grimy gopher guts . . .

"Stop it!" I said. "I hate that song and you know it! Besides, you shouldn't be promoting violence to your little sister, anyway! It's wrong!"

April shrugged and turned away. "Take what you can get," she said.

"You're a terrible role model!" I yelled as she walked towards the garage door, car keys in hand.

"That's nice. You want a ride to school?"

"I'll walk, thanks," I glared at her.

April looked down at my knee-high stacked boots, which were no more comfortable than the ballet slippers from the day before. "You're gonna walk in those?"

"Excuse me, but supermodels walk down slippery runways all the time in six-inch stilettos. I'm pretty sure I'll survive the experience." I shook my hair out over my shoulder, trying to get in the habit of looking like Mariah, who had probably never once had to grow out her bangs. She probably just *willed* her hair to look fabulous.

"Do you have a twitch or something?" May asked me as she came downstairs, looking 500 percent more miserable than she's looked before. I hadn't thought that was even possible. Her dirty blonde hair had no body or volume whatsoever, and her skin looked really pale in that "Maybe you should read this pamphlet about anemia" way. If it wasn't so expensive, I would've totally offered to let her use my tinted moisturizer.

But all I said was, "What twitch?"

"Your twitch. You keep doing that thing with your hair."

"I'm tossing my hair," I told her.

May just groaned. "Tossing is for salad, not hair."

April jangled her car keys again. "Okay, last time. Does anyone else want a ride to school?"

"Why are you going so early anyway?" May asked her, digging in the bag of bagels. She frowned a little, then peeked in the bag. "Oh, *gross*, who put the onion bagel in here? If there's *one* onion bagel, then they're *all* onion bagels."

April was distracted long enough to drop her guard, and I flew into her brain like a bee. An angry bee. An angry bee with a grudge.

"Ohhhh," I grinned after a few seconds. "I know why April wants to go to school so early."

"Shut up, June."

May glanced from me to her, then back. "Why?"

"Because she wants to get there early so she doesn't have to see Jooooooolian." I giggled at her and then scooted away before she could shove me.

May sank her teeth into the bagel and ripped off a huge chunk. "Cwazy," she said through a mouthful of bread. "I thot we were in wuv wiff him."

"We are not in love with him," April said hotly. "I am going to school in a car, and you're both welcome to join me. Although I'm starting to question that last part."

"If your brain could blush right now, it would," I told her. "You're so translucent it's asinine."

May swallowed. "Where are you getting these words?" she asked me. "Seriously, last week it was 'shut up' and 'nuh-uh,' and now you're all polysyllabic and shit."

I just shrugged. No point in telling her that I had ended up seated next to this kid in my bio class who was trying to get to the National Spelling Bee Championship. Michael knew thousands of words and their definitions and kept chanting them over and over in his head. At the rate he was going, I was probably gonna end up at the spelling bee championship, too.

I just continued to glare at April, who was glaring right back. "I guess we all have our secrets," I said.

"Guess so," April shot back.

Great big globs of greasy . . .

I gave her one last dirty look before going to get my iPod and my bag. It was too small to hold all my books, which meant that I had to carry a couple of extra texts. "You know," May said as she watched me gather them up, "they make these things called backpacks now. You should check them out."

"And look like Miss Dork over here?" I said, nodding towards April. "No, thanks. I'd rather stagger."

"Of *course* you would," April laughed. "May, you wanna ride?"

May's thoughts flitted towards me. *Probably should walk with June, but . . .*

"I'm fourteen, not four!" I snapped. "You don't have to watch out for me!"

"Stop reading my brain," May replied calmly. "There are terrible things lurking in there. Some people don't make it out alive."

"You are *so* weird."

"Thanks."

April cleared her throat. "The bus? Is leaving."

"Bye," I said pointedly.

"*Vaya con Dios*," May told me, then grabbed her bag. "Shotgun!"

April shrugged. "Suit yourself, June. Have fun limping to school."

I hate when she's right.

A painful twenty minutes later, I hobbled into my first-period bio class with all the grace of a wounded moose. *Supermodels do this all the time*, I thought to myself as I eased into a chair. *You gotta smile through the pain. Make it work.*

If there was one thing I could do, it was make it work. I hadn't suffered through two lame sisters for nothing, after all.

The whole class was boring, even for someone with special gifts like myself. Reading the teachers' minds was starting to get repetitive, especially when all they thought about was mundane things like grocery shopping or picking their own kids up from school or how to bisect two parallel lines. Sometimes people's thoughts feel like a dusty room, especially at eight o'clock in the morning, and I yawned and sat back in my chair, writing down the notes a minute ahead of the lecture and probably violating every one of April's stupid "do no harm" rules. Whatever.

That's right. For once in my life, school was easy. Big fat hairy deal, though. I'd take excitement over easy any day.

By the fifteen-minute snack break, I was ready for the day to be over. Maybe May would take me off-campus with her, or at least forge a note saying I went home with a stomachache or something. I could always read her mind and get some blackmail material. It would be—

—outta here.

I turned around, nearly hitting some sophomore in the face with my hair. "Oops, sorry," I said to her, then realized that it was the girl that had almost been impaled on the hood of our minivan. The one with the black hair that could seriously use some deep conditioning. She looked sort of shocked that I was even talking to her, but I guess I couldn't blame her. "Uh, that whole thing was my sister's fault," I said quickly, but then I saw Mariah disappear out the door and I ran to catch up.

I hurried down the hall and around the corner to where she and Jessica and Daphne were standing outside under a eucalyptus tree, passing a bottle of water among the three of them. Jessica's hair was in such a high ponytail that it looked painful, and Daphne had overplucked her eyebrows, which made her seem like she was in a constant state of surprise.

It was an unfortunate look for both of them, I'll just say that.

I was trying to decide if I should go up to them or not when I got Mariah's thoughts again. *Hey, it's Calendar Girl.*

She recognized me.

Game on.

"Hey," I said, walking over to them and not even looking at Jessica and Daphne. Their thoughts were already in my brain and, to be honest, they didn't warrant repeating. "What's up?"

"Nothing," Mariah replied. "How's your calendar sister?" She looked at Jessica and Daphne. "Her sisters are named April and May. How lame is that?"

I let that comment slide, only because it *was* pretty lame. My parents had a lot to answer for, as far as I was concerned.

"Who are you? March?" Jessica asked. It was a pretty lame joke, considering she already knew my name. But then again, she always had a nasal sound to her voice that made everything she said sound snide. Even her thoughts had the same tone, which was annoying as all heck.

"No," I said, then stood up a bit taller. "I'm June." I looked at her coolly, the way May looks at people when she wants to scare them. "I'm sorry, remind me who you are again?"

Daphne snorted a laugh and Jessica flushed a bit before recovering. She tugged on the cap sleeve of her T-shirt, the one that Alexander McQueen designed for Target. I recognized it because I had the same one. "I'm Mariah's friend," she said to me, then added in her thoughts, *Even if she is a total bitch*.

I had to laugh. "*Sure* you're her friend. If you say so." Then I turned back to Mariah before Jessica could say—or think—anything else. "So what are you up to?"

Mariah gestured over her shoulder down the hill, where roads and cars and freedom exists. "We were just talking about maybe leaving early. You know, taking a personal day?"

I had managed to tune Daphne and Jessica's anger down low enough so that they sounded like snippy little bees in my ear. No actual words, but plenty of emotion. (I had fine-tuned this skill the past three nights in a row with the homeless guy down the street from our house. I had to do *something* if I was ever gonna get any sleep), but Daphne broke through first. "We were talking about it," Daphne interrupted. "*We* were. The *three* of us."

"Four's a crowd," Jessica added.

"Actually, it's *three's* a crowd," I corrected her. "Besides . . . Jessica, right? I thought you hated Mariah."

Jessica's eyes widened, and Mariah looked at her. "*What*?"

I shrugged. "Just something I heard. I don't know, maybe it's not true. Rumors can be so nasty, I know." I tried to look sympathetic. "Lies can do terrible things."

Oh my God, I had never had this kind of power in my life! I totally understood why superheroes sometimes turned evil and got the crazy eyes. Jessica and Daphne's minds were already going haywire, and I couldn't sort out their thoughts quickly enough to figure out who hated me more.

But like I said, I'd take excitement over easy any day.

"So you're ditching?" I asked Mariah as the two other girls shifted their shoulder bags uncomfortably. "Cool."

"Yeah, guess so." She looked down at my boots, and I swear to God, I would have walked fifty more miles in those boots if it meant that she would notice them. "You wanna come?"

"Yeah, sure," I said. *Play it cool, June*, I told myself. *You are not a puppy in a pet store. Don't look eager.* "I guess so."

Mariah grinned. "Cool."

My heart swelled when she said that, almost like it was pushing against my ribs. This was it—this was the start of my new life without my parents or crazy sisters trying to tell me what to do. It was freedom like I had never had before, and I already wanted more.

"Wait, she's coming with us?" Daphne glared at me. "Who the hell is *she*? She's just some stupid freshman."

I have to tell you, after reading Daphne's mind for the past three minutes, that was the nicest thing she had said about me yet. And besides, she and Jessica were only sophomores, the same as Mariah. They weren't even a full year older than me. Puh-lease.

"Whatever," I shrugged, then turned to my brand new friend. "But Mariah? You should know that Daphne told everyone that you stuffed your bra last year."

Bull's-eye.

All three girls looked like they had swallowed a bird or something, their eyes were so big. Mariah was the first to recover. "You did *what*?" she snapped at Daphne.

Daphne held up her hands just like people do when they're being robbed at gunpoint. "I didn't say anything!" she cried. "I swear, ask Jessica!"

Jessica looked like she wanted to throw up, and she started to squeeze her empty water bottle so it made this really loud cracking sound, like bones crunching. Not a pleasant soundtrack to the conversation.

"Well, how would I have known, then?" I asked innocently. "I'm new here. All I know is what I hear."

Mariah glared at both of her now ex-friends. If there's one thing I've learned from being a fourteen-year-old girl, it's that entire social structures can be dismantled and rebuilt in less than thirty seconds. It's kind of like playing Jenga every single day, only with people's lives instead of wooden pegs.

"You two can *go to hell*," Mariah said to them. She looked taller and stronger now, and I felt a bit of a rolling sensation, like I had gotten on a roller coaster that I hadn't meant to ride. Her brain kind of sounded like the inside of May's when she was mad, all swear words and swirling anger wrapped up in shrillness.

I made a note to never piss Mariah off . . . and to not read her mind if I ever did.

"So are we still ditching?" I asked, eager to get off campus so that Jessica and Daphne didn't decide to stab me with their ballpoint pens in the middle of fourth period. I would have to figure out a way to ask April if she saw me bleeding on the floor at all in the near future, and I was gonna have to figure out how to ask that question delicately. "I think the bell's gonna ring soon," I continued. "We should probably go."

Mariah didn't take her eyes off Daphne. "Yeah," she said tightly. "We're going."

"June!" A voice rang out, and I didn't even have to turn around to know that it was April.

"Oh, great," I muttered, then turned around and glared at my sister. She was stalking towards me angrily, her backpack slung over one shoulder and her shapeless cardigan flapping around her like wings.

"It's my sister," I told Mariah. "Give me a minute, I'll be right back."

The minute I was close enough, April grabbed me by the elbow and dragged me away from the three girls. "Excuse me for a minute," she muttered through clenched teeth. "I need to borrow my little, *innocent* sister here."

"What are you doing?" I hissed as soon as I was away from everyone. "What is your problem?"

"Those are both excellent questions!" April said, dropping my arm and putting her hands on her hips. "In fact, they're so excellent that I was going to ask you the exact same ones."

"Well, I asked you first!"

"*June*. Don't even."

"What?" I said. "I didn't do anything wrong!"

"You totally turned those girls against each other! I saw you do it!"

"You were spying on me?"

"Look," April huffed. "This is not my ideal situation, either, okay? But it is what it is and you cannot—you absolutely *cannot*—play with people's lives this way! We talked about this!"

"But they *did* say those things—!" I started to protest.

"No, they didn't!" April said. "You heard them *think* those things! There's a huge difference! You're lying to get what you want, and that is so wrong that there isn't enough time in the day to tell you how wrong that is!"

"No, I told the *truth*," I countered. "I said that I heard it from somewhere. I can't help it if I heard it from Jessica's and Daphne's minds! And Mariah shouldn't be friends with girls like that!"

"And by the way," April continued like I hadn't said anything, "you are definitely not ditching with Mariah."

"What are you, my second mother? I wasn't even going to!"

April rapped herself in the head. "June? Don't lie to me, too."

It was all so unfair that I felt like I could explode. "Oh, whatever," I shot back. "You with your creepy visions that you won't tell me about! Well, I know *lots* of things, too, more than you do! I also know that May ditches all the time, and you never tried to stop *her* before! It's not my fault you have to be the goody-goody sister! If I wanna be friends with Mariah, if I wanna ditch with Mariah, I'm going to, and you can't stop me."

April narrowed her blue eyes. "Try me."

I took a step closer to my oldest sister. "Try me back," I said quietly, "and I'll tell Mom that you're gonna sleep with that guy."

That did it. April blinked twice, and she looked at me. "You would, too."

"Maybe." The roller coaster I had gotten on was still ascending towards the sky, making me feel a bit nauseated, but there was no going back now.

"Look, Junie," April said. "I'm telling you, please do not ditch with Mariah. Please."

"Tell me why."

"I-I just don't think it's a good idea."

"You know what, April? That's my job now. I'm the one who hears the ideas, not you."

And I turned in my beautiful boots and went back to Mariah. Jessica and Daphne had slunk off to wherever ex-communicated friends go (probably into the library like all the other losers), and I shook my hair and smiled at her. "Sorry," I said. "My sister gets all weird sometimes."

"So does my brother," Mariah agreed. "So you're up for it."

I could feel April glaring into me, thinking, *Don't do it, don't do it, don't do it.*

"Of course I am," I said. "Let's go."

Junie, don't do it, don't—

I tuned her out. "C'mon," I said to Mariah. "Let's get out of here."

chapter 10

"I should be wearing yellow CAUTION tape, I'm that bonkers."

april

The night after June ditched school, I slept terribly. I couldn't even tell if I was seeing the future of a bunch of strangers or just dreaming. The red light kept returning again and again, flashing quietly in the back of my brain, and I hoped that it wasn't a brain tumor. I wasn't sure if I could go to a doctor and explain the problem without being sent off to the loony bin. "Hi, doctor, yes, I've been seeing the future and for some reason I have an imminent sense of dread following me around everywhere, and it's not just because I'm sixteen years old and worried about college applications. Should I just take some Tylenol?"

Yeah. No.

Sometimes I wondered if June went through the same thing, lying in bed and listening to a million voices all around her. Sometimes I wished I was the mindreader so I could know what the hell my sisters and everyone else were thinking all the time so I wouldn't have to guess at it.

I guess I had power envy.

I was even more annoyed because I had been so busy worrying about my sisters that I was too distracted to write my paper for English. We're reading *The Myth of the Cave,* the thing that Plato wrote, and I had read it the night before, but couldn't remember a thing about it other than there were some shadows and people were chained together.

Here's the thing: I know I'm supposed to be the smart one. And it's true, I like school and all that, but sometimes I wish I could just fail. I wish I could stand up and scream, "Why are we even reading this? Why does Plato *always* use metaphors? Why can't *anyone* just say what they mean?!"

I realize I might be letting my personal issues crowd the situation, but still. June has it so lucky sometimes. No one expects her to be brilliant, and of course what can she do? Read minds and be brilliant. The irony just kills me.

(Of course, I already knew that I was gonna get a 94 percent on the paper that I had yet to write, but that was beside the point.)

My mom was already up and having her tea by the kitchen window when I tiptoed downstairs early that morning. She always gets up way before the three of us—she says it's her "me time"—but that only started after my dad moved out. I guess she had a lot more time after he left, and she had to organize it somehow. Otherwise the day just gets too long.

When I saw her, I did what I had done every day since I first started seeing the future: I looked through my mom's day, waiting for something terrible to pop up. I searched for aneurysms, strokes, sharp objects, fired employees who came back to the office for one last shot at revenge. I looked for anything I could find and once again, came up with nothing.

I do that every day with my sisters, too. I know I can't see everything that happens, but damn it, I'm trying. The only thing I don't know is what will happen when I *do* see something terrible. I'm trying not to imagine it.

But my mom's day was mundane, the same as all the other days. Work, grocery store, bills, and when she saw me and smiled, I smiled back, relieved to have something to smile about.

"Hi," she said. "You're up early. Want some tea?"

"Is it caffeinated?"

"Nope. It's herbal and all-natural and good for you."

"Pass. It tastes like goldfish food."

"I thought so." She sipped again before setting the cup down. "April? Can I talk to you about something?"

Shit. Why did this not come up when I scanned for potential problems? I was in no mood to have this conversation, the are-you-girls okay discussion. I had already had it a few times with my mom and once with my dad on the phone. He had cleared his throat a lot, and I remember wishing I knew what he was going to say because it was so awkward to wait through the pauses.

Be careful what you wish for. That's what I would advise.

"I'm fine, Mom," I told her as I started to peel an orange. "I swear. Me and May and June, we're all fine."

"No, I know," she said. "You girls, you're wonderful. It's just that . . . I've been noticing that May seems to be disappearing more and more often."

I dropped the orange as I whirled around in surprise. "What?" I said in a voice barely above a whisper. "You noticed *what*?"

Well, that settles it. I'm the crappiest future-predictor the world has even known. I bet that psychic cat on the Third Street Promenade has more success than I do.

"I just mean," my mom continued, looking as calm as I didn't feel, "she seems to be spending a lot more time in her room lately."

Oh.

"Oh," I said. "Um, yeah, I don't know. You know May. She's just weird sometimes. She likes her space."

"No, she always has," my mom agreed. "And I understand. It's just . . . I know she's really disappointed about having to delay her trip to Houston to see your dad."

"Yeah, she is."

"Do you think everything's okay with her, though? Besides that? I know she's been having a rough time adjusting to your dad and I being apart."

I knew my mom was thinking about the tequila incident, when May got smashed and created a chain of events that led to us moving here. But was she *okay*? How in the world was I supposed to answer this one? *None of us are okay*, I wanted to tell my mom. *Not in the slightest*.

But instead I just said, "I'm sure she's fine, Mom. June and I would know." If that wasn't the truth, I don't know what was. "She's not a big social butterfly. She's not even a social *caterpillar*."

My mom laughed and then wrapped one arm around my waist and gave me a hug. "Well, okay," she said. " I know it's unfair to say that you're the oldest, but . . . you're the oldest. Keep an eye on your sisters, all right?"

"Mom, believe me," I told her, hugging her back before pulling away. "I'm watching them all the time."

* * *

I managed to finish my Plato paper during fourth period, since I knew the teacher would be too busy talking about the quadratic equation to notice me, and at lunchtime, I ran to the computer lab to print it out as soon as lunch started. It wasn't my best work, that was for sure, but it would have to do.

The halls were pretty empty as I walked towards my locker, since most everyone else had gone to lunch. I wondered if I'd be doing that with my old friends at my old school, leaving campus and eating french fries or fried rice or sandwiches. I hadn't really talked to anyone since we moved away. I couldn't even imagine the conversation. "Yeah, my summer was awesome. By the way, I have crazy brain capabilities now. And you?"

There were only two people in the hall as I approached my locker, some girl and a guy. Great. Instead of one fleeting moment of peace and quiet, I get to witness nasty hallway making out. Only as I got closer, I realized that it wasn't just any girl. It was Avery, the black-haired girl that May had almost hit with the car. "Great," I muttered to myself, pulling my hair in front of my face so that she wouldn't see me. I kept wondering if I should apologize to her or something, but what could I say? *Sorry my invisible sister almost hit you with the car?*

But it didn't look like Avery had any interest in me at all. She was pinned up against the wall by some guy who was breathing on her neck. I'm no hall monitor, but it didn't look comfortable. She was smiling, though, so maybe it was? I don't know; I had bigger problems to deal with than Avery's ability to find quality guys.

I was just coming around the corner when I saw something just behind my eyes, a flash of brown liquid flying up towards the ceiling, a gasp and a shout before it was gone again.

"What the hell was—?" I started to mutter to myself, but just then I turned the corner and slammed into someone much bigger than I was. That someone was carrying coffee and as we ran into each other, it flew out of his hand and the coffee went up in a smooth arc, almost like it was in slow motion.

I screamed and hugged my paper to my chest.

The person gasped and swore.

Oh. Got it now. Sometimes the visions don't make sense until they actually happen, which is an unfortunate side effect.

"Oh my gosh, I am so sorry!" I cried, realizing the coffee has spewed everywhere *except* on my backpack, thank God. (I had library books in there and I *hate* paying fines.) "Are you okay?" I asked. "Was it hot? Did you burn yourself?" I flipped through my brain like it was a deck of cards, looking for emergency rooms, burn units, skin grafts.

"Wow, you're high-strung," the person said, adjusting his filthy-looking baseball cap, and I looked up and realized that it was Julian.

Oh, thanks, Brain, I thought bitterly. *Thank you* so *much.*

Julian just stood there, wiping coffee off his jacket sleeve. I could barely see his face, his hat was pulled down so low, but when I finally made eye contact, I could tell he was not thrilled. His eyes snapped from me to the coffee puddle on the ground, then back to me, and I watched as he used his free hand to tuck his hair behind his ears. It looked sort of soft and straight, like maybe he had just washed it. I wondered what kind of shampoo he used, what it smelled—

Focus, April.

"I'm totally sorry!" I said again. "I really am!"

"Would you relax? It wasn't even hot. It was just cafeteria coffee." Julian wiped his black sweatshirt and then shook the coffee drops off his hand. "What are you, ADD or something? You seem like you're about to go off the rails."

I could only stand there in shock, opening and closing my mouth.

I had never heard this guy do anything more than grunt, and now he was talking to me? Granted, it's not like he was saying sweet nothings or anything, but still.

"No, I'm not, as a matter of fact," I finally said when I got my voice back. "I'm not ADD; I'm just a considerate person. Unlike *some* people who still use Styrofoam cups."

Whoa. Bitch Snark April was here and ready to play.

He just waited a few seconds before making a "whatever" noise and walking away, leaving the cup on the gray tiled floor where it rolled around in a coffee puddle. "Yeah, okay, never mind," he said. "See you."

Wait a minute. He *littered*?

I didn't care what my brain had told me: There was no way in hell that I would *ever* sleep with a litterbug.

No. Way. In. Hell.

"Hey!" I yelled after him. "You going to pick that up, you freaking litterbug?"

"Freaking," he repeated with a grin. "Wow. You're a rebel."

"Yeah, just like *you*," I shot back. "Leaving trash on the floor in a high school. Oooh, way to be an individual." I motioned to the A on his hat, that overused symbol for anarchy. "What, first you throw trash around and then you take over the government? Sounds like a fantastic plan." I waggled my fingers at him, which, yeah, looked about as stupid as it sounds, but it was too late to undo it.

Julian started to say something, but I was on a roll and it was too late to stop me. "And you know what else?" I said. "You need to get out of my way when I'm at my locker because you're always crowding me with your stupid *everything*! All the time! You're always around! Just leave me alone, okay? God, you and Plato and everyone else are so freaking—yeah, I said 'freaking,' by the way, get over it—*annoying*!"

Julian's eyes grew wider as he stared at me while I ranted, and pretty soon I realized that my pulse was racing and I was breathing hard. "What?" I said, glaring back at him. "Do you want an encore?"

Julian was silent for a minute and then he said, "*Myth of the Cave*, right?"

"What?"

"The Plato thing."

My heart was still moving the angry blood through my veins. "Yeah, what about it?" I said. "It's ridiculous."

Julian nodded. "You're a junior."

"Yeah."

"Yeah. I read that last year." He rubbed his hand over his hat. "This is my brother's hat, by the way."

"Oh." I wasn't sure what to say to that. "So you're not an anarchist?"

"I'm not that motivated." He smirked, and I noticed he had kind of an adorable smirk, if smirks can be considered adorable. "But I did steal it from my brother when I went to visit him last year."

"Oh." I sighed and motioned to the floor. "Are you gonna pick that up or do I have to do it?"

Julian glanced down at it, then back at me. "You got some issues, you know that?"

"As a matter of fact, Julian," I said. "I *do* know that, but thank you for noticing."

"You know my name?"

I froze halfway to picking up the cup. *Think fast, think fast, think fast.*

"I, uh, I heard your friend call you—"

"I don't have any friends."

Damnit.

"Look," I said, hurling the cup into the trash as I turned around, "you honestly want to know why I know your name? I'll tell you why! It's because I'm psychic! So there!"

The air froze between us as the words fell out of my mouth. I had never said the word "psychic" out loud before, not even to May and June. I stood still and waited for Julian's reaction. I waited for the straitjackets, the news cameras, whatever was about to happen. I hoped I wouldn't cry.

But I saw nothing coming for me, and then Julian just laughed. "Wow," he said, "you're crazier than I am."

He didn't believe me. He thought I was joking. I had a sudden flash of him sitting at his desk in math two periods later and chuckling to himself, remembering our conversation.

Apparently he had never heard that whole thing about how there's truth in humor.

"Yeah, well," I said. "You have no *idea* how crazy I am. I should be wearing yellow CAUTION tape, I'm that bonkers."

He laughed again. He had a really deep, hearty laugh. "So what's *your* name?"

"April."

Julian nodded. "Well, I'm sorry I littered, April."

"Well, I'm sorry I yelled at you."

I shifted my backpack from one shoulder to the other. At this point, it was getting uncomfortable with us just standing there in the hallway while everyone else in the world was eating lunch. Or maybe it was just uncomfortable the way he was looking at me all quizzically.

"And I'm also sorry that I never said thank you," he went on. "When you shoved me during the earthquake. I didn't say . . . shit, this is embarrassing."

I just looked at him, trying to read what was going on behind his dark brown eyes, terrified that he would know what I was. Why did *June* get to be the mindreader? I didn't know Thing One about trying to figure out what guys were thinking!

"Thanks," he finally huffed. "Thanks for not letting a five-hundred-pound light fall on me, even though I probably could have sued the school and made a million dollars."

"That's the weirdest thank-you I've ever received."

"Yeah, well."

"You're welcome," I added quickly. "No problem."

We stood there for a minute, a perfect portrait of awkwardness. I searched desperately for a distraction, for something that would end the uncomfortable silence.

I was sitting on the grass with Julian, eating lunch. And I was smiling.

"What the hell?" I started to say before I could stop myself, just as Julian said, "Soo . . . you eating lunch?"

I just looked back at him. "Are you asking me to eat lunch with you?"

"Um, you know, not unless you wanna sit with your friends or—"

I paused for a second, then admitted the truth. "I don't have any friends."

Julian grinned. "Yeah, like I said, me neither." He looked at the students milling around us. "Not many people worth being friends with."

"Yeah, okay, lunch. But that's it," I added, quickly remembering the vision I had had. "Just lunch. No funny business."

Julian raised an eyebrow. "I'll cancel the parade and fireworks, then."

I laughed despite myself. "Good. I hate big scenes."

* * *

If you had told me that Julian brown-bagged his lunch, I wouldn't have believed it.

But there he was, sitting on the grass in front of our school, opening up an old shopping bag and pulling out a sandwich. "You bring your lunch?" I said. "Really?"

"So do you," he pointed out, motioning to my Tupperware filled with carrots and hummus. "At least, I think that's lunch," he added. "What is that?"

"Hummus," I said. "It's very healthy and packed with protein."

"Has someone pre-chewed it for you?"

"That's disgusting!" I said. "Oh my God, that is vile. And who are you to talk? You're eating a sandwich on *white bread*."

"It's delicious," he said before taking a huge bite. "Deeeee-licious."

"White bread can kill you."

Julian waited until swallowing before answering. "April," he said, "high school could kill me. So could driving on the freeway, crossing the street, or flying in a plane. I'll take my chances on the white bread." He took another bite and then added, "Let me guess. You're the oldest."

"Yeah. How'd you know?"

"'Cause you're so bossy."

"Well, you'd be bossy, too," I muttered. My hummus looked completely unappetizing now, so I stuck with the carrots. "Having to keep track of everything all the time."

"What?"

"Nothing."

"I'm serious. Pushing me out of the way—"

"You thanked me for that," I argued.

"And now you're telling me what bread to eat?" Julian smiled out of the left corner of his mouth. "Bossy McBosserson."

I rolled my eyes and tossed a carrot at him. It hit him in the shoulder, but he didn't flinch or move away. "Well, *you* must be an only child," I said to him. "Seeing as how you have the emotional capability of a gopher."

Julian smirked. "Guilty as charged, except for the gopher part."

"Well, then you wouldn't get it. All the responsibility involved, especially when—" I stopped myself from saying, *Especially when you can see what's going to happen to them.*

"Especially what?"

"Nothing."

"No, you were gonna say something."

"It was nothing," I insisted. "You know, you and my sister May would really get along. You both like artificial flavoring and being rude."

"She sounds like my kind of girl."

I glared at him. "Don't even."

"Fine. So I guess it's just you and me then."

I choked on my carrot, and Julian had to thump me on the back while I hacked up carrot bits. "Jesus, you okay?" he said. "Don't choke to death. They'll blame me for it, you know they will."

My eyes were watering as I nodded. "M'fine," I said. But even as I spoke, I was getting flashes of Julian's future: him sitting at home, drawing in a composition book, headphones tight over his ears; kissing his mom good-night as she slept on the sofa, her work shoes still on her feet; Julian sitting next to me at the movies, laughing about—

Waitaminuteagain. Was I seeing us on a *date*?!

Good God, this whole "seeing the future" thing was the worst occurrence of my entire lifetime.

I glanced back up at him, and I must have looked scary because he actually drew back a bit. "What?" he said. "Do you need the Heimlich?"

"No, I . . ." I shook my head, rattling the visions around in my brain. I tried to refocus on where we were, looking at blades of grass and then the parking lot that was just over the hill, but I couldn't stay focused. The visions were so clear, some of the clearest ones I had ever had, and I realized that the closer I got to Julian, the more I would see about him.

That's wonderful, I thought. *Just wonderful.*

"I'm fine," I told him. "Seriously. A piece of carrot just went down the wrong way."

"Well, don't die on me or anything."

I smiled despite myself, but then made sure to keep a healthy distance between us. I was pretty sure my ultimate vision wasn't going to happen right there at lunch, but I wasn't willing to take any chances.

Instead, I got a different vision this time.

The red came back slowly, crowding into my line of sight little by little until it was all I could see. I could hear sirens now, and it took a few seconds before I realized they were in my head and nowhere else. *The red light was flashing around and around, and now Julian was standing there, hands in his pockets, the red light reflecting off the features of his face. A police officer walked up to him as the sirens became so loud that they hurt my ears.*

Oh my God. Oh my God.

"April?" Julian was saying. "April, what? Are you okay? Are you choking on another carrot?"

"I, uh, I have to go," I said quickly, scrambling to my feet. My muscles were all shaky, and I knew I had to get away. Julian wasn't safe, wasn't okay, wasn't *right*.

I should have known that the minute I saw him with a styrofoam coffee cup.

"Wait, what—?"

"I have to hand in my paper," I said as I crammed my Tupperware into my backpack. My stomach was growling, but I ignored it. There was something bad happening here, and I wanted to get away as fast as possible. I could eat my stupid carrots and hummus later. "I'll see you later."

"Well . . . okay," he said, looking sort of bummed as I hurried away, but I didn't turn around to say goodbye again.

It took me until the end of sixth period to stop shaking. The visions were getting worse, I realized. First the red, then the sirens, now Julian. I tried to stop seeing it, but it kept playing over and over like a bad movie, reminding me that something terrible was on its way, and I could do nothing to stop it.

chapter 11

"What's the point of crying if you can't even see the tears?"

may

School always sucked for me. I mean, even in first grade, I was the kid who was like, "We're here all day long? Every day? For the next *twelve years*? You're kidding me."

But now? Now that I could literally disappear into thin air and go wherever I wanted in the entire world?

School had officially become hell on earth.

What good is a power if you can't always control it?

I had to make it bearable somehow, so I started to figure out where I could disappear without anyone noticing. At lunch, while every one else tried to look all cool eating their PB&J sandwiches that their moms had made for them, I got to leave campus, walk three blocks to the local 7-Eleven and get a delicious snack that consisted entirely of preservatives. (I'm already anticipating the day when April sees what I'm doing and has a health-based meltdown about it. "Do you know what preservatives can do to the human body?" she always says, and I'm just like, "If they can preserve food, they can probably preserve me, too.")

I also figured out that right before the bell rings, I could disappear and get a head start out the door. It wasn't even about getting to my next class on time, it was just about getting out of the last one as fast as possible. I couldn't ditch, mostly because my older, bossier sister was probably watching me like a hawk, but I could do other things.

And I did them all.

* * *

April came into my room on Thursday after school while I was lying on my bed, editing my online photo album on my laptop. I know my sisters think I have, like, wish-fulfillment issues or something, but I just like looking at the pictures. After being in school all day, escapism is necessary, and France seems like a great place to start.

"Hey," April said.

"Hey hey," I replied, pulling one headphone out of my ear. "What's up, buttercup?"

"Who's the guy?"

"What guy?"

"The one that's coming over tonight."

I frowned. "I have no idea. Why don't you tell me, Madame Aprilini? You're the psychic one."

She rolled her eyes. "He's wearing a lot of clothes from Stanford. Does that help?"

I felt my heart pinball around in my ribcage. "Henry?" I said before I could stop myself. "What do you mean, we're not . . . I didn't . . ."

"Apparently he's coming over to tutor you?"

"But we didn't plan it!" I sputtered. "What sort of stalker creepazoid does that?"

April grinned wickedly at me. "You're blushing."

"No, I'm just turning red with fury because I loathe the ground he walks on. There's a difference." I put my headphone back in my ear, but she came over and pulled it out again. "Excuse me," I said, "you're violating my safety zone. Physically *and* emotionally."

"You ain't seen nothing yet," she said, then plopped down next to me, stretching out her legs on my dark purple bedspread. (I had dyed it myself in the washing machine, which had sort of wreaked havoc on everyone's else laundry for the next week. Live and learn.) "So?" April prodded. "The guy?"

"Can't you just predict it and leave me alone?" I asked. "C'mon, April, this is my happy place. You're ruining it."

"His name's Henry," June told her as she walked past my now open bedroom door. "He's her history tutor."

"It's called the right to privacy, June!" I yelled after her. "Look it up!"

April just rolled her eyes at June. I don't know what happened between them, but something did. There's been a lot of bitchface between the two of them, and whenever one of them enters a room, the other leaves. "So," she said. "Henry. He's cute."

"Yeah, if you like that cocker spaniel look."

"Is he nice?"

I didn't even look up from my computer. "Oh, he's just the best," I intoned. "After we study together, we're gonna go to the soda fountain and share a malted. It'll be dreamy! What about you? Have you banged Julian yet?"

June poked her head back in the room. "No, she's using her psychic powers to avoid him," she announced.

I nodded. "*Nice*. Way to go, April. That won't end badly or anything."

"Look, this is way different," she said as she glared at June. "You have a guy who's coming over to tutor you. I have a psychic vision with no basis in actual reality. There's no legitimate suitor potential."

"Stop reading Jane Austen. You sound like *Emma* crossed with *Star Trek*."

April shook her light blond hair in a move that almost resembled June, except that April didn't do it on purpose. "Whatever, no, I don't."

I needed a subject change, since thinking about Henry was filling me with Stanford-colored rage. "Hey," I asked April. "Am I going to Paris?"

"What?"

"Am. I going. To Paris?"

"What are you talking about?"

"That's what I'm asking you. You can see the future, tell me where I'll be in five or ten years."

"You know it doesn't work like that," April said. "I can't pick and choose what things to see."

"What about London, then? Do you at least see London?"

"I see London, I see France!" June started to chant from the bathroom. "I see—!"

"I see someone getting choked with their toothbrush!" April yelled at her. June stopped singing immediately.

"Let's get back to the important issue," I said. "Have you banged that guy yet?"

"Really, May, that's just rude."

I smirked. "I'll take that as a no, then."

"Look, I'm probably wrong, anyway."

I laughed. "Yeah, because you've been so wrong before. You *wish* you were wrong."

June came back into my room, now delicately patting a powder puff across her face. "So your tutor is coming here? To our house? Tonight?"

I spun around and fixed her with my death stare. "If you *even* read his mind—"

June just shrugged. "I cannot control the great inner workings of my glorious brain."

"Wait," April interrupted before I could go for June's throat. "Oh, crap, why didn't I see this?"

"What?" I asked. I suddenly felt a little sick. Every time April has a vision it seems to lead to disaster, and I didn't even want to think about the sort of disaster that could happen when Henry and I were around each other. It would probably lead to someone missing a limb. "Does one of us wind up in the emergency room or something?"

"No, it's not that," April said. She suddenly looked uncomfortable. "It's Thursday. Mom has her date tonight."

It felt like all the air went out of the room when she said that, but then I realized that was just me disappearing again. "C'mon, May," June said, already looking wary. "Don't kid around."

April had her frantic face on, her eyes darting towards the door. "May!" she hissed. "It's Mom—she's coming up! Get back here!"

Five seconds later, I was sitting on the bed next to April, with June standing next to us, clenching her puff in her fingers. "Oh!" my mom said when she saw us. "Look at you girls, it's like you were expecting me."

"Hi, we're fine," April said. Only she didn't look fine at all. She looked like a nervous Chihuahua. Next to me, June giggled and I dug my elbow into her arm, silently telling her to be quiet.

"Um, girls," my mom said again, and then she sat down in the black beanbag chair I keep in the corner of my room. "I wanted to tell you, and I'm sorry it's taken me so long. But I've just been trying to figure out the best way to tell you this—"

Oh, God, this was agony. I couldn't watch another version of the "Girls, we have something to tell you" speech, so I cut right to the chase. "Are you going on a date or something?" I asked her.

April made a tiny yelping noise that, again, sounded very Chihuahua-like.

My mom looked, well, shocked as hell. "Um, yes," she said. "Yes, I am. Tonight. His name is Chad—"

Of course his name was Chad. Of *course* it was. Nothing sounds douchier than Chad.

"—and he works in the office with me and he's very nice. But I want you girls to know that it is just a date. That's *all* it is."

The three of us stared silently back at her, and suddenly June shivered.

"And he's coming over tonight at six to take me to dinner," my mom added.

"Is he paying?" June asked.

"Um, I don't know, Junie Bee. Maybe, I—"

"He should pay," June said. "If he doesn't . . ." She mimed drop-kicking someone, and our mom laughed.

"So June is okay with it," she said. "What about you, May?"

It took all of my strength to not disappear. I could feel my heart squeezing itself tight, my ribs shimmering with energy, the roots of my hair quivering in anticipation, but I held on tight and tried not to ache with the effort.

"It's fine," I lied. "Whatever. You're a single woman. Go forth."

My mom smiled and looked at April, who just nodded. "Totally fine," she said. "Did you tell Dad?"

I gotta hand it to my sister sometimes—she knows how to ask the good questions.

But then she raced on before my mom could answer. "Because I really think he'd be okay with it," April continued. "I mean, really, Mom. He would be. I'm *positive*."

The three of us smiled at my mother. "I'll talk to your father," she said. "It's not your job to worry about that." She paused. "So this is okay?"

We nodded as one.

"So why do you all look robotic all of a sudden?" she asked.

Someone had to think fast and let's face it, I was the perfect candidate. "Hey, guess what?" I said. "There's this guy coming over tonight. He's my educational enhancer—"

April snorted. "Tutor."

"—and he's gonna enhance my European history skills tonight at seven using our kitchen table and probably a Snapple, too. If I'm feeling generous."

"I think he likes Sprite better," April said quietly. "Just a hunch."

My mom just blinked at me. "*You* have a boy coming over?"

"She doesn't like him," June said quickly, avoiding my glare. "Don't worry, Mom."

My mom smiled a little. "And you know this because . . . ?"

"Because I told her," I said, cutting June off before she could open her mouth again. "It was a moment of weakness. I think someone spiked my drink with a truth serum."

My mom grinned and got up to kiss the top of my head. I still like it when she does that, even though I can't tell her. "Fine," she said, "but April's in charge."

"Must be a day that ends in Y," June muttered.

"And I'll be home by nine thirty at the latest," she continued before kissing April and June, too. "I'll call if we get stuck in construction traffic or something."

We waited until my mom went into her bedroom before collapsing in various states around the room. "That almost killed me," I muttered. "I thought I was gonna disappear right in front of her."

"I love how I get to supervise your education enhancement date," April giggled. "This is gonna be the easiest thing I've ever done in my life. *Breathing* will be harder that this."

June was still quiet, though, gazing off into space. "Stop it," I told her. "You're spying in someone's brain. Knock it off."

"No, I'm not," she said automatically.

"Whatever. Liar," I said, but she didn't even bother to defend herself, so I left it alone. It's no fun when June doesn't react.

April was lying down on the floor now, her hands over her eyes. "I know this much," she said, then sat up and looked at us. "We are gonna screen this Chad guy like he's never been screened before."

"Homeland Security's got nothing on us," June agreed, then gave me a shove as she walked past. "I'm out," she said. "The mindreader needs a nap."

* * *

At five fifty-nine, the three of us were carefully arranged around the living room. April had the remote, and June's legs were slung over the chair. But I don't think any of us could have said what we were watching on TV. We were just waiting for Chad.

Ten seconds before the doorbell rang, April suddenly sat up and said, "Showtime," and we were at the front door before my mom even got downstairs.

"Girls, you don't need to meet him like an army," she said, shoving us back. "He's not gonna attack us."

June and I looked to April for confirmation on that last part, and she just nodded and pulled us back so my mom could open the door.

Chad, I'm sorry to tell you, looked totally normal. I don't know what I was expecting—fangs or too much body hair or terrible cologne—but he just looked like any guy you'd see at Starbucks. "Hi," he said. "You must be Carolyn's daughters."

"No," I said. "We're just extras. She hired us from the agency."

"Oh my God," April muttered, just as my mother shoved me backwards and blocked me from the doorway. They work as a team sometimes, April and my mother.

My mother smiled and brought him into the foyer, where my sisters and I eyed him warily. "I recognize you girls from the pictures on your mother's desk at work," Chad said. "She's always talking about how proud she is of you."

June, a sucker for any compliment, no matter how clichéd, beamed like the sun. "Who does she talk about most?" she asked. "April, May, or me?"

"I'm April," April interrupted, stepping in front of June. "Hi. It's nice to meet you."

Why does she always have to be such a freaking goody-goody? It makes it that much harder for me to be . . . well, *me*.

My mom introduced the three of us, and when it got to my turn, I shook his hand and said, "It's nice to meet you," and then felt the pinky finger on my left hand start to tingle.

I shot a look to June and imagined myself disappearing. June raised her eyebrows and then slowly nodded. "Got it," she mouthed, then cleared her throat. "Hey, Mom, can we go watch TV? It's an *America's Next Top Model* marathon, and I want to see where that one girl pours beer on that other girl's weave. It's a classic."

April coughed to cover her laugh.

My mother looked at us, then back to Chad. "These are my daughters," she told him. "Feel free to run screaming."

No time like the present, I wanted to say, but I knew my mom would ground me for a million years. And besides, I was too busy worrying about my left hand, which was starting to vanish no matter how much I concentrated on keeping it in my hoodie pocket.

But Chad just grinned and said, "No, no, my kids like that show, too. Nice to meet you girls."

June literally jumped at the sound of April's and my thoughts screaming out of our brains, and I didn't have to be like June to know that April was thinking the same thing I was. *Kids? Chad has kids!? We could potentially have step-brothers or step-sisters?*

"It was really nice meeting you, too," April said as we almost stampeded over one another in our rush to get out of the foyer. "Have fun tonight."

"Kiss-ass," I hissed as soon as we were out of earshot. "Do you want a bunch of snot-nosed kids moving in here and making us share rooms and chore lists and quality time?"

"It's a first date, not a wedding," April whispered back. "You and June are such drama queens."

"Hey, I practically went deaf from the sound of *your* thoughts, too," June huffed. "It was like a train whistle. Now who's the drama queen, huh?"

"I'm not a drama queen; I'm just the oldest. It's hard enough watching out for you two, much less—"

"Do you think he has any sons?" June asked. "Like, cute ones?"

April and I stared at her in horror.

"What?" she demanded. "Don't judge me, I'm just asking! It'd be nice to have a brother, so I didn't have to deal with you two all the time!"

I threw my hands—well, hand by this point—up in the air and faced my sisters. "Can we just vet this guy already?" I demanded. "Before he takes our mother and dumps her body in a river or something equally terrible?"

April just sighed. "He's a nice guy," she told us. "I saw it. He has a daughter who looks about thirteen and a son a few years younger, and he's taking them out for pizza tomorrow night. He's a good dad."

"How great for them," I muttered, but there was a stabbing pain in my stomach when I said it, and I felt the whoosh of air and watched my sisters blink and then look around for me.

"Okay, May, you do your thing," June sighed. "April and I will do the hard work. You just float and be all creepy and invisible. We've got this."

I burned with fury, but stayed hidden. *He's a good dad.* The words almost sounded like they were mocking me, like April had said it on purpose, even though I knew she hadn't. Chad probably wouldn't have cancelled a trip to Houston. I hated Chad now. Screw him and his kids and their pizza time. If my mom was lame enough to date him, that was her stupid problem. They didn't need a chapero—

Oh my God, I was a genius.

"I can follow them!" I cried, snapping back to earth so fast that I accidentally stumbled into April. "Sorry, ow. But I can follow them! I can be all invisible and see what happens!"

"Now that's stalker-y to the tenth power," June said. "You wanna follow our mom and Date Guy? What if they kiss? Oh my God." She shivered again. "That is like my worst nightmare. What if there's slurping noises? Oh, ew ew ew." She hopped up and down and waved her hands in front of her, wrinkling her nose like she smelled something terrible.

"They do *not* kiss," April said definitively. "They—uh oh."

"Uh oh what?" I demanded. "Uh-oh what?"

"They're going out for Mexican. You know Mom's allergic to avocados." April raised her eyebrows. "Oh, crap."

I rolled my eyes. "April, *please*, your language. My delicate ears."

"Oh, wait, no, she's fine." April's forehead smoothed out, and she looked relieved. "There's no guacamole or anything. Phew, okay, anyway. She's just gonna have the enchiladas and a glass of wine and—"

"If Chad drinks and drives, then I have to follow them," I interrupted. "It's my family duty."

"—and Chad has a Coke," April continued. "There is no drinking and driving, and I don't see you anywhere in the backseat, May. So there."

I thought quickly. "Well, if I were invisible, you couldn't see me, anyway. So there." I stuck my tongue out at her.

"Oh, *real* mature—"

"Can you both just shut up for a minute?" June said. "I'm trying to see if Chad's a date rapist. *God.*" Her eyes moved fast, her fingers absentmindedly tapping out a rhythm on her jeans. "Okay," she said slowly. "Not a date rapist. He thinks his dry cleaner's is ripping him off. He keeps meaning to take his car in for an oil change."

"Well, that settles it," I said. "Our mom can't ride in a car like that. It's a death trap."

June just sighed. "I'm sorry to tell you this, but he's completely honorable. A little dorky, but so's Mom."

April shrugged and then shoved her hair over her shoulders. "Well, that's that," she said. "Dating season has begun."

"Wait, so you're both okay with this?" I said, gaping at my sisters. "It hasn't even been six months since we moved here! She didn't even ask us if it was okay until *two hours ago*, and you're just gonna lie down?!"

June just looked at me. "You," she said, "need to take a pill."

"Does your best buddy Mariah have one I can borrow?" I shot back.

June pretended to listen for something. "What? Did anyone else hear that? Is someone talking? They must be invisible because I can't even see them, that's how insignificant they are!"

"Dammit, I am not a WWF referee!" April cried, stepping in between us again. "Stop doing this! You two are so freaking annoying."

June startled. "Why'd you just think of Julian?"

April actually blushed. "I didn't."

"Yes, you did. You just thought of him." June grinned slyly. "You *liiiiiike* him."

I looked at April. "Feel free to hurt her. I won't say a word about it to anyone."

Our mom suddenly poked her head into the room. "Girls, we're gonna go," she said. "And May, we'll talk later about appropriate venues for sarcasm." She eyed me meaningfully.

I sighed. "I can't help it if my talents are unappreciated in this particular venue."

"Have fun, Mom," April said.

"If he likes it, he should put a ring on it," June added. "Think like Beyoncé."

My mom laughed and ran her hand down June's hair before grabbing her purse. "Okay, girlies, have a good night. Do not call me unless the house burns down or one of you breaks a bone."

"What about a concussion?" I said. "Should we just text you in that case?"

Another meaningful glare from my mom and then she was gone.

Five minutes later, I was upstairs, lying on my bed and looking at my Paris pictures. I had only really started collecting them after we moved here, when all I wanted to do was go somewhere else, anywhere else. I was just about to flip back to the beginning and look at them again when April flounced past my room. "Henry's here, May!"

I glanced at the clock by my bed. "Wait, no, he's not. It's only six forty-five."

The doorbell rang.

"Told you so!" April's voice called out as she retreated to her room and her beloved homework. "I love how you always think I'm wrong."

"Guess what else I'm thinking," I muttered, but then I trudged downstairs and went to meet Henry.

He was standing in the foyer where Chad had been only moments earlier, carrying a big Stanford backpack that was stuffed so full that its seams were stretching. "Oh, wow, what a surprise," I said. "What, did you come over to spread your college propaganda to the neighbors?"

"I thought I'd surprise you," he replied. He attempted to smile at me, but it fell off his face when I didn't respond. His hair was really messy, too, like he had driven over with the windows rolled down. What a rebel.

"You know," he continued, "seeing as how we . . . we sort of argued, and then you ran off and never came back."

"I think you also forgot about the part where you insulted my very existence. That was a high point for me."

Henry at least looked a bit guilty. "Yeah, well, I'm also obligated to tutor you for at least five more sessions."

"My heart just skipped a beat," I muttered. "And you know, you didn't have to bring every single book you own. We have books here, too. My sister April collects them. I'm sure we could have supplemented."

"Your sister said I could just go into the kitchen, so . . ."

"Which one?"

"Um, I think your kitchen—"

I rolled my eyes. "Don't be so literal. I meant which sister? There's a couple of them floating around here."

Henry laughed a little. "Oh. Oh yeah, um, the dark-haired one, sort of shorter than you."

"That's June," I said. "April's the other one. She's upstairs. Another way to tell them apart is that June's annoying and April's boring."

"I heard that!" June cried from the living room.

I looked at Henry. "See what I mean?"

"Yeah, I have a sister, too," he said. "I get it."

I looked towards the kitchen. I was suddenly in no mood to think about history or Henry or my sisters or my mom or Chad. My brain was too full already. "Follow me," I said. "The wonders of history await."

After we settled at the table with water for me and a Sprite for him—I see what you did there, April—I looked at the mammoth textbook and sighed. "So how long does this have to go on for?"

"An hour? An hour and a half? I don't know, I've never tutored anyone before."

"That's becoming pretty obvious," I said. "I guess we're both screwed now." I glanced down at my feet just to make sure that they were both staying where they belonged, but then I saw Henry's shoe. "Dude," I said, leaning in closer. "Oh my God. Dude."

"What?" Henry followed my gaze. "What, did I track dirt in?"

I was already laughing so hard I could barely talk. "Do your shoelaces say STANFORD on them?"

Henry bristled. "They're just shoelaces," he tried to defend himself.

"AHAHAHA!" I had to put my head down on the table while I composed myself. "Look, Henry," I said as soon as I could breathe again, "if you ever need someone to tutor you in how to be cool, feel free to ask. I can help you."

Henry just muttered something about college educations being the foundation of a solid adult life, then flipped open his textbook. "So," he said. "What do you know about Robespierre?"

"Lame," I replied, still wiping my eyes. "What kind of name is Robespierre, anyway? He was just asking to be beheaded with a name like that."

Henry just looked pleased. "So you know he was beheaded?"

"I'm good on the gory stuff."

"So then you also know that Marie Antoinette was . . . ?" Henry waited patiently for me to finish the sentence.

I just blinked at him. " . . . played by Kirsten Dunst in the movie?"

Henry sighed.

I grinned and settled back into my chair. "Well, I'm not *wrong*," I insisted. "Half-credit."

We spent ten minutes sitting there, Henry trying to get me excited about the French Revolution and me not getting excited about the French Revolution. I was so bored that I even thought about disappearing, just to make things more interesting, but I erased the thought before June heard it or April saw it happening. I was bored, not suicidal.

"So when Robespierre . . ." Henry continued, but I interrupted him with another loud sigh.

"Can we take a break?"

"It's only been ten minutes, and you haven't gotten one question right yet," Henry pointed out. To his credit, he didn't even seem too annoyed with me, which meant I wasn't trying hard enough.

"All the more reason to take a break," I told him. "I'm stressed. This isn't a good frame of mind for productive studying."

"You sound like my sister," Henry said.

April came hurrying into the kitchen just then. "Hi, don't mind me, I'm just getting some water," she said, shooting me a mom-like glare before adding, "I'm May's sister April."

"Hi," Henry waved.

"Uh, April, you're killing my learning buzz. You see what just happened?" I said to Henry. "She came in, and I forgot everything that I had learned so far."

"You can't forget what you don't know," Henry said.

April grinned as she poured herself some apple juice. "Henry," she laughed, "I don't know what they pay you to do this, but I know it's not enough."

Henry shrugged, blushing a little. "It's volunteer work for my college application."

April glanced over at him, taking in his outfit, backpack, and ridiculous shoelaces. "Let me guess where you're applying."

"It's one of the best schools in the country," Henry said. "And they've got a golf team that—"

"April," I interrupted, not wanting to even enter a golf discussion, "you got your juice. Mission accomplished. Now can you please leave?"

She started to leave, but then doubled back and grabbed the roll of paper towels off the counter and put them down between Henry and me. "Here," she said, then winked at me. "Trust me."

"You *really* didn't have to do that," I told her. "I mean it."

April grinned. "Oh, that's nothing. Just you wait."

Henry looked between us, frowning a little. "Thanks," he finally said. "It, uh, never hurts to have paper towels."

"Yeah, they'll be good for soaking up the bloodshed," I muttered. "Are you leaving now, April?"

"Ta ta," she waved. "Have fun!"

I rolled my eyes and turned back to Henry, shoving my hair out of my face just as he was lifting up his can of Sprite.

I hate when my sister is right. I hate it so much.

My arm hit Henry's, and the Sprite went flying over both of us.

"Oh, shit!" I cried as it fell over my jeans and the floor and the table. "Oh, sorry!"

"It's a good thing your sister brought the paper towels," Henry said. "What a mess."

"Don't worry, we've got more Sprites in the garage." I was already blushing from mortification. "Here, hand me some."

He started to mop up the table while I attacked the sticky floor. "Well, at least it didn't land on the textbook," Henry said. "That's good."

"How wonderful," I replied. "Maybe I could spill it again."

Henry laughed, and when he went to take the paper towel from me, our hands met and our fingers touched. "Sorry!" I said, pulling away fast, just as Henry said, "Sorry!" and yanked his hand back.

Guess what disappeared soon afterwards?

You got it.

I rammed my now-missing left hand into my hoodie pocket, burrowing it deep so that Henry wouldn't notice I was now one hook short of a pirate. Then I laughed nervously. "Wow," I said. "That was . . . "

"Yeah," Henry said, then cleared his throat again. "So. Robespierre."

"Beheaded," I said automatically. "Missing a body part. I feel for the guy." I sat back in my chair and silently willed my feet to stay where they were.

I could feel them for the next ten minutes, getting closer to disappearing every time Henry leaned forward to make a point or pick up the highlighter. It was probably the least productive tutoring session ever. He could have been teaching me basic math for all the good it was doing. All my effort was going into not disappearing, and besides my hand and my feet, I was doing a great job of hanging on. It's too bad they didn't give grades out for mind-body control, because I'd be rocking a 4.0 GPA in that subject.

"Are you getting this?" Henry asked after a while.

"Yeah, why?"

"You're not being sarcastic or making comments."

I smiled. "No, this is fascinating. I'm just fascinated. This is me being fascinated."

"Ah, there we go," Henry said. "That's more like it."

"Do I sound like one of 'those girls' now?"

And poof, there went my feet.

I swear to God, I've never been conscious of the back of my neck before, but I was pretty sure it was starting to go, too. I was trying not to panic, and I forced myself to think fast. "Wow, it's cold in here," I said. "Do you think you could grab the blanket off the back of the couch for me?"

Henry looked at me. He was wearing jeans and a T-shirt. "It's, like, seventy degrees outside."

"Yes, but . . . I'm very sensitive to temperatures." I was nowhere near cold, and the idea of having a blanket on top of me was miserable. June was right—why couldn't one of us (i.e. me) have been able to fly instead?

"Well, okay," Henry said, and he came back a minute later with the blanket. "Here. You're not trying to give yourself heatstroke so you'll pass out and miss tutoring, are you?"

I took the blanket with my one hand and quickly spread it over my legs. "I *wish* it was heatstroke," I said as I felt my ankle vanish.

Who needs an ankle, anyway?

"So after . . ." Henry started to say, leaning forward to push the book back in front of me, and I automatically pulled back, just in case

I got overwhelmed and my nose disappeared. He actually smelled kind of good, like autumn leaves or—

"Ew."

Henry and I both looked up as June came into the room, wrinkling her nose at me.

The brat had been reading my mind.

"June!" I said, so loud that it startled Henry a bit. "Can I do something for you? Lobotomy, perhaps?"

"Relax, I'm just thirsty. Hi, Henry," June added, waving at him. "How's it going?"

"June!" I nearly shouted. "This is not your personal tutoring session. Quench the thirst and leave."

"Hi, June," Henry said.

Why was he nicer to my sisters than he was to me? He didn't even say hi the first day we met!

"No need to be jealous," June mumbled, tossing her dark hair overdramatically as she reached for the Brita inside the fridge. She can't even pour water without making sure that people notice her.

"Don't feed the animals," I told Henry, giving my sister the evil eye. "It only encourages them."

June ignored my comment for the time being. "Aren't you a little warm?" she said, eyeing the blanket. "Or do you just like wearing polyester and wool together?"

"I'm fine," I said stiffly, sending her the mental image of all my missing parts.

June widened her eyes, then giggled to herself and pretended to look for a glass in the dishwasher. Henry's back was to her, so he couldn't see her. But I could.

Unfortunately.

"He likes you!" she mouthed at me, then pretended to make kissy faces before pointing at him and grinning.

"And then when the Revolution started. . ." Henry droned. He had no idea that my sister was reading his mind.

I widened my eyes at June and gritted my teeth just as the thumb on my good hand started to tingle.

June must have seen it happen in my mind. "Oops," she said. "Bad timing, huh?"

"What?" Henry asked, glancing up.

"Nothing," I said with a grimace. "June, can you leave? Please?" *Before my entire head disappears?*

"I'm just getting water," June insisted. "Slow your roll."

Henry laughed. "My sister says that all the time."

June just nodded towards Henry, then gave me the thumbs-up signal and a wink.

I'm missing two feet, an ankle, and one hand, I thought, *but I will find a way to kick your ass. Try me.*

June pretended to look scared as she poured her water, then made a big deal out of rinsing her glass and putting it in the dishwasher. By now, I was blushing so furiously that I thought the blood vessels in my cheeks would burst, and I kept my eyes on the textbook, not even daring to look at Henry.

This was easily the most mortifying experience of my life.

"So," I said as soon as June disappeared upstairs, "those are my sisters. I'm sorry you had to witness that. They must have escaped from their cage. It won't happen again."

Henry just laughed. "That's cool," he said. "My sister's pretty crazy. I'm used to it."

"Really, I think I can one-up you in the crazy category."

"Yeah, well, do either of your sisters have a loser boyfriend like mine does?"

"I don't think so, but I will happily set them up with one if it keeps them away from me." I shoved the textbook away from me. "Where can I get a loser boyfriend? eBay? Or do I just have to hang out in a McDonald's parking lot?"

Henry grimaced when I shoved the book away. "I'll pay you to take hers," he said. "No, I'm kidding. I wouldn't want to do that to either of your sisters."

"That bad, huh?"

"Yeah." Henry eyed me carefully. "You sure you're not too hot wearing that blanket and hoodie? You look a little . . . warm."

"No, I'm fine," I said. I was sweltering. "Just fine." I smiled with my mouth closed, just in case a front tooth had disappeared on me. "So . . . loser boyfriend?"

"Oh, yeah. He's an asshole. He's supposed to be a senior, but he flunked junior year. And now I think he dropped out. He doesn't even care about her."

"Wow," I said. "That kinda sucks."

"Yeah." Henry started wiping the condensation off the side of his empty can of Sprite. "Your sisters seem pretty normal compared to mine. I tried talking to her, but . . ." Henry shrugged. "You know."

I hoped that June wasn't listening or April hadn't seen this coming. They'd never stop talking about how my history tutor thought they were the bee's knees. "I guess my sisters aren't so bad," I admitted. "But we don't sell normal too well."

And as if to prove my point, my right knee went. I was so busy talking about Henry's stupid sister that I wasn't concentrating on keeping everything where they should be. "Oh, shit!" I cried before I could stop myself, which nearly gave Henry a heart attack.

"What, what is it?" he asked.

"I . . . I just can't believe that there's so much about European history that I don't know!" I lied. I clapped my hand over my left kneecap, trying to keep it in place through sheer force of will. It was trembling under my skin, like ripples on water. "Will the royal lineages *ever* end? Keep going, so much to learn!"

I hung in there for another ten minutes, gripping my arms tightly around my chest just in case my boobs decided to do a vanishing act, too. (Not that anyone would notice if they disappeared. They were barely present even before all this shit started to happen.) I watched the clock on the microwave as it ticked the minutes away, nodding and "Uh-huh"-ing to Henry's comments as I tried to get through the rest of the session.

The clocked flipped to eight, and I let out a huge sigh of relief. "Wow, eight o'clock already?" I said, interrupting Henry just as he started talking about some treaty. "God, I'm exhausted, aren't you?"

Henry looked over his shoulder at the clock. "Sure you don't wanna go until eight thirty?"

"My brain is fried," I told him. I wondered if I stood up, would I look like Swiss cheese, with holes where all the important parts should be? "Can't learn with a fried brain. It's probably unethical."

The front door started to click open. "Hi!" my mom yelled. "I'm home!"

"Oh, Christ," I muttered, covering my eyes with my one good hand.

"Hi, you must be Henry," my mom said, her heels clacking on

the floor as she came into the kitchen. "I'm May's mother; it's so nice to meet you."

"Oh, hi, Mrs. Stephenson, it's nice to meet you." I should have known that Henry would know how to do the Mom dance.

It may have been my imagination, but I thought I saw my mom bristle at being called Mrs. Stephenson. She had gone back to her maiden name after the divorce, which had sort of hurt my feelings. I don't know why. I guess it was just weird to have a mom with a different last name.

Not that I wasn't becoming adept at handling weirdness.

"Henry was just finishing up," I told my mom. "And leaving."

"You're a trooper, Henry," my mom said, grinning at him. "May doesn't do well with history."

"I just find reality difficult enough," I defended myself, not realizing how true the words were until they were out of my mouth.

"That's okay," he said. "I'll see you in school tomorrow, May?"

I nodded at him. "Sure."

My mom looked over at me. "May," she said slowly, "wouldn't it be nice if you walked your friend to the door?" She raised an eyebrow.

Oh, God. Oh, God. I have never had a panic attack before, but there's a first time for everything.

Henry raised his eyebrows at me so that his forehead wrinkled, and then shook his head and sighed before he grabbed his bag. "I can see myself out, Mrs. Stephenson."

The minute he was gone and the door shut behind him, my mom looked over at me. "Why," she asked, "are you wearing all those clothes and blankets? Are you cold? Are you getting sick?"

She reached out to touch my forehead, but I ducked away. "No, I'm fine. I just got a little cold sitting here."

We needed a subject change. Fast.

"So how was Chad?" I asked. "Was he dreamy?"

My mom shrugged. "Fine. He paid for dinner, so June will be happy about that."

"April will be thrilled, too."

"Yeah, you're right. And what about you?" My mom eyed me. "What about you and Henry?"

"Mooooom," I said. "He's just a tutor."

"All right," she said. "But keep me updated, okay? Your mom likes to be in the loop."

"So Chad was just fine?"

My mom paused, and when she looked over at me, she was smiling the same evil smile that I sometimes use. "He had a piece of spinach stuck right here," she said, pointing to her upper incisor, "and he talked so much that I couldn't even get a word in edgewise to tell him."

I started to laugh. "Are you serious?"

My mom was laughing, too. "Unfortunately."

That was easily the best news I had had in days.

"I'm gonna go upstairs and check on your sisters and change," my mom said. "You okay down here?"

"Peachy." I was practically shaking from the effort of keeping it together, and I gritted my teeth together. *Hang on*, I thought to myself.

My mom paused. "You sure you're okay? You look a little . . . ?"

"Flushed?"

"Tense."

"Well, studying will do that to you."

She laughed and made her way upstairs. I sat there, listening to her footsteps as she went into June's room, then April's, then hers.

The second the door shut, I was dashing upstairs. It was really weird to run and look down and not see feet, and I bolted for the bathroom, locking the door behind me.

When I turned around, I couldn't see myself in the mirror at all.

I'm not sure how long I was there, but it was a while. I tried to talk myself into coming back, but it wouldn't work. And I laid on the floor, full of frustration and not much else. I probably would have cried, except that I never cry. It's just not my thing.

And besides, what's the point of crying if you can't even see the tears?

After a long time, June started knocking. "May," she whined through the door. "I have to get ready for bed."

I ignored her.

"Come *onnnn*," she moaned. "Seriously. I have to cleanse and *moisturize*!"

And suddenly I was back in my skin, angry at being interrupted, angry that I couldn't control it, angry that it even *was*.

"Oh, well, God forbid you can't cleanse and moisturize!" I shot back, yanking the door open. June flounced in past me.

"It's important to have a daily routine," she told me, then glanced over. "It wouldn't hurt you. No offense."

"Yeah, well, I think anyone that spends that much on moisturizer is a moron. *No offense*."

"I hope you enjoy having crow's feet when you're older," she retorted. "So did you have fun lying in here and being all miserable?"

"Hey!" I said. "You can't spy on me! I was—"

"I didn't spy!" June protested. "It's not like it's hard to figure out that you'd be moping in here." She tied her hair in a messy bun and then pulled out all her little toiletry items and lined them up on the sink.

Sometimes I think June's biggest goal in life is to be in a Neutrogena commercial.

"You know what else?" June said, but didn't wait for me to answer. "You know earlier? When Mom was telling us about her date?"

"Yeah, of course. It was only, like, three hours ago."

"And remember when you said, 'Are you going on a date or something?' and she looked at you?"

"You shuddered," I said. "I remember that."

June looked over at me, and there was something in her hazel eyes that I hadn't seen in months. She was scared, I realized.

"What, June?" I said again. "What is it?"

We probably would have stayed like that for a few more seconds, if April hadn't woken up screaming.

chapter 12

"I can't see anything."

june

My liquid cleanser clattered onto the floor as May and I flew out of the bathroom at the same time, both of us charging down the hall. I think May even disappeared for a few seconds, I'm not sure, but we both arrived in April's room at the same time. She looked like she had fallen asleep while studying in bed, her books scattered everywhere, and now her eyes were white and wide, her shoulders jerking with her breath.

"What?" I gasped. "What is it? What'd you see?"

April shook her head. "Dr-dream," she managed to say. "Just a dream. Sorry."

I was already crawling up on the bed next to her. "It's red," I told her. "Your brain, your thoughts, everything's red." I think my voice was shaking a little, and I couldn't see past all the color in April's mind. "What's red? What is it? What's that noise?"

May tried to pull me back, but our mom arrived in the doorway before I could move. "April?" she said. "Honey, what is it? What's wrong?"

"I'm fine," April said. "Really, I am, it was just a crazy dream."

I shook my head. She was pushing me out, thinking of everything under the sun to keep me away. It almost physically hurt, that's how forceful the thoughts were. "Stop it," I whispered. "I can't see anything. Stop *doing* that."

"June." My mom came into the room and put herself between April and me, gathering April up as she put one hand on my cheek. "June, honey, give her some space."

I stood there and looked at April, who just looked back at me with those same scary ice-blue eyes. She had seen something, and she was cutting me out of it.

I think even May knew it, too.

"April," I said urgently. "Come on. *Tell me*."

May came over to the bed and sat down next to me, pulling me back away from April. "It's fine, June," she said. "Just leave her alone. It's nothing."

I just tugged myself away from her and scooted to the end of the bed. I didn't know how to explain how upset April was, but I could feel it. It was like hearing the scary music on a movie but not being able to see the picture, and I couldn't believe that my sister wouldn't tell me what was wrong. She was my sister! Wasn't that the deal between siblings? Especially *us*?

April was still panting a little, and our mom rubbed her arm and looked down at her. "You okay?" she murmured.

"Fine," April said. "Really, it was just stupid."

"Liar," I whispered, soft enough so that only I could hear it. May put her arm around my shoulders and squeezed, which is not something she normally does. I guess I looked pretty emotional.

I didn't want anyone to touch me, though, not when they were just going to lie to me. I shrugged May's arm off and got down from the bed. "Whatever," I spat. "I'm going back to sleep. Have fun figuring out your *issues*, April."

"June—" my mom started to say, but April sat up and disentangled herself from my mom's arms. "I'm fine," she said. "Really, Mom, I'm okay. June's just pissed about something else."

My mom looked at her warily. "You sure?"

April nodded. "I'm fine," she said for what seemed like the millionth time. "I had a Coke before I went to bed. Stupid idea."

She was lying. I knew it.

She was lying *to me*.

But what April didn't know was that I had secrets, too.

When I first started reading minds, I got a lot of mixed signals. It still happens sometimes, like when I thought this guy Travis was thinking about bra shopping, but it was actually the girl next to him. (*That* was a weird moment for sure.) Even when I heard the things that Jessica and Daphne were thinking about Mariah throughout the day, I thought they were coming from someone else.

What a bitch.

She thinks she's so great. Everyone knows she totally stuffed her bra last year. What a joke.

But when I heard my mom's thoughts as she announced that she had a date that evening, I knew what I was hearing wasn't a mistake.

She was surprised that May knew she had a date. She thought it was weird. And then she thought how much May reminded her of her mother, our grandmother.

And she thought how much it seemed like her mom was always able to read her mind.

I couldn't go to sleep for the longest time, even after April calmed down and everyone else went to bed. My brain felt like it was hooked up to a battery or something, it was so twitchy. So I waited until both my sisters were fast asleep, their minds all trippy and weird from dreams (May dreams about a rhinoceros sometimes, that's how weird she is), and then I got out of bed and tiptoed down the hall to my mom's room.

The light was still on under her door. "Mom?" I whispered, using one knuckle to knock. "You there?"

"June?" she called, and I pushed the door open. She was reading in bed, and the bed looked all huge and empty when it was just her in there. She still slept on the same side that she always did, and I wondered if my dad did the same thing in Houston.

The thought made my heart feel lonely, like when you see a sad movie but you can't cry in front of your friends or something. It sort of hurt.

"Hi," I said, standing in the doorway.

She took off her reading glasses and set the book down. "Hi, babe. What's up?"

"The roof," I said automatically, a total May line. "I couldn't sleep."

She sighed and beckoned me over, and I climbed up on the bed next to her and put my head in her lap, just like I used to do when I was a little kid. "Did April freak you out?" she asked quietly.

"No." A lot of things had freaked me out, but it wasn't like I could tell her.

"You sure? Things are weird right now, Junie Bee, aren't they?"

I nodded. "*Really* weird. Can I ask you a question?"

She stroked my bangs back from my face. "Sure. Fire away."

"What was Grandma like?"

Her hand froze in my hair, and I glanced up. There was confusion and sadness and genuine curiosity. *Why is she asking me this?*

"I'm just curious," I said. "We never talk about her, and today we were talking about family trees at school." A total lie, but whatever. These were desperate times.

My mom took a deep breath. "She died when I was fifteen," she told me. "It was very difficult. I didn't have brothers, or even sisters like you do, and your grandfather was . . . What do you girls always say? Old-school?"

I grinned. "Old-school, yeah."

"Well, that was him. He wasn't a man who talked a lot about his feelings. Or my feelings."

"Is that why you always want us to talk and share and be all bond-y?"

"Part of it, yes."

"So, okay, but what was Grandma *like*?"

My mom paused even longer this time, and I saw three people, three women's faces. "Did she have sisters?" I asked, then added, "Or brothers?" before it looked too suspicious.

"Yes, she did, actually. Two sisters, just like you."

"And what were they like?" I was starting to get a prickly feeling under my skin. I wondered if this was what May felt like whenever she disappeared, like the line between two worlds was being erased.

"I . . . I don't really know. I never saw one of them. Your grandma said she was a hermit, but I don't think she was serious. Anyway, she lived off the coast of Maine somewhere. And the other sister, she was really bossy. A know-it-all. Grandma didn't like her very much, but she was always visiting, anyway."

The prickly feeling picked up some steam. "And Grandma was . . . ?"

"A lot like you, actually. The youngest. Funny. Always up to something. She liked to be wherever the action was." My mom rested her hand on top of my head, and I could tell she was thinking again. "She was very intuitive," she said. "She was a wonderful mother in that way. She seemed to always know just how I felt and what to do about it. She always knew what to say to make someone feel better, or help in some way."

I thought about how I ratted out Jessica and Daphne, and my stomach flipped. "Oh," I said. And then, despite my flippy stomach, I asked, "How did she die?"

My mom didn't seem to notice how high my voice was. "Heart attack. She was way too young for it, but that's what happened."

I thought for a minute. "Maybe her heart was just too big, you know? Like, if she had all that intuition, maybe she just couldn't handle feeling what everyone else was feeling all the time."

Oops, I scared her, my mom thought, and I quickly rolled over and smiled at her, even though my insides were trembling. "Was she pretty like me, too?" I grinned.

"Not as gorgeous as you," my mom laughed. "But yes, she was beautiful."

"Mom?"

"Hmm?"

"Why'd you name us April, May, and June?"

"You know why. Those are the months that you were born."

"Yeah, but everybody always makes fun of us. You couldn't have been more creative?"

"Have a baby every thirteen months for three years and tell me how creative *you* feel," she replied, but then stopped herself. "Actually, I take that back. Do *not* have three babies in three years, not until you're at least thirty-five."

"You could have named me after Grandma," I offered.

My mom paused. "You'd want to be named Gladys?"

I wrinkled my nose. "Ew. No. Mom?"

"Yeah?"

"I love you."

"I love you, too, Junie Bee." My mom kissed my forehead. "Go to bed."

And I did.

* * *

The next morning, I was over it. I didn't even bother to wait for my sisters or beg a ride off of April to school. I walked instead, glad to be by myself and surrounded by random thoughts. (You'd be amazed at how many people driving to work each morning hate their jobs.)

I didn't even see my sisters until the snack break, and even then, it was by accident. I was looking for Mariah, but instead I saw April and May standing by May's locker, their heads together as they talked. May looked concerned and worried, and April just looked as tense as she normally did. But as soon as I saw them, both April and May suddenly stood up straight and looked towards me.

April had seen me approaching, obviously. Their thoughts were all muddled up now as they stared at me, thinking about homework and Stanford and lunches on the grass, nothing that made any real sense. "Whatever," I said as I breezed past them. "You have issues."

"You're not ditching today again, are you?" April asked.

"You would know," I replied.

"Let me rephrase," May interrupted. "You're not ditching today again."

I just glared at her. "Your moral high road is not all that high, you know."

"We're talking about *you*, not me," May said, tugging on her black T-shirt. "And I'm not ditching."

This was kind of the part where I was glad I was the mindreader, not my sisters. Because honestly? Ditching wasn't really that awesome. I mean, it was Mariah and me and her boyfriend, Blake, who wasn't exactly the cool rebel boyfriend that you see in the movies. He was sort of . . . I don't know. He was different. He didn't really talk a lot or wear his seatbelt or respect Mariah's personal space. And all we did was just go to Del Taco and then back to Mariah's house, where we watched *Scary Movie* while Blake and Mariah made out on the couch. Mariah giggled and kept trying to push him away at first, but Blake was what April would call "goal-oriented." "C'mon," he kept saying, laughing at first and then insistent, and finally Mariah giggled and said, "Fine." Then they went up to her room while I sat on the couch and watched the movie from the beginning so I wouldn't have to think about the thoughts floating down from upstairs.

Because . . . ew.

But at least it was better than going to gym.

"June," April said again, shaking me out of my thoughts. "You better not be ditching."

I shrugged. "If I am, I am. You can't stop me."

April seethed in fury, but all she said was, "Promise me you'll say no."

"What?" I said, but then I saw Mariah standing towards the edge of the campus. She was in the spot where we had ditched before, far away enough that it was easy to slip away, and close enough that it didn't look conspicuous. "Adios," I told my sisters, then hurried over to her.

"Hey!" I said. "Are you ditching again?"

Mariah laughed a little. "Maybe. You in?"

"Duh," I said, tossing my hair over my shoulder. "I'll go if you'll go."

God, I need a cigarette, Mariah thought, but all she said was, "So I'm having this party next Friday."

I tried to stay calm, but inside? I was *dying*. This was the party she'd been planning for in her head the other day. "Cool," I said. "Who's going?"

"Everyone," she shrugged. "My mom's going out of town with my stepdad. I don't know—some romantic getaway shit. So the house is ours." The romantic getaway thing kept rattling around in her brain like a pinball, though, kind of like the way April kept thinking about red lights, or May thought about crimson and Stanf—

Wait. I didn't care what my sisters thought anymore. I was being invited to a party. There were bigger and better things happening to me than my sisters' lamebrains.

"So what kind of party is it?" I asked.

Mariah raised an eyebrow. "It's the kind of party where people get trashed." *Hasn't she ever been to a party before?*

I began backtracking furiously. "Good," I said. "Because the parties where I used to live were so stupid. They actually played board games." I decided to leave out the detail where I was the one who brought Scattergories.

"Board games?" Mariah scoffed. "Good thing you moved."

I was going to a party! Just like in the movies!

My real life was finally starting, all because of some crazy mindreading skills

It was about time.

"Yeah," I agreed. "Good thing."

chapter 13

"This was a MacGyver-style mission."

I've seen things that I never want to see for the rest of my life.

May knows, too. I mean, I had to tell *someone* about the vision I had that night, and my brain was already too fuzzy and weird to keep the whole secret. Besides, it's not like I could tell June what I had seen.

I knew I wasn't dreaming when I had the vision. Dreams never make any sense; they always have strange things like a school of fish swimming through your living room or something. Every time I saw the future happening, it always made sense. There was never anything odd or surreal.

I wish that it had been a dream that night.

I saw the red lights again. This time I knew they were emergency lights, ambulance or police cars or something. The sirens were there, too, louder than they had ever been, and I saw Julian standing there just like I had before.

The only difference?

This time, I saw June there, too.

I told May about June in the hall the next day. But I didn't tell her about Julian.

After school for the next few days, I tried to get more information.

I sat at my desk and stared at a lemon-and-rose-scented candle that ended up giving me a headache, trying to meditate myself into some sort of hypnosis. June found that hysterical. "Dinner's ready, Dalai Lama," June announced one evening, but she didn't understand, and how could she? I didn't even know what to tell her. "Yeah, June, bad news, it looks like you're going to be in an accident involving lots of emergency crews and sirens." I mean, no. I can't do that. Not until I know more.

I've seen that vision a hundred times since, but there was nothing new. It always stopped just after I saw June's face, so I couldn't even tell if she was hurt or injured or—

No. I wouldn't even think that last part.

So when I finally saw Julian on the following Monday, standing by our lockers and flipping through the combo lock like he didn't care what numbers he stopped on, I stormed over to him, my eyes on fire.

"Do you know my sister?" I demanded.

"What?" He glanced down at me, his hair falling in his eyes even as he kept spinning the lock.

"Do you? Know? My sister?"

"Who's your sister?"

"You tell me."

Julian just looked down at me like I had two heads. "Seriously," he said, "you're insane. You're the craziest girl I've ever met, and that's saying something."

"I don't doubt it for a second," I replied. "But this is all you need to know. Stay away from her."

"From who?"

"My sister!"

Julian finally got his locker open and practically knocked the guy behind him in the head as he swung the door open. "Sorry, dude," he said, then turned back to me and leaned against our lockers. "I will gladly and happily stay away from your sister. I will stay away from your whole damn family if they're anything like you. The only problem, Genius, is that I don't know *who the hell you're talking about.*"

I glanced around and saw June coming in through the front doors, arm-in-arm with Mariah. "Well, crap," I muttered, pointing towards the girls. "That's her. *Her.*"

Julian followed my gaze and then started to laugh. "That girl is your sister? You're related to *Mariah*? Which one of you is adopted?"

"No, the other one. The one that isn't carrying any STDs and doesn't look like she's going to end up on *Judge Judy*."

"Frickin' love *Judge Judy*," Julian said. "She's awesome."

"Hey, buddy! Eyes on the prize!" I snapped my fingers in his face. "You don't *talk* to June, you don't *look* at her, you never acknowledge her presence. Got it?"

June walked past us as I spoke, giving me the evil eye without breaking her conversation with Mariah. I made eye contact with her and held it for a few seconds, trying to look threatening and big sister-ish, but a vision suddenly got in the way, and I instinctively clutched at my locker, trying not to fall down.

June and Mariah were at a party. June was wearing her pink skirt and a pair of red shoes I had never seen before. She looked cute, flushed, happy, and Mariah looked wasted. It was crowded and hot, and a straight-A report card was stuck to the refrigerator door. Friday night. Someone was yelling in the background about some girl being drunk in the bathroom.

"I'm *so* going," June whispered to me as she walked by, giving me a triumphant smile as I came back to the present day. I glared at her, but she was already floating up the hallway. She did that on purpose, reading my mind like that. What a brat.

Julian, blessed with ignorance, just shut his locker without taking anything out, chuckling to himself. "So you're giving *me* the 'stay away from my sister' lecture, and meanwhile she's walking through the halls with Mariah Bradden? That's pretty classic."

I faltered a bit. "Wh—You know Mariah?"

Julian shook his head. "I was wrong earlier. The only person crazier than you is Mariah."

"Oh, well, that's just *great*," I muttered. "What, are you dating her? Did you date her?"

Julian held up his hands. "Not guilty on all counts, Judge Judy. I just . . . know things."

"Things?"

"Yeah, things. Like she's not on the honor roll."

"I suspect that even my grandmother could have figured that out," I snapped. "What else?"

Julian rolled his eyes. "She's got this boyfriend, okay? And he's sort of an asshole."

"No one is 'sort of an asshole,'" I pointed out. "It's an all-or-nothing description."

"Then he's officially an asshole. He used to go here, but he got expelled." Julian paused for a minute before adding, "Blake and I used to be friends. We hung out a lot, but . . ."

"But . . . ?" I prompted.

Julian suddenly stopped walking and turned to look at me. "He's sketchy, okay? I just don't trust him."

This was worse than I feared. "Define sketchy," I said, and when

Julian hesitated, I added, "My sister is hanging out with his girlfriend. How damn sketchy is he, Julian?"

Julian took a deep breath and ran his hand through his hair. "Sketchy like he gets a kick out of sleeping with other girls even while he's with Mariah."

I almost fell over again. "That's not sketchy," I said. "That's cheating."

"Yeah, I know. But he knows what he's doing, and he knows how to do it. He gets off on it. He outlined the whole thing for me one night when we were both smashed, and that's when I stopped hanging out with him. So all the energy you just spent yelling at me? You'd be better off yelling at him. That's all I'm saying."

"I don't know Blake," I admitted. "But my sister ditched school with Mariah the other day."

Julian whistled under his breath. "Stupid move. Blake probably drove them."

"I know, right?" I hugged my books closer to my chest. "I should have stopped her. I should have dragged her—"

"Well, you didn't know," Julian said, and I bit my tongue before I could tell him that yes, I definitely had known.

I knew lots of things now.

My brain started to work fast, putting all the tiny pieces together. Something bad was going to happen with June and Julian. June was friends with Mariah now, no matter how hard I tried to stop that from happening. Mariah apparently had Blake, the idiot boyfriend. There was a party on Friday night. Bad things tended to happen at parties. Maybe Julian would be at the party that night. Maybe the bad thing was going to happen *that night.*

Before I could really panic, I got another flash of Julian and me at the movies. We were sharing popcorn and it was dark, and the people behind us were talking.

Suddenly I had a plan.

"Hey," I said to him. "Are you gonna ask me out?"

Julian's mouth opened, then closed, then opened again. "I, uh . . ." he coughed. "You're really not one for a smooth transition, are you?"

"If you're not, it's cool," I continued. "But I just need to know." I had no time for subtlety or nuance.

Julian laughed a little and ran his hand through his hair. "You're one of those take-charge girls, aren't you?"

"Dude, you have no idea."

"Well, I, uh, I was gonna ask you if you wanted to do something stupid and clichéd, like the movies, but now I'm afraid you're gonna punch me."

I guess I was a bit tense. I tried to relax, but my brain was still going at warp speed. Tiny flashes of Julian were popping up everywhere: eating, sleeping, yelling at someone when they cut him off in traffic, his face once again illuminated by red lights. "I'm not gonna punch you," I said. "Not unless you look at my sister."

"So do you want to go to the movies?"

"Friday's great for me."

"Really?" He sounded surprised. "That's, uh, okay, cool. Friday night."

I eyed him. "If we go to the movies, you should know that I don't like to miss the previews."

"Imagine my surprise."

"And no blow-'em-up action crap with cheesy dialogue. I like movies with plot. And subtitles."

He paused, then smiled. "So you like to go to the movies to read. Of course."

"*No*, I just like to enhance my cultural awareness."

Julian laughed out loud, that deep hearty laugh again. "What a load of pretentious bullshit."

"Excuse me?" I reared back, putting my hands on my hips. "Have you ever asked a girl out on a date before? Because I'm not exactly an expert on getting asked out by guys, but I have a feeling you're doing it all wrong."

Julian paused for only a second, but it was enough. "Oh," I said. "You *haven't* asked a girl out before."

"Bad idea to call you out on your pretentious bullshit?"

"Yeah. Not advised."

"Noted. But," he added, "you haven't really been nice about me asking you out yet."

"I said yes," I protested. "That's about as nice as it gets."

Julian paused, then smiled. "You were serious about the subtitle thing, weren't—?"

"Oh so very serious," I said. "Look at me. This is my Serious Face."

Julian narrowed his dark eyes at me and then nodded. "Serious Face committed to memory. Not that I've ever seen anything but Serious Face, though."

I fidgeted a little. My mom hadn't met him yet. My sisters were gonna launch themselves into orbit the minute they figured this out, and I was just starting to realize that I was about to go out on my very first date. Breakfast wasn't sitting well in my stomach.

But all I said was, "So. How does this work?"

Julian shrugged. "I think I have to pick you up and pay for shit."

I sighed. "Do I have to wear heels and look cute? 'Cause I really don't have time to do all that."

"Hell, I don't care. I've already seen you look like this"—he gestured to my jeans and sneakers"—so it's not like you have to impress me."

That wasn't exactly what I was hoping to hear, but at least I didn't have to worry about tottering around in kitten heels in front of him while I was supposed to be saving my little sister's life. I'm just one person, after all. "You should probably meet my mom when you pick me up," I said.

"Is she gonna give me the Serious Face, too?"

"Along with the Serious Talk and the Serious Life-Threatening if you don't bring me home in one piece."

"Awesome."

I had to laugh at that. "So Friday. This Friday, right?"

"What's your obsession with Friday?"

"Fridays are my favorite." They weren't. I like Thursdays better because then you still get the anticipation of Fridays, but that wasn't important at the moment. "You plus me plus movie equals date?"

"Multiplied by your mom's Serious Talk."

"Exponentially," I added, then looked up at him. He was gazing down at me sort of oddly, and it made me uncomfortable, like when I knew that June was reading my mind. "Are you going to ask for my number?" I said. "You know, so I can tell you where I live?"

He pulled his phone out of his pocket, and I gave him my cell number, making sure he entered it correctly before I let him put it away. "Wow," he said when I was done checking. "You are the most control-freaky girl I've ever met."

"I'm also the second-craziest," I told him, then gathered up my bag. "Consider yourself warned."

* * *

I don't know how anybody can date another person without having the power of foresight. (That's what I called it in my head. The Power of Foresight. It sounds a lot more impressive than "Girl Who Can See the Future" or even worse, "Girl with Superpowers.")

But if I hadn't already seen my and Julian's date from start to finish, I would have been a nervous wreck in the days leading up to Friday. As it was, I still found it hard enough to keep my sisters at bay, June especially. Lucky for me, she was too busy running around with Mariah, going shopping with her or talking to her on IM or the phone. I didn't really want my sister hanging around Mariah, the girl whom Julian dubbed "the craziest girl," but I didn't know how to stop her, either. I kept tabs on June, though, watching through the day to see what she would be doing. She ate a lot of Del Taco and hung out at Mariah's house, as far as I could tell, and Blake wasn't in the picture for the next few days. I didn't even want to know where he was. I hoped he was in a Russian work camp or on the coast of Antarctica, but I wasn't that lucky.

But really? June's life looked sort of boring.

And I was determined to make sure it stayed that way. I had already seen flashes of June at the party, and as far as I could tell, she was fine. I even saw her going into the bathroom to help someone who was sick, so that was great news. June could be Florence Nightingale if she wanted. Just as long as she was safe.

The Friday afternoon before my date with Julian, I came home from school and washed my hair and shaved my legs, going extra-slow so I wouldn't nick myself. Not that I had seen Julian touching my legs (oh my God I would die), and not that I had seen us getting into any kind of situation that involved the emergency room, or a swimming pool either, but shaving my legs just felt like the kind of thing I should do before my first date. I was pretty sure that was one of the rules involved.

I already knew that Julian was going to pick me up at seven oh-three (the three minutes late was because he got stuck behind a bus at a red light on the way to my house. The lights in this neighborhood last forever sometimes.) We were going to see the new French film at the one arthouse movie theater that was twenty minutes away. I also knew that around the forty-three-minute mark, Julian was going to try and hold my hand, so I had already planned to knock the popcorn over and create a diversion. It made me feel better to have a game-plan. I had to start seeing Julian's future more, trying to look for June in it. I had no time for surprises now. Surprises only reminded me of everything I couldn't see.

But most importantly, I had to keep Julian away from the party.

After I got out of the shower, I put on jeans and my nicest sweater, the V-neck gray one that was soft and hadn't pilled up too much on the sides. I also cleaned the dirt off my sneakers and used some of June's hair stuff to make sure that my cowlick in the front stayed down. I even wore a bit of tinted lipgloss that tasted like watermelon. I looked nice, I had to admit. Respectable. The kind of girl who didn't look like she had the Power of Foresight.

And then around six thirty that evening, I put the next part of my plan into action.

I sauntered upstairs to May's room. She was wearing a black

hoodie and jeans, lying on her purple bedspread with her European history text wide open, twirling her pen between her fingers. "Woe to those who enter," she said without looking up.

"I'll take my chances," I told her.

"It's your funeral."

I ignored her and sat down on the edge of her bed. "May," I began. "Favoritest sister ever."

"No." She didn't even look up at me. "Whatever it is, no."

"Can't I just admire your—"

"No."

I sighed. "Okay, I need the biggest favor in the world."

"I never would have guessed."

"It involves June."

"This just keeps getting better." May calmly turned a page in her book.

"She's going to a party tonight with Mariah and . . ." I paused nervously. "I need you to follow her."

May just looked up at me with her bluish-green eyes. She and our dad have the same color eyes. It's kind of eerie now. "And how exactly am I supposed to—*oh no*."

"May, c'mon—"

"No. No way. You want me to turn invisible and follow our little sister? That is *not* cool. The ethics police are gonna haul you off to jail."

"There's no such thing."

"Then citizen's arrest it is."

"May! This is our sister we're talking about! She could be in danger!"

"Yeah, but April, you don't know that!" she exclaimed, tossing her book aside as she sat up. "Maybe she was getting a speeding ticket when you saw that vision!"

"She can't even *drive*! May, just come on. I can't go. You're the only one who can watch her."

May just laughed. "Excuse me? Excuse me?! Who here is the future predictor? Show of hands?" She looked around the room and then back at me. "Oh, *thaaat's* right. You. You're the one. Can't you just conjure up a little vision, a sneak preview?"

"Do you think I haven't tried? All I know is that June wears that stupid pink skirt and red heels, and Mariah is wasted."

May snorted. "I could have predicted that."

"Well, that's all I'm getting."

"So she's probably fine."

"But what if she's not? What if tonight is the night where there's an accident or something happens and—?"

"And what exactly am I, May Stephenson, a fifteen-year-old girl who lives in the fricking suburbs, going to do to stop fate?" May put her hands on her hips. "You tell me that. Do you ever see that happening?"

I paused. "No."

"Of course you don't. This is so wrong, April." She flopped back onto her pillow. "I'm pretty sure this violates every single moral and ethical rule in the book."

I pulled out my ace in the hole.

"What about when Mom and Chad went on their date?" I asked her. "I practically had to restrain you from following them. What's so different now? This is just June, not Mom."

May paused before asking, "And what am I supposed to tell Mom about where I'm going?"

I thought fast. "I don't know. Tutoring with Henry? You're so smart. You'll think of something."

"Don't even flatter me." She sighed and turned back to her book, but then back at me, looking me up and down. "Where are *you* going?"

Shit.

"Um, the movies."

"With who?"

"How do you know I'm going with someone?"

"Because it's Friday night." May spoke like she was talking to someone especially slow. "And you never, ever go out to the movies." And then her eyes became huge. "Shut up, tonight's the night, isn't it?"

"What? What are you—?"

"You're going with Julian, aren't you?"

I could feel myself blushing. "Yes, but that's—"

"Is tonight the big smoocheroo?"

I took a deep breath. "No, as a matter of fact, it's not. He is going to be very polite and courteous."

"Well, that's no fun."

I waited a minute before telling her. "Look," I said. "This is the part you don't know. When I had that dream, that vision, when I saw June and the lights? I also saw Julian, too. He was there."

May sat up on her bed again. "Are you serious?"

"Yes."

I could see May adding everything up in her head, her eyes widening as the pieces came together. "So you're going out with him for the sole purpose of making sure that he stays away from June?"

"I already made him swear he wouldn't even look at her, but this is just extra insurance."

May just shook her head. "April, that is so low. This is way lower than me secretly following June."

"Hey, it's not like I have a choice!" I bristled. "I'm trying to protect our sister, and if this is what I have to do . . ."

"So you're going to lie to a guy and pretend to like him and go on a date with him—"

"He was already gonna ask me out!" I protested. "I saw us at the movies. I just . . . moved it forward."

"You're *using* him. And now you're using me, too!"

"I'm not using him or you!" I cried. "It's not that I don't . . . I just . . ."

May raised an eyebrow. "So you like him?"

Oh God. Not May, too. June's matchmaking mindreading was enough of a pain.

"On the list of Complicated Things," I told her, "this is just below quantum physics and the theory of relativity. I'm just trying to make sure everything is okay."

"And so in doing that, you'll make lovey-dovey eyes at Julian while I'm at a party, being literally invisible and watching our little sister puke up the contents of someone's liquor cabinet. Won't it just be *romantic*?" She fluttered her eyelashes before pretending to gag herself.

"June's not gonna puke," I said. "She doesn't get sick. Trust me. I've seen that much. So you'll do it? For June?"

May hesitated before saying, "You owe me so much." May can look really scary—almost dangerous—when she wants to.

I grinned anyway and hugged her, even as she tugged herself away. "*So much*," she repeated.

"You can have anything," I promised, relieved I'd found a way to make sure everything was going to be all right. "My firstborn child, even."

"What kind of crappy deal is that?" she frowned. "What am I gonna do with a baby? 'Oh, here, May, I'm so grateful that I'm gonna give you something that screams and cries and poops.' Yuck. Just give me money instead. Or a first-class ticket to Paris. Not your theoretical baby."

June came bounding up the stairs then. "What baby?" she said. "Whose baby?"

"Were you reading our minds again?" I demanded. "Were you?"

She just rolled her eyes. "Whatevs, Miss Paranoid. And no, I wasn't, I was talking to Mariah on the phone downstairs, and frankly, I'm more interested in hearing what she thinks than what you think." June clapped her hands together like an adorable seal. "So get this. Mariah's worried about me coming to the party tonight because she thinks I'll look cuter than her! Hee! So whose baby are we talking about?"

May just laughed and opened her computer. I could tell she was thinking hard, keeping June out of her mind.

"It was just a metaphor about when I have kids," I told June.

June's eyes lit up. "So you and Julian did it already?"

"Don't you think you would know by now if I had?" I asked her. "How many choruses of 'Greasy Grimy Gopher Guts' do you think I can sing that would distract from *those* thoughts?"

June nodded thoughtfully. "Good point. I, on the other hand, need to iron my skirt."

May waved June away, but I stopped her in the doorway. "So you're going to that party tonight?"

"Duh. Mariah's picking me up in twenty minutes."

"Mariah's picking you up for a party at her house?"

June smirked at me. "Yep. Isn't that a *nice* thing to do, don't you think?"

"I think it's a waste of natural resources. And you're telling Mom . . . ?"

"That Mariah and I are going to the movies and then for food afterwards."

"You know you have to be home by eleven."

"Who says I won't be?" June smiled. "And you know Mom always falls asleep by ten, anyway."

I looked back at May for help, but she ignored me. "She's singing 'Frere Jacques,'" June informed me. "She's too busy blocking me out to talk right now."

May just laughed to herself and clicked her computer keys with unnecessary force as we both headed out of her dimly lit room.

Fifteen minutes later June came bounding back out of her own room, wearing the pink skirt and black tights and shiny red shoes. "What do you think?" she said, twirling in the doorway to my room.

I froze. I had been thinking about Julian, wondering if maybe I should put on a necklace or something, wondering if that's what girls were supposed to do on dates, and I couldn't stop my thoughts fast enough.

"Shut. Up," June squealed. "You have a date with that guy?" She giggled and covered her mouth. "Shut up, shut up, *shut up*! Tell me everything."

"I can't do both," I pointed out.

"Stop being so literal!" Then she looked me up and down. "You're wearing jeans on your date?"

"I always wear jeans." I glanced in the wall mirror at my outfit. Next to June, I looked like I was going to dig up potatoes in a field. "I like my jeans. We can't all pull off the pink-skirt look, June. It's not for everyone."

"I love this skirt!" she said, crowding me out of the way so she could look at her own reflection. "It puts a little hustle in my bustle, if you get what I'm saying."

"It's also perfect for being puked on by idiots," May added, wandering in. I could tell she was still pissed about what I was making her do.

June just sighed. "April, is anyone gonna puke on me?"

"No. But just . . ." I hesitated and both my sisters looked at me. "Just be careful, okay? Don't be stupid."

June rolled her eyes. "Thanks, *Mom*, I know. So where's your date tonight? What are you doing? Did you kiss him yet?"

"We're going to see the new Jeunet film—"

"Nerd," June said.

"You're going to the new Jeunet film?!" May cried, and I winced. It was sort of salt in the wound, considering that she's the Francophile and I was forcing her to spend the night watching people she hates get trashed. "Hate my life," she sighed.

"And what else are you doing?" June said. "Are you going hiking or something? You're wearing shoes with rubber soles."

"They're practical."

June shook her head. "You're hopeless."

"Says the girl wearing cotton candy for a skirt," I shot back. "Look, just promise me that you'll call me or Mom if you need a ride—"

"Duh again," she sighed. "God, why does everyone think I'm incapable of taking care of myself?"

"No comment," May muttered.

"Whoa, Mom thoughts approaching," June said suddenly, and ten seconds later we could hear my mom on the stairs. "Hey, girls?" she said, then saw me and June wearing nicer-than-usual clothes. "Hey, where's the party?" she grinned. "You two look so nice!"

May snorted a laugh through her nose.

"There's no party!" June said quickly. "I'm just going out with Mariah to the movies and then maybe for food. And home by eleven, I know, I know."

My mom looked surprised that June brought up the curfew before she did, but then she just looked to me. "And what about you?"

I sighed inwardly. "There's this guy, Julian? And he goes to school with us, his locker is above mine, and he asked me to go to the movies tonight? If that's okay?"

There was something dancing in my mom's eyes that I couldn't quite understand. "A boy asked you out?" she said. "And you're just telling me now?"

Now both my sisters' eyes were on me. Great.

"Well," I said, "I sort of asked him out first?"

"You did?" June squealed, then slapped my arm. "You *cougar*!"

I glared at her, then looked at my mom, who was now obviously biting back a smile. "And this Julian boy, he's nice?"

"No, he's an ax murderer," May spoke up. "April's going to rehabilitate him. It's her volunteer project for school."

All of us except for May rolled our eyes. "He's nice," I assured my mom. "Trust me."

My mom nodded. "So I assume he's going to pick you up so I can meet him?" It wasn't really a question the way she said it, and I was glad I had figured this part out earlier.

"He'll be here around seven, give or take three minutes," I said, then cleared my throat and prayed May wouldn't kill me for this next part. "And May has plans, too."

May almost fell off the bed, but she recovered long enough to say robotically, "Yes, I'm going to do homework with Henry. It will be lovely and exactly how I imagined spending yet another Friday night. Oh, I'm so happy. What joy, what rapture."

My mom just smiled. "Well, it's good you're finally taking an interest in schoolwork."

June coughed to hide her giggle.

"I just can't believe that all three of my girls are going out and doing their own things." Now my mom's voice was sort of wobbly. "You're growing up so fast, it makes me so happy!"

All three of us immediately rushed over to her. "Mom, don't cry!" June said. "If you cry, I'll cry, and I'm wearing DiorShow mascara. It can't run; it's too expensive. Every tear would cost, like, five dollars."

"Oh, for the love of God," May muttered, then elbowed her way in to hug our mom. "Mom, do you want us to stay home tonight? Are you gonna be lonely?"

Yes! I suddenly thought. May was a genius. We could stop this whole thing if we all just stayed home and—

"No, no, that's ridiculous," my mom said. "Don't worry about me. I'm just glad you girls are adjusting and moving on and making friends. You'll see, one day you might be moms and then you'll understand."

I doubted that, but I just gave her a squeezeshe kissed me back and patted my hair down. "You look lovely," she said. "I'm sure Julian will appreciate it."

"Well, we'll see," I said. "Who knows what could happen?"

Our mom went into her room soon afterwards, changing out of her work clothes, and May and June went back to their rooms. I glanced again at my mirror, making sure I looked all right. Not that it mattered, though. This was a MacGyver-style mission, I reminded myself, not a date-date.

"April?" June called from her room. "Can you come here a minute?"

"What is it?" I said, following her voice.

She was standing in front of her dresser, digging through one of the drawers, but she stopped long enough to give me a withering glance. "So I'm still pissed at you," she said, "but I just can't let this happen."

"Let what happen?"

She sighed "Seriously, April? Your first date and you're wearing a *sports bra*?"

I glanced down at my chest. "What?" I said. "I don't really have anything else!"

June shook her head. "I swear to God," she muttered, then pulled out something puffy and pink and lacy. There were tiny pink bows at the bottom of the straps and lace outlining the cups. "Here," she said, thrusting it at me. "Put this on and thank me later."

"Where did you get this?" I said. "This is, like, the girliest thing I've ever seen."

"Well, it's a *bra*, so I hope so. I'm sorry, I won't let you rock the uniboob look on a date."

I took the bra from her. "Thanks," I said.

"No problem." She grinned at me. "Remember every detail for me, okay? I wanna live vicariously."

I took a deep breath and let it out slowly. "Anything," I said, "for you."

chapter 14

"There are few things worse than being all alone in a crowd."

I was going to kill my sisters.

I know I have a bad night ahead of me when I'd rather be studying European history with Henry. Hell, I would have sat through a Powerpoint lecture about Stanford rather than follow June to some stupid high school party. I know my little sister, after all. She's seen all the movies, heard all the stories, and was probably convinced that going to a real high school party would change her life.

Ha.

I also thought April was being overcautious and freaked out. I mean, she couldn't even predict an earthquake. How does she know that what she sees is even going to happen? It didn't make sense, and worse, I didn't know how to argue with her. So I said yes, I'll go, I'll spy on our little sister.

What a ridiculously bad mistake.

The first inkling I got that told me I had made the wrong decision was when Mariah's boyfriend pulled up to the curb. I had pretended to leave for Henry's five minutes earlier, but instead I just disappeared and waited in the bushes for my secret ride. I got stabbed by a few thorny branches by the time the car finally arrived, and when June came dashing out the front door, I ran after her like a total stalker and slid into the car just before the door shut.

How was this even my life?

The car apparently had been busy collecting rust and weird engine noises. "Hi!" June cried to her friend, hugging her over the front seat while I curled up in the corner and silently cursed April. I already knew that June couldn't read my mind when I was invisible, which was lucky for both of us at this point.

"Hi, Blake," June added, but Blake just nodded at her and continued to smoke his cigarette as he pulled out of our driveway and careened down the street.

I was 97 percent sure that Blake had been stoned when he took his driving test. That's just an educated guess.

Mariah and June buzzed about something. Well, June blabbered on for a while. Mariah wasn't exactly a chatterbox, but it was obvious she liked having someone like June around, someone who thought she could do no wrong. "Yeah," Mariah said every so often, but as soon as we got to the first red light, Blake leaned over and kissed her, interrupting June's manic chatterings. Well, he didn't really kiss her so much as attempt to give her a tonsillectomy with his tongue. I haven't kissed a guy, so I'm not a romantic virtuoso or anything, but that just didn't look sexy. Or even comfortable.

I glanced over at June, almost not wanting to see her face. She looked a little awkward and really young, even though we're only thirteen months apart. Why couldn't she have been a nerd like April, or a loser loner like me? Why did she want to be like these people? I know I'm not cool, but at least I don't have moronic friends.

Mariah turned around to look at June. "You wanna stop and get food first?" she asked. "We're gonna go to Del Taco."

"Cool, yeah," June said, happy to be included once more. "Hey, Blake, did you take the GED today?"

"Nope."

I was pretty sure we had just hit the creative apex of Blake's vocabulary.

Mariah put her hand on his arm, but he ignored her. "He was passed out this morning," she said affectionately. "He even slept through me calling him."

By now, I was convinced that Blake had been dropped on his head as a child, and that this was possibly the best thing that woud ever happen to him.

"Oh," June said. "So when are you taking the test?"

Blake shrugged and hit the gas when the light turned yellow. "Whenever. Nothing's set in stone."

"Yeah, no kidding, Blake," she replied. "No freaking kidding."

I have to say, I'm pretty amazed that Blake didn't drop out of school sooner than he did. When we got to the Del Taco drive-thru, he tried to count out exact change, and it practically gave me a migraine to listen to him mutter. I could tell June was annoyed, too, and I couldn't imagine what it would be like to have to hear Blake's thoughts. It was probably like being put under heavy sedation or hit in the head with a billy club.

"Here," June finally said, thrusting a five-dollar bill over the front seat. "It's on me. Keep the change."

Blake didn't even say thank you.

I lowered my invisible head against the front seat and banged it against the cracked pleather interior. There were a bunch of *Road & Track* magazines under my invisible feet, along with another magazine that had a girl in a red bikini on the cover. I wasn't expecting *Popular Science* or the *Wall Street Journal*, but this was ridiculous.

As soon as we got to the party and June opened the door, I scrambled out the door past her, grateful to be out of the car. That relief only lasted for about ten seconds, though, as I realized that I was actually at a party where I didn't know anyone.

I was invisible, of course, but there are few things worse than being all alone in a crowd of people. Not only that, but from what I could see of the party, it looked like the red-cup, beer-swilling, idiots-attending party of my nightmares.

Next to me, though, June beamed. "Awesome," I heard her whisper.

Kill me now, I thought miserably.

It was packed inside the small house, and it smelled like beer and sweat and hair-styling products from all the girls there. The music was playing really loud, some top-40 song that I hated and would probably never get out of my head, and I watched as June and Mariah held hands and went into the kitchen. I followed because I literally had nothing better to do at this party.

The house was pretty nice, I had to admit. It wasn't like MTV *Cribs*, but it had an upstairs and a downstairs and a kitchen big enough to fit all of my stupid-ass classmates. Most of them were in there now, but I didn't know anyone's names. They all looked sort of familiar, but not in a friend way, more like the way commercial actors seem familiar. Just because you recognize people doesn't mean you know them.

There was a china cabinet near the living room, holding a bunch of Hummel figurines and some crystal swan sculptures. It was safe here, as out of the way as an invisible person could get, and I absent-mindedly chewed on a cuticle as I watched June make her way outside, hot on Mariah's heels. *This isn't so bad*, I thought to myself. *It's just a party. Who cares about these people, anyway?*

Thirty minutes later, I was ready to go drown myself in the keg.

June was fine, of course, just like I knew she would be. She had a beer, and I watched to see if she was gonna puke or maybe climb onto the roof and proclaim that she could fly. But she was just giggly on the couch, talking to a boy that I didn't recognize. When she got up to leave, she took her cup with her, and I was pretty sure that April had drilled her on never leaving her drink unattended. April had given me the same lecture last year, but it wasn't like anyone was inviting me to parties back then.

Or now.

What did look especially inviting was the beer June had. I'm not a huge beer person, but I was so tired of watching everyone else have fun that I wanted some for myself. Someone had put the music on repeat so the same annoying song kept blasting out, and I finally made the executive decision that June would be fine.

Then I went to get my beer.

I managed to snag a cup before anyone noticed, then I crept upstairs to the part of the house where no one could see me drink it. It was much quieter and cooler up there, and I took a few sips of my warm beer and let out a sigh as my body came back to earth.

This was way better.

I wandered around, washing my hands in the bathroom before going across the hall and into an empty bedroom. It was dark, and I reached for the lights before realizing that there were people in the room. Two people in fact.

Two people. In a room. With the lights off. You do the math.

I almost started to stammer apologies before I realized that I had gone invisible once again, surprised right out of my skin. There was a rumbling male voice, coaxing and dangerous at the same time, a wolf in sheep's clothing. "C'mon," he was saying. "C'mon, it's fine. She's downstairs."

It was Blake.

I stood in the doorway, my eyes probably ready to fall right out of their sockets.

"No, wait, I can't," the girl was saying. And the girl was definitely *not* Mariah. Whoever she was, she already sounded pretty trashed. And I didn't know what was happening, but something told me that it wasn't good. Not at all.

I slammed my fist into the lightswitch before disappearing again, both literally and figuratively. I knew there was no way anyone could see me, but I still ducked back into the hallway, listening to the confused voices in the room. "What the fuck?" Blake muttered, and a few seconds later, Avery came out of the room, pulling her shirt up on her shoulder and her black hair all tangled. Her eyes were big and drunk, and Blake came storming out of the room past her, pounding down the stairs, unhappy that someone had thrown the light on his little game.

Asshole.

I wandered into another room, still hanging onto my plastic cup. This was way better, I realized. There was no one in here so I just left the lights off, and I could see June through the window—she was sitting outside on the grass with Mariah and another girl, talking fast and furious about something. Or someone, more likely. June looked happy, but it wasn't the happy face that she gets when she sees kittens or new shoes. This was the happy face she put on when our dad said he was moving to Houston, when June said, "Oh my God, can we have horses?" with a huge smile on her face, a smile big enough for everyone else to share.

It was sort of weird how her happy face just made me sad.

Before I could start to feel bad for my sister, though, the light suddenly turned on and I whirled around.

It was Henry.

"What the hell?" we both yelled at the same time.

"What are you doing here?" he demanded.

"Me?" I cried. "What are *you* doing here? Is this even your kind of scene?"

"Well, yeah," he said, "considering this is my *bedroom*."

Whoa, Nellie.

I glanced around and saw numerous Stanford pennants on the wall and a crimson comforter on the bed. There was a neatly organized desk with some pencils in a Stanford mug by the light and all of his textbooks stacked into a neat pile.

"Wait a minute," I said. "This is your house?"

He nodded tersely.

"Oh my God, Mariah's your sister?" I clapped my hand over my mouth. "How is that possible? Are you even biologically related or is this a step-kid thing?"

Henry let out a huge sigh and came into the room. "You know, I think I have more questions than you do," he said. "Like, why are you in my room?"

"Oh, that. Well, that's, um, that's pretty funny." I was starting to walk away from the window in case June saw me, but I tripped over a shoe and sloshed a little beer on the floor and a stack of—

"My *National Geographics*!" Henry cried. "Oh my God, what are you doing?"

"Oops, sorry," I said, then giggled. I never giggle, though. It must have been the beer. There were so many yellow magazines in a stack along the floor against the wall that it looked like a small skyline. "Yeah, you can never have too many of those, can you?"

"It's a subscription," Henry said, bending to blot the beer off one of them with a tissue. "Now can you get out?"

Instead, I just sat down on the bed. Again, it must have been the beer. "No," I said. "I'm sorry, I just followed my little sister to this party because our older sister made me and it sucks. No offense, of course. So wow, Mariah's your sister, huh? What's that like?"

"Like being in hell with someone you hate," Henry replied.

"Henry!" I gasped. "Did you just make a non-Stanford-related joke?" I pretended to be shocked as I drained the last of my beer. Thank God at least one of these clowns knew how to pump a keg. "That was a great effort!"

I saw a small smile toy at the edge of Henry's mouth. "Do you want another one?" he asked.

"Another joke?"

"No, another beer."

I guess I must have been tipping the cup a little too far back into my mouth, trying to get the last drop.

"I do," I said, "but I can't go back downstairs. My sister doesn't know I'm here. I'm spying on her. Ssshh." I put my finger to my lips. "It's a secret."

This time, Henry actually smiled, and he came back a minute later with two red cups. "Wow, two of them?" I said. "Henry, you spoil me!"

"One's for me," he said. "Don't get greedy."

"I'm just grateful," I said, then took a long sip. This one was ice cold, which was nice considering that his room was starting to feel really warm. For a second I realized I'd never actually been in a boy's bedroom before. "So. You and Mariah are brother and sister. You never even said anything."

Henry sat down in his desk chair and shrugged. "You didn't ask."

"Well, it wasn't a question about European history, so I wasn't sure if it was allowed."

"You can ask me about Stanford, too," he said, and this time we laughed together.

I wondered if April had seen this happening, me and Henry drinking beer and actually getting along.

"Okay," I said. "Here's a question. What's so great about Stanford?"

"It's somewhere new," he replied. "It's somewhere not here."

"Well, I mean, I'm not the biggest fan of your sister"—words couldn't describe how much I disliked Mariah—"but are your parents lame or something?"

And miracle of miracles, Henry started talking. He told me about his parents, how his dad got remarried and moved up to San Francisco and had twins with his new wife. "Mariah hates them," he said. "She won't go visit. She just hangs out with Blake."

"It's hard when it's your sister," I agreed. "I mean, my sisters make me crazy and everything. . . ." It took a few extra seconds to get the words out. ". . . But they're my sisters."

"Yeah," Henry said with a sigh in agreement.

And somewhere in my heart, I missed my dad.

There was a sudden commotion downstairs, people laughing and screaming about something, and I remembered what I was supposed to be doing. "Oh, um, hey, not to jet on you, but I should probably go check on my sister. But will you be . . . around? Later?"

Henry shoved his hands in his pockets and nodded. "Probably. Considering I live here."

I smiled despite myself and ran downstairs to check on June, making sure that Henry wasn't following me as I hit the stairs. By the time I got into the kitchen, I was invisible again. Thank God I was learning how to control this. Not that it mattered at a party full of drunk people, though. They would probably just think I was hired entertainment as I flickered on and off like a broken bulb.

There was a huge crowd of people in the kitchen, and I figured out pretty quickly that it was a drunken game of Truth or Dare, with Blake and Mariah towards the middle of the crowd. Yeah, because *that* relationship was gonna end well. I was feeling sort of fuzzy around the edges, but I was definitely sober enough to stay away from that game. It would only lead to trouble.

Instead I scanned for June, but I didn't see her. Maybe she was outside. I was just about to go looking for her when I heard Mariah yell, "Henrrryyyyy!" and start giggling hysterically. "Henry! It's my brother! Henry, truth or dare!"

I whirled around and saw Henry trying to throw away our red cups from upstairs. Of course he was recycling them. God forbid if any trash gets left in his neatnik room. He looked half-annoyed and half-pained at his sister's screech, and he tossed the cups in the bag so hard that I thought they would bounce back.

"Truth or dare?" Mariah cried again. "I'll choose for you! Truth!" She took a huge sip of something that was definitely not beer, then hiccupped and wiped her mouth with her hand.

She is really just a class act.

"Truth!" she said again. "That girl you're always tutoring. Do you want to fuck her?" She giggled hysterically at her question, and suddenly everyone was staring at Henry.

Myself included.

I could feel my heart starting to do flippy things, and I wasn't sure if it was the beer or just good old-fashioned adrenaline that made me want to throw up. I kind of wished I wasn't there, but at the same time, I didn't want to leave. I was standing right next to Henry now, so close that I could practically count his eyelashes, and he had no clue that I was there.

Nobody did.

"Tell the truth!" Mariah screamed.

Henry swallowed hard, and then his eyes got hard and steely. "Hell no," he said. "Not *her*." And then he disappeared back upstairs.

I was suddenly glad I was invisible. If I hadn't been, then I probably would have started crying. Then again, if Henry *had* been able to see me, I wouldn't have known what an asshole he really was. But now I knew.

After all, he had said it right to my face.

I mean, it wasn't like I was planning on makin' babies with the guy, but did he have to say it like that? Like the mere idea of me made him ill?

There were a couple of guys in the dining room setting up vodka shots, and I headed in that direction. June came flying past me, having no clue that I was right there, yelling, "What'd I miss? What'd I miss?" at Mariah. I just stalked right past her and made myself visible as I went through the doorway. Just like I thought: people were so drunk and the house was so crowded that even when they *could* see me?

No one saw me at all.

chapter 15

"You have got to be kidding me."

You know, I have to say, not that the party wasn't exciting, but I kept waiting for it to be different.

Don't get me wrong, though. It was definitely awesome, just not quite what I was expecting. I guess every time you see a party scene in a movie, there's always something happening, like an impromptu dance party or someone so drunk that they agree to shave their head. You can always tell that it's a party that will *change! their! lives!* and I wanted that.

Then again, those people in the movies aren't also mindreaders. I guess that's sort of a bummer for me.

"You smoke?" Lilian asked me. She was one of Mariah's friends, but she didn't go to our school. I would say half of the people didn't go to our school, and I would know this because I'm observant. Lilian had pale skin and a hard face, like her hobbies included boxing and looking menacing, and I shook my head at the Camel Lights she offered.

"No, thanks," I said. I know smoking kills and all that, but also, you get these really weird pucker lines around your mouth. And I haven't been using moisturizer every night since I was ten for no reason. "But go ahead," I added. "I don't care."

It was sort of stressful to keep a conversation going with people I didn't really know. If you weren't talking to someone, you were standing there looking like a moron, so I kept trying to keep the conversation going. Somehow I ended up standing near this bucktoothed guy named Derek I recognized from homeroom. I had now heard about Derek's mom's prizewinning rabbits for twenty minutes, even though I hate rabbits and Derek sort of spits when he talks.

In the movies, they never talk about prizewinning rabbits at parties. Still, at least I wasn't hanging around by myself like that Avery girl. She kept floating from group to group, but it wasn't like she was a super chatterbox. I half-wanted to sic Derek on her, but he was sort of a nice guy and that would have been mean. (And also? He kind of looked like a rabbit. Funny that.)

Still, the music was crazy loud, so forceful that I could practically feel it move my eardrums, and I made sure to have my beer with me at all times. The red plastic cups were ubiquitous (my newest word from spelling bee guy). And every so often, someone would spill or slosh, and everyone nearby would scream. Mariah, in particular, thought it was hilarious, draping herself over my shoulders and giggling uncontrollably. She already smelled like beer, but that was okay because she was my friend. And that's what friends do—have fun at parties and drink and watch everyone else do the same thing.

At least, that's what they do in the movies.

"Heeeeeeey," Mariah slurred at me as the night wore on. Her eyes were hazy, and I put my hand on her elbow to catch her before she tumbled to the ground. "Oops!" she giggled. "Stay upright."

"Yeah," I grinned, still hanging onto her. I was still sipping my beer from time to time, not letting it out of my sight. (April gave me a lecture about the danger of roofies last year that seared itself into my brain.) "Having fun?"

Mariah smiled sleepily. "I love my house. And my friends. And my boy. Where's my boy?"

I glanced around. "I dunno. I haven't seen him in a while."

"That's cool," she said. She was hanging onto me again, clinging as some people stampeded past. I recognized this guy Matthew from my geometry class, and Arthur from history. I kinda wanted to say hi, but I didn't know them. Not really, not like you would know someone well enough to say hello.

"So you know," Mariah said as we stumbled together towards the grass. "My dad has a beach house."

"Really?" I said, nearly dropping her on the ground. "Where?"

"Cabo."

"A beach house in Cabo?" A beach house in Cabo! It's seriously my dream to go to a beach house in Cabo. I just didn't realize that until Mariah said it. But now that I knew? Totally my new goal.

"You should come," Mariah said, falling down next to me. "You and Blake and me. It'll be awesome."

"Your dad doesn't care that you bring your boyfriend to Mexico?" I asked.

"Whatever. He's not around. He doesn't even go down there." Mariah frowned and waved her hand around, dismissing the idea. But her brain was saying, *Fuck him, fuck him, fuck him,* really really fast, like she didn't even know she was saying it, and I leaned back a bit, just in case her thoughts became contagious. I wasn't quite sure who we were talking about, Blake or her dad, and really, I didn't care.

Just put me in a bikini and get me to Cabo.

"That'd be amazing," I said to her, handing her my beer so she could finish it. (Beer tastes gross. What's the point of having two older sisters if no one tells me this stuff?)

"Amaaaaaaaaayzing," Mariah repeated, just as Blake came out the back door, his eyes sort of wild and weird. "Blake!" Mariah screamed, and he looked sort of embarrassed that she knew his name, but came over anyway, flopping down next to us. His brain was all about light, lights being turned on, lights so bright that I couldn't see anyone else in the room, and I decided that Blake was either super drunk or super high and that maybe now was a good time to start socializing again. It was either that or watch them make out and listen to their thoughts. Ew.

Unfortunately, though, Derek cornered me again. "Hey!" he grinned when he saw me step inside. "Miss me?" His front teeth glimmered in the dim light.

I almost snapped back, but I bit my tongue because I could tell from his thoughts that I made him really nervous, the kind of nervous you get when you're talking to someone you like and your mouth gets dry and you say every stupid thing in your head. It wasn't the way Blake thought of Mariah. In fact, Blake didn't really think about Mariah at all.

So I spent another half hour on the couch with Derek, leaning back as far as possible and listening to the thoughts around me. It's kind of fun to hear people's brains get drunker and drunker, like someone hit the slo-mo button. I even giggled when Julie Hincks started to fantasize about sticking her tongue down Derek's throat. That girl had to be totally wasted. There was no other logical explanation.

By the time I was able to extricate myself from Derek, something had happened in the kitchen. I ran in as soon as I heard shrieks of laughter, beelining right for Mariah. "What'd I miss, what'd I miss?"

I cried. But she was giggling too hard, and her brain was pretty much mush. Instead, she just grabbed my shoulders and kept laughing, and pretty soon I was laughing with her, too. Is this what they meant by a contact high? I wasn't sure. "Cabo!" she squealed in my ear, and suddenly everything felt amazing. This was what I had wanted. I wanted friends, I wanted parties, I wanted music and people, and I wanted to be myself.

And I finally had it.

Unfortunately, I also had to pee.

I managed to hold it until I just couldn't anymore, and then I found the first-floor bathroom. The door was shut, and I banged on it impatiently. "Hurry up!" I cried. "There's a line!"

There wasn't, but whatever. I seriously had to go.

Avery walked past, holding a red plastic cup and looking sort of puffy-eyed. "Oh, hey," she said.

"Hey," I replied, trying not to hop up and down like a four-year-old. "How are you? How's work?" When she looked confused, I added, "My sisters and I saw you at Best Buy, remember?"

"Oh yeah," she said. "It's fine, whatever. Hey, have you seen Mariah around? Is she with Blake?"

Visions of Mariah and Blake flashed through her mind, the two of them making out like the world was ending. I winced a little at the vision. "Uh, I think they're—she's outside," I said. "I'm not sure."

"Cool," she said. "You might want to find a different restroom, by the way. It's gonna be occupied for a while."

I pounded on the door again and asked, "How do you know?"

A voice inside the bathroom yelled, "Go away!" and I froze as Avery drifted away.

I knew that voice.

Ignoring Avery, I yanked the door open and stepped inside. Someone was hunched over the toilet, moaning softly to herself, and when she looked up at me, my eyes almost fell out of my head.

"Oh my God," I groaned. "You have *got* to be kidding me."

chapter 16

"This isn't make-believe! This is it!"

april

Okay, not to sound selfish, but there is one nice thing about having divorced parents who live apart. When a guy comes over to pick you up for a date, he only has to meet one of them. I hadn't ever thought about that aspect before, mostly because there wasn't a chance in hell that a boy would need to meet my parents for any date-related reasons, but now that the opportunity was here, I realized it was a bonus.

But again, this was not a date. This was a fact-finding experience. Operation: Save June and Whatever Other Yahoos Were at the Party.

I have to say, my mom was a pretty smooth operator. My sisters had just left when Julian arrived, and my mom shook Julian's hand and didn't act weird or say things like, "I have a gun and I know how to use it, Buster," or whatever overprotective parents say to their daughters' dates. (And just so you know, she doesn't have a gun. We aren't even allowed to shoot rubber bands at each other.)

Luckily, Julian went with the flow. He wasn't even wearing his Anarchy hat, either, and his dark hair looked kind of tousled and cute. He shook my mom's hand back, introduced himself, and called her "ma'am" which I found hilarious. I had already seen this little meeting going well, but I was never sure what my visions were missing. My brain couldn't see everything, which made the holes in my visions seem that much bigger. I never knew what would fall through the cracks.

"So you're going to the movies?" my mom asked him. "That'll be nice. April never gets to go to the movies."

See what I mean? Like that. I had not seen *that* comment coming. Now Julian would think I was some sort of turtle-hermit hybrid.

I gave my mom the death glare behind Julian's back as I shrugged into my coat. She just smiled and said, "Well, have fun, you two. April, home by midnight, okay?"

"Okay," I said.

"Call if you need anything. You have your cell phone?"

I waved it at her, and Julian very nicely held my coat so I could put my other arm into it. I got a bit tangled up, and it quickly devolved into a *Three Stooges* moment. But it was still a thoughtful gesture.

And my mom smiled so hard I thought the lower half of her face would fall off.

"Bye," I said as Julian went to open the front door. I gave my mom a hug and hissed in her ear, "'April never gets to go to the movies'? Really???"

"Oh, relax," she whispered back. "There's a boy holding a door open for you. Go."

I waved goodbye to her as we went out the door, and when she waved back, I saw her evening lying ahead of her. She would eat cheese and crackers, standing up at the counter because there was no one to sit with her at the table. Then she'd watch MTV because it made her think of us, her girls, all of whom were growing up and going away. She'd go to bed at ten and sleep on the left side, just like she always did. She would turn up the volume on her cell phone and put it right by her head, just in case we called, but I already knew that when I got home that night, she would be asleep and her phone wouldn't ring once.

"Earth to you," Julian said as he held the car door open for me. "Where'd you go? Your eyes got weird for a second."

"Just trying to remember if I unplugged the iron upstairs," I said, and bit back the sad feeling that ached in my throat. "So who taught you about opening doors?"

"My mom," he said. "She sort of threatened to take away my car if I didn't treat you well."

"Really?"

"Oh, yeah. She said that if I wasn't a gentleman, she'd take the car and I'd have to ride my bike and then we'd see how many dates I'd get." He laughed to himself as he started the engine. "Of course, I've had the car for a year, and you're the first girl that's been in it."

"Oh," I said. I didn't know whether to feel honored or weirded-out. We were on a date, an *actual* date. It was finally sinking in. I glanced around. Julian's car wasn't filthy, but it was obviously a guy's car. He didn't even have an air freshener or a trash bag. "Well, if it helps, I can call your mom and tell her that you were very nice to me."

Julian laughed and started backing out of the driveway. "The night's not over yet."

I just smiled and fastened my seatbelt. "Don't worry," I said. "I've got a good feeling about it."

The movie was only half-crowded, and we found seats towards the back just as the lights started to dim. "I suppose you're one of those people who doesn't like it when other people talk during the previews," he whispered as he settled the popcorn between us.

"Ssshh," I replied, which made him laugh. He really did have a nice laugh, and I had to remind myself that Julian equalled trouble.

No matter how nice his laugh was.

Afterwards, we walked over to this café for coffee, and he paid for that, too, even buying me an extra shot of espresso. "You're so not gonna sleep tonight," he said as the barista handed me my drink. I just smiled and didn't bother to explain that that was the point, that the last thing I wanted to do was sleep and have that dream and see his and June's faces again. I'd take espresso-induced insomnia any day.

"So," I said once we stole a table by the window. "What'd you think of the movie?"

Julian sipped his coffee thoughtfully. "I guess I just have one question."

"Hmmm?"

"What the hell was that?"

I practically spit cappuccino all over him. "THAT was French magical realism!" I cried. "Did we even see the same movie? Did you fall asleep?"

"No, because I was too busy *reading* my movie." He glanced at me. "Uh-oh. You liked it, didn't you?"

"I loved it," I said, and it was the truth. I felt even worse for making May follow June to the party, since she probably would have loved it, too. "You didn't?"

"April, it was completely unrealistic."

"It was a metaphor!"

"Next time, we're seeing one of the *Saw* films."

"Oh, yeah," I scoffed. "Your mom threatens to take your car away from you if you don't open a door for me, and you want to take me to a movie where people disembowel each other? Ha. You're a comedian."

Julian grinned, and I suddenly realized that we were talking about our second date. He was going to ask me out again, and I wasn't sure if I knew that because of the vision I was having or because of the way Julian's face looked when he smiled at me.

"So," he said. "If I promise we don't see a disemboweling film, wanna do it again?"

I started tearing my napkin into shreds. "Uh," I said, sounding like the village idiot. "Yeah, it's just . . ."

Julian sat back in his chair and ran his hand through his dark hair. "Oh."

"No, no, it's not that," I said quickly. "It's just . . ." I took a deep breath and tried to figure out how to tell him something without telling him anything. "Things have been sort of weird. At my house."

"Yeah?"

I nodded. "Yeah, my parents, they, uh, they got divorced a couple of months ago. That's why we moved here. And then it's just been all strange. Really strange. I mean, I can't even explain how strange things have been, so just trust me on this."

"Strange like the movie we just saw?"

"Not even. Strange like . . ."

I wanted to tell him so bad. I wanted to say everything, that my sisters and I were blessed or cursed or haunted or whatever, that we were *something*. I needed someone else to carry the burden before I dropped it and everything fell apart.

I took a deep breath. "Um, my sisters and I, we have this—"

Cream everywhere, dripping down the side of the condiment bar in fat, oily drops, leaking all over people's shoes , , ,

"Oh, no!" I said without thinking, and two seconds later, some guy knocked over the creamer container and sure enough, cream everywhere.

Julian looked at me when I said that, then turned around to follow my gaze just in time to see the accident. "Oh, that sucks," he sighed. "Good thing I already filled up."

But the vision reminded me that I hadn't watched May or June in almost an hour. Julian was leaning over to hand the guy some of our napkins, and I glanced down and closed my eyes and looked hard. But all I could see was June standing in the kitchen, laughing next to Mariah, looking happy. It was the same thing I had seen all week, the same stupid vision that refused to confirm my worst fears, and I took a deep breath and let it go.

June was fine. May was fine. I couldn't see either of them. Everything had to be fine.

"You okay?" Julian said, leaning in to look at me.

"I'm fine," I said automatically.

"You know, you get this really weird look on your face sometimes," he said. "It's like you're watching TV."

"Really?" I said before I could help myself. "That's what I look like?" I blushed. I couldn't believe he'd been studying my face that closely.

"Yep." Julian sat back and reached for his coffee. "So your parents got divorced and now things are strange. Why does that mean you can't go to the movies again?"

I squirmed a little in my seat. "You know, you're very direct," I told him, trying to buy time.

He raised an eyebrow. "You know a better way to be, Bossy McBosserson?"

I smiled despite myself, and Julian smiled back. "I can go to the movies," I said. "I just . . . it's just so complicated. Life is so crazy right now. I don't even know who I am."

Julian just laughed. "April, no one knows who they are. Everyone's life is crazy. Look at me, I'm completely screwed up."

"Way to sell the second date," I said.

"You know what I mean."

He was right, I did know. I searched frantically, looking for a second date with Julian, but before I could get too far, Julian started talking again.

"I like you," he said. "How's that for direct? You're the first girl to ever give me shit about my styrofoam coffee cup and my white bread and the first girl who wasn't scared of me, or didn't accuse me of being some crazy goth freak just because I wore black or whatever. And I don't know what your deal is, but I don't give a damn that your parents are divorced or your life is strange. I don't care."

"You say that now."

"I do. I am. I'm saying it now. I'll even read another movie with you."

I wanted to tell him so bad right then, but how do you say, "Good news, I've seen the future, and you and I have sex. I don't know when, and I don't know how. But we will, so just be patient." I couldn't say that, and I didn't know what to say. So I just looked at Julian, and he looked at me.

"Fine," he said. "You want to decide this by having a staring contest? That's cool."

I laughed, but didn't blink. He didn't, either, and we held each other's gazes for such a long time that my eyes started to water. "Ha, you're losing," he said. "Second date, here I come."

It was so relaxing looking into his eyes, like I didn't have to worry about anything anymore, like everything would work itself out and—

Julian's nose wrinkling, a sudden loud sneeze.

"You're a bully," I laughed. "And you're going to lose, my friend."

"No, I'm not . . . oh, shi—AAACHIIOOO!"

I squealed in triumph, raising my arms over my head. "Victory is mine!" I cried, and some people turned around to stare. "Yes! Man the confetti cannons and cue the orchestra!"

Julian started to laugh, but he didn't sound nearly as happy as I was. "Wow," he said. "I don't think a girl has ever actually celebrated not having a second date with me."

Oops.

I dropped my arms back in my lap. I had forgotten we were actually competing about something, and I looked at Julian as he looked away. "I'm sorry," I said. "I just like to win. I didn't think—"

"It's cool." He swallowed the rest of his coffee. "Really, it's—"

"Wait," I said. "Just wait a minute." I dropped my head in my hands, waiting for something, anything. But all I got was the kiss again, replaying again and again like a taunt, and when I looked back up at him, Julian was staring at me, waiting for an answer.

"I don't know how I feel," I said slowly. "But I think that there's something between us." But was it a bad something? Why was he part of the vision with June and the red lights and my terrible sense of dread?

"There are a lot of somethings between a lot of people," he told me.

"Believe me, I know. But you have to realize that I have a lot going on right now."

Julian nodded seriously. "Okay."

I took another deep breath. "And my sisters mean more to me than anything in the world."

"That's one of the things I like best about you."

I paused, sort of taken aback by that. "Really?"

"Yeah. The other day, when you yelled at me to stay away from your sister? You looked like one of those bears that you see on the Discovery Channel." He paused before adding, "It was kind of hot. Not gonna lie."

"Well, yeah, okay, I was a little out of line with the yelling," I said. "But if we can go slow, like super-super 'oh look, I'm a turtle' slow, then . . ."

"Then . . . ?"

"Then okay, we can hang out again. But no horror movies!" I added quickly.

Julian smiled so wide that even my heart could see it. "Cool," he said. "My mom's totally gonna let me keep my car."

"Hey," I said. "The date's not over." But then I blew my argument by yawning.

"Yeah, it is," Julian said, and he stood up and put his hand out to me. "C'mon. Curfew is only two short hours away."

"I live fifteen minutes away."

"There could be traffic."

"There's not," I said automatically.

"And you know this because . . . ?"

"I just do." I stuck my tongue out at him to lessen the truth of what I had said.

"Can I ask you something more difficult?"

"Okay."

He held the door open for me when we went outside, and the autumn fog rolled in from the ocean and made me shiver. "How come I have to stay away from your sister, but not from you?" he asked me.

I froze. This was another moment I hadn't seen coming. "Um . . ."

"Is this one of those strange things that you can't explain?"

I could tell he was being sarcastic, but I still nodded and grabbed onto the opportunity. "Well," I said, "the truth is, June's actually a robot. I know," I hurried on as he started laughing. "We don't tell many people that because of all the prejudice surrounding robots in our society, but it's true. And sometimes her microchip goes wonky, and she goes on a killing spree. It's awkward, but now you know."

Julian looked down at me, still laughing. "Remember how I said you were the second-craziest girl I know?"

"It's hard to forget something like that."

"Well, you're slowly making your way up to first place."

"Good," I grinned. "I told you, I hate to lose."

When he dropped me off back at home, he opened the car door for me and even walked me to the front door, hands shoved deep in his hoodie pockets. "So," he said.

"So," I echoed, looking towards my front door. "Thanks for everything. I had a really nice time."

He would get home just fine and then he would check on his mom, who was asleep on the couch because she gave him the bedroom in their single bedroom apartment. He would eat some Golden Grahams and then put his dish in the sink and go to his room and close the door. He would smile to himself, and he would look so happy that it would make me wonder why I hadn't kissed him tonight.

"Yeah, me too," he said. "I even liked the movie."

"You're such a liar."

He paused before saying, "Yeah, I am," and we both laughed. "So maybe I can call you this weekend?"

He would call me tomorrow at one thirty-four p.m.

"Sure," I said. "That'd be nice."

"Cool, okay." He smiled again and started to walk backwards down our driveway before he realized something. "Oh!" he said. "One thing!"

I already had my key in the lock, but I turned around. "Yeah?"

"My mom would kick my ass if I didn't tell you this."

I smiled. "Okay. What?"

"You looked very *you* tonight."

"Excuse me?" I said. "Is that a compliment?"

"I just mean . . ." Julian scuffed his toe along the cement steps, and I could see the faintest hint of a blush creeping into his cheeks. "You looked really happy tonight. You've never acted like that before. It just seems like you're always on guard and tonight . . ." He looked up at me, and our eyes locked into another staring contest. "I just liked being with the real you."

The words hit so hard that all I could do was keep staring at him, and before I could respond, he hurried off. I stood there until his car drove off, watching him leave. And when I got inside, the light over the stove was the only thing on in the kitchen, and all I could hear was my heart pounding in my chest.

I knew my mom was asleep upstairs, so I went to peek in her door. "Mom?" I whispered.

"Hmmmph?"

"Mom, I'm home."

She rolled over and squinted. It was so dark that I could barely see her. "Have fun?" she mumbled.

My heart was still thudding. "Yeah," I said. "It was cool." But I couldn't find the word to describe how it really felt. I don't think that word has been invented yet.

"Good," my mom yawned.

"Go back to sleep," I told her, but she was already rolling back over. She was tired, I knew. And I also knew that our neighbor's car backfiring would wake her up at five thirty in the morning, and she wouldn't be able to get back to sleep. So I closed the door and went into my room.

Julian said he liked being with the real me.

And the world still turned.

I sat on my bed for a long time, trying to figure out where all the pieces would go, and it wasn't until my cell phone rang that I moved, going to dig it out of my purse. I saw myself in the mirror as I did that, and I realized I had the dumbest, goofiest smile on my face. I wondered how long it had been there and how long it would stay, but it fell away when I saw the caller ID.

It was June.

"Hello?" I said, flipping the phone open. "Junie?"

"Hi," she said, and her voice was icy.

"June, are you okay? Where are you?"

"I'm at the party." She was. I could hear the noise in the background, loud thumping music and people being obnoxious. May was probably miserable.

"Are you okay?" I asked June again, my giddiness getting obliterated by nerves all over again. "Is everything all right?"

"Oh, I'm fine," she said, but her voice was still clipped and haughty, and I could feel her fury coming down the line.

"So what—?"

"*I'm* totally fine," June interrupted. "It's May who's wasted."

I got to Mariah's house in less than six minutes, speeding through a yellow light for the first time in my life. I had left a note for my mom under her bedroom door just in case she woke up. But she was snoring when I left, and I hadn't seen her waking up until the backfiring car.

June had given me Mariah's address and said, "Don't miss the left-hand turn," before hanging up on me, and I was getting the sick sense of dread in my stomach, the same one I got when my parents sat us down last summer, the same one I got when the earthquake hit and I shoved Julian out of the way without realizing what I was doing.

Things were going to change tonight. I didn't have to see the future to know it was coming.

When I got to Mariah's house, May was sitting on the curb, and June was standing behind her, arms crossed with a look of fury on her face that almost made me scared of her. Henry was sitting next to May, patting her shoulder awkwardly while she hung her head, hair falling towards the gutter. The front door to Mariah's house was wide open, and I could see enough of the inside to know that it was trashed. There were already some empty beer bottles in the small patch of grass that led to the front door.

It wasn't a good scene, let me just put it that way.

"What happened?" I said after parking and leaping out of the car. "Are you okay?"

June just laughed. "Yeah," she said. "You were right about one thing. I didn't get puked on tonight."

Knock it off, I thought. *We don't want Henry to know—*

"Oh, whatever," June said out loud. "That wouldn't even be the worst thing that happened tonight."

I squatted down by May, who was holding a bottle of water. "Hi," I said to Henry, ignoring June for the moment. "What are you doing here?"

"This is where he lives," June interrupted Henry before he could even speak. "He's Mariah's *brother*. Another interesting piece of information. Can we go home, please?"

May groaned and held her head. "June, please, just shut up."

"You wish."

"Are you gonna puke again?" I asked May.

"There's nothing left," she muttered. She was still sort of slurring, but I could tell that she wasn't as drunk as she probably had been earlier. I haven't ever been drunk, and I'm not really a partier (news flash, I know). But I've seen enough movies and TV shows to know what it looks like. "Did you tell Mom?"

I shook my head. "No, she's asleep." I looked up at June. "What about you? Are you—?"

"Do *not* talk to me," June snapped. "I called you for a ride and that's it."

Henry was still awkwardly patting May's shoulder. "Do you want some more water?" he asked her.

"No, thanks," she said, then groaned again and dropped her head into her hands. "Is someone dangling me upside down? It feels like I'm upside-down."

"Fantastic," I muttered, while June rolled her eyes before glaring at me again.

"April, let's go."

I looked back up at June, prepared to snap back at her, but she cut me off. "No," she said. "You do not get to say *anything* to me."

Henry was looking among the three of us warily. "I think she's okay, April," he said to me. "She spent a lot of time puking."

May moaned into her hands.

"Yeah, it was *spectacular*," June said, her voice heavy with sarcasm. "Seriously, one of the best things that's ever happened to me." She paused before adding, "And what a *delightful* surprise to see my sister May here."

May looked up, and for a split second, we shared a guilty glance. June knew what we had done. "Sorry," May said to me.

"You better not be apologizing to April!" June snapped. "The only apologies that I want to hear better be—"

"Let's get out of here," I said, cutting her off before she started blabbing in front of Henry and whoever was drunkenly stumbling down the front steps. "C'mon, let's go home."

June started to walk towards the car. "I hope she pukes all over the front seat," she said as she stalked away.

Henry and I gingerly helped May stand up. "Oh, wow," she said. "Wow."

"Okay, she might still be a *little* drunk," Henry whispered.

"Wooooow."

"Yeah," I agreed. "Okay. Thanks for taking care of her."

"June did most of the work," Henry admitted. "I just brought her outside."

I looked back at my youngest sister, who was sitting in the backseat with her arms crossed, not looking at any of us. "Well, thanks anyway," I said.

May looked up at him and yanked her arm away from his hand. "Don't touch me," she snapped. "You're an asshole."

Henry looked a bit surprised. But he let go of her, and May half-collapsed, half-slid into the front seat. "A total asshole," she muttered.

"Oh, good," June said from the backseat. "She's an *angry* drunk."

"That asshole is named after a king, did you know that?" May glanced up at me as I buckled the seatbelt around her. "Stupid kings."

"Oh my God," I muttered, then started to load her into the front seat. "You're going to die of embarrassment tomorrow, I know that much."

"Yep," she agreed, then spent thirty seconds trying to move her dirty blond hair out of her face before giving up. "Take me home, I'm broken."

I leaned in and said, "If you puke in my car, I will end you," before slamming the door and going around to the driver's seat.

We hadn't made it a block down the street before June said, "What the hell, April?"

Her voice was flat and cold and would have been scary if she hadn't been my baby sister. "Oh, *what*," I shot back, looking at her in the rearview mirror. "What? Yeah, okay, so May followed you because I was worried."

"Are you kidding me?" she screeched. "It was just last week that you were giving me the big 'we have to be ethical and not lie' speech! What happened to that? Now who's the liar?"

"I thought something could happen to you!" I yelled back.

"You *thought*? Or you *knew*?"

"Guys, *please* shut up," May said, rubbing her forehead and wincing.

"Deal with it," June shot back. "This is your own fault. And I'm pissed at you, too!"

"I would have never guessed," May mumbled.

"What happened?" I asked them, glaring at May as I spoke.

She shrugged and rested her head against the window. "It was just a couple of beers. And the clear stuff."

"Vodka?" I said. "You're wasted on vodka?"

"Please never say that word again."

"Do you know how many bad stories involve vodka?" I screeched, which made her wince again.

"*I'll* tell you what happened," June said, shoving herself between the two front seats. "*I'll* tell you how your brilliant plan worked out, April. May here decided to help herself to some 'happy drinky drinks'—which I believe is what she called them while puking—"

"They were actually *sad* drinky drinks," May interrupted.

"—and after a few hours of this, I go into the bathroom, and guess who I found on the floor?"

"Oh my God, May," I muttered, shaking my head. That explained why I thought everything was fine. I couldn't see her when she was invisible. The only flaw in my supposedly excellent plan.

"So you *did* ask her to follow me!" June was so angry, I could hear her voice shaking. "Do you even *realize* how much you both completely ruined this night for me? Mariah is probably never going to invite me to ditch with her again, and we were really starting to become friends. Real friends. Can you believe it? I guess probably not since neither of *you* seem to have any. And now I can see why. Because you're total hypocrites."

"June," May started to say, holding her head in her hands, but June cut her off.

"Don't you dare," she said, and I was almost a little scared of June's voice. "I know, May. I *know*."

May winced as she tried to turn around. "You know what?"

Oh no, I suddenly realized. *Oh no.*

"I know about you and the tequila! I know that you're the reason we had to move because you went into your 'poor me' mode and got trashed! You were remembering it the whole time you were getting sick in Mariah's bathroom. But what if Mom finds out about tonight, huh? Where are we gonna move *next*, May? What else are you two going to ruin for me?"

"June!" I cried. "We were just worried. We thought—"

"Fuck you."

It was like she had slapped me, her words were so fast and strong. Even May looked up in surprise, first at me and then turning around to look at June.

That did it. Now I was pissed, too.

I jerked the car over by the side of the park that was near our house. It was completely empty, save for the fluorescent lights that lit the playground area, and I unbuckled my seatbelt and twisted around to face June. "You have absolutely no idea what you're doing," I said to her, my voice low and angry. "You have *no idea*."

"I know better than anyone," she shot back. "No one can lie to me. I just never thought my own sisters would. I know way more than either one of you."

"Oh, yeah?" I sneered. "Like what? Please, enlighten me! What do you know that's so great?"

June smiled smugly. "I know that Mom's mom was a mind-reader."

May and I both stared at her.

"And she had two sisters, too," June continued. "One of them became a hermit in Maine and the other one"—here she glared at me—"was really bossy all the time. Mom called her a 'know-it-all.'"

"Mom told you this?" I said, my voice barely above a whisper. "Did you . . . did you tell her? About us?"

"No, I'm not stupid. I just asked her about Grandma," she said. "And she told me that Grandma always seemed to know what she was thinking. And if you think *that's* a coincidence," she said, interrupting my thoughts before they were full formed, "you're an idiot."

May looked between us before saying, "But I don't want to go to Maine."

I was too surprised to respond. Could this really be true?

"I told you!" June yelled. "No one can lie to me! I can see everything they're thinking! I just wish I hadn't tiptoed around you and May! I should have read your minds, too, because then I would have known what traitors my own sisters were!"

May sank back into the car seat and sighed loudly.

"And you're not even sorry, are you?" June continued. "Believe me, I'm trying to find an apology, and I can't even hear—"

"You're not gonna get an apology!" I screamed at her, shocking her into silence. I had been right. The burden was too heavy and now it was falling to pieces. "You have no idea what I've seen!"

"I did just now."

"And that doesn't scare you?" I demanded. "You and sirens and red lights? That doesn't scare the absolute crap out of you?"

June shrugged, her bravado firmly in place. "It doesn't mean anything. You don't even know what it means. I can tell. And if it was so important to you," she added, "why'd you send May to be invisible and stalk me? Why didn't you do your own dirty work?"

May sighed heavily. "Because she was keeping Julian away from you."

"May!" I screeched.

"Well, what?" May snapped. "It's true. Don't pretend to be all innocent." She turned back to June. "She saw Julian in the vision about you, and she's trying to keep him away so nothing happens."

June's mouth fell open as she looked to me, and I felt about as big as a blade of grass. "You used some guy?" she gasped.

"Oh, don't *even*," I told her. But I knew she was right, and I was starting to feel really miserable and confused about this whole night. "You're the one who's been using people's thoughts against them, ruining their friendships!" I insisted. "I told you this was dangerous. I told you that we needed to stay together and not—"

"*You're* the one that divided us!" June yelled back.

"God, we're so screwed up," May whispered, covering her face with her hands.

"This could have been great!" June shouted. "This could have been amazing! And instead of dealing with it, you ruined *everything*!"

"Amazing?" I repeated slowly as the anger traveled from my stomach to my throat to my mouth. "What *exactly* did you think was going to happen? This isn't television, June! This isn't a movie! Giles and

Buffy aren't gonna appear and show us how to deal with our wonderful new powers!"

"April—" May started to say, uncovering her eyes with one hand to grab my arm, but I shook her off.

"Some fricking owl is not gonna come sailing in through your bedroom window with a letter from Hogwarts!" I continued to rant. "There's no Dumbledore! The Cullens aren't gonna show up and invite you to come with them in Forks! There's nothing! This isn't make-believe! *This is it*! It's us and it's *only* us!"

June's eyes were filling with tears, but her voice didn't even shake when she spoke. "It's *always* only been us," she whispered. "And it's not working anymore."

I fell back against my seat and tried to catch my breath. June's words were like a fist into my stomach, hitting so hard that it burned. Maybe she was right. My sisters and I had spent all night lying to innocent people, and I tried not to think of Julian's laugh, how he had watched my eyes with his, how he had trusted me.

May stared out the windshield as the reality of June's words settled around us. My stomach hurt, my throat hurt, everything hurt. And next to me, May was biting her lower lip. "She's right, April," she said after a minute. "We're kind of falling apart."

I watched a car drive past us, unable to speak.

"I want to go home," June said. "I want this day to be over."

I turned the key in the ignition with numb fingers, then put it into drive. The silence in the car on the way home was as bad as the silence after our parents announced their divorce, as heavy and melancholy as dark clouds.

Our mom was still asleep as we climbed the stairs, and one by one, we all shut our bedroom doors behind us. *A house divided*, I thought as I looked in the mirror. The last time I had seen myself, Julian had just told me he liked being with the real me.

But he hadn't really seen me at all.

I sent thought after thought towards June as I lay in bed that night. *I'm sorry I'm sorry I'm sorry I'm sorry*. But she never opened her door, never left her room, and when I started to cry, I didn't know if she was listening or not.

chapter 17

"A liar is a liar is a liar."

The pain.

Oh, the pain.

I woke up when the morning—actually, *afternoon*—sun hit me in the face. That's what it felt like, too, like it was hitting me, bludgeoning right through my skull and into the soft, sensitive place in my brain.

"Uuuuuuuggggggghhhhhh," I muttered. It sounded nonhuman, like an animal had made that noise while dying on the side of the road, and I rolled over and looked at the clock by my bed: one thirty-seven p.m. Saturday was almost half over, which seemed appropriate. I wanted this day to be done as soon as possible.

I lay there for a while, trying to breathe without moving any part of my body that hurt, and when that didn't work, I tried being invisible for a while. I looked down at my messy bed, not seeing my body anywhere, but it still ached. And finally I reappeared and sighed.

If being invisible couldn't even save me from a hangover, what good was it?

I listened to my sisters as they went up and down the stairs, slamming doors and then opening them with a *whoosh!* I wasn't the mind-reader or the future-teller, but I knew my sisters well enough to know that they were pissed at each other and also at me. They weren't talking, and the house was oddly quiet. I hadn't even heard June's chicken alarm go off (which, I'm not gonna lie, was so far the best thing that had happened to me that morning).

By the time I made it downstairs, I was ready to maim anyone who made a loud noise or looked at me for too long. "Oh, hi, sweetie," my mom said to me as she sailed through the kitchen. "Sleepyhead today, huh?"

"Something like that, yeah," I said, wincing as she kissed the back of my head. The guilt I felt was nearly as bad as the hangover. I had thought maybe one of my sisters would rat me out, but that would mean turning themselves in, too. I guess a liar is a liar is a liar.

"Well, up and at 'em," my mom continued, not noticing that I was clinging to the kitchen counter with both hands. I would have clung longer, but then I realized that my left foot was going again. (And why always the left foot? Why not my right earlobe or both kneecaps? God, what I wouldn't give for an owner's manual or an FAQ or something.)

"I'm gonna go back upstairs and, uh, straighten up my room," I said to my mom. "It's a disaster."

She looked at me. "You're seriously going to clean your room on a Saturday?"

"Um, yeah?"

My mom just grinned. "Good. Try to put some of your good influence on your sisters while you're at it."

"Yeah, maybe not," I muttered as I went back upstairs.

April was standing by my bed when I got back upstairs, arms crossed and tapping her foot. "And a happy hello to you, too," I muttered, crawling back towards my bed. "Now get out."

"Just to make it clear," April glared at me, "I'm not talking to you."

"Really? Because current evidence proves otherwise."

"I'm only talking to you right now because I want to find out what happened last night and June's not talking to me."

"We should have followed her more often, then," I said, and was rewarded with the sound of June's bedroom door slamming shut.

"She's reading our minds like an encyclopedia right now," April informed me.

"And you know this because . . . ?"

"You really think she's *not*?"

April had a point. "Well, that's just wonderful," I muttered, then pulled the covers over my head. "When are you gonna start not speaking to me? Please say now."

"Tell me what happened last night."

I pulled the blankets away long enough to scowl at her. "Why? You're the one who sees the future? You didn't see any of it?"

"Start talking."

"Get out." The last thing I wanted to do was relive my embarrassment in front of April, the Perfect Child.

"May—"

"What?" I yelled back, then winced. "Seriously, April, just get out. All I want to do is disappear."

"Yeah, pretty handy trick for you," she shot back. "Maybe if you had stuck to this plan, we wouldn't be in this situation now!"

"What? The one where we're not speaking to each other? Sounds ideal to me." I burrowed into my pillow.

"You were supposed to watch June, and instead you could have been hurt, too!"

"I *am* hurt!" I hissed at her. "My brain is about three sizes too big for my skull right now. And June was *fine*. Or she *was*, until you made me follow her and it all went to hell. It's your fault, not mine."

I knew this wasn't true, but I wasn't in the mood to play fair.

"So I was the one who made you drink and puke on someone's lawn?"

I pointed towards my bedroom door. "Would you just GET OUT ALREADY?" I winced again as my voice made my head pound.

"Fine," she said, then spun on her heel. "Gladly. Happily."

As soon as she left (leaving the door wide open, what a brat), I let myself melt away and lay there for a few minutes, looking at the crack in the ceiling. I thought about getting up and following my sisters around, unbeknownst to them, but after last night, the idea didn't sound fun at all.

My phone started to ring on my nightstand, and I came back long enough to stretch an arm out of the blanket and look at the caller ID.

Shit.

I waited until the third ring to answer it. "What," I croaked.

"Uh, hi," Henry said.

"God, is everyone a morning person?" I groaned.

Henry just laughed his nervous laugh. "I was calling to see how you were feeling."

"Guess."

"Not so great?"

I uncovered my eyes and looked towards the bedroom door, trying to see if my mom was coming. I was so used to April or June giving me the heads-up that I felt like I was missing some important piece of armor.

"May?" Henry said. "You there?"

"Yep."

"So how *are* you feeling?"

"Like a Mack truck carrying a bunch of angry chickens ran me over."

"Really?"

"Twice."

"Oh, wow. That's not good."

"You're very astute, Henry." I rolled onto my side and pulled the blankets over my head. I really felt like running Henry over with a truck at that point, after the way he had said, "Hell no, not *her*," at the party last night. The words had been in my brain all night, mixed in with alcohol fumes and dizzy spells. *Hell no. Not her.*

It was enough to make me want to be sick again.

"So you don't wanna study today?"

"Henry, let me ask you a question. Are you always an asshole to girls, or is it just me? Do I bring out that special side of you?"

It kind of sounded like Henry did a spittake of whatever he was drinking.

"Because if it's just me," I continued, "you can go crawl back into whatever hole you came from."

There was a pause before he said, "As opposed to puking in a gutter?"

"That's what I thought," I said. "Ciao ciao, mon ami." I started to hang up the phone, but Henry's tin voice hummed through the receiver.

"Wait, May, don't hang up! I'm sorry, just don't hang up!"

My thumb hovered over the "end" button. "You're sorry?"

"I . . . I feel really bad. I should have watched out for you last night. Mariah's parties, the people there aren't always the greatest."

"Yeah, I know. In fact, I'm talking to one of them right now," I shot back. It was sort of nice to know that even when it felt like my brain was about to rupture out of my head, it still worked.

I could practically see Henry bristle on the other end of the line. He was probably wearing his Stanford hooded sweatshirt, playing with the drawstrings the way he always did whenever he was tutoring me. "Is that all you're sorry for?" I asked quietly.

"God, May, yes!" he finally said. "I called you up to apologize. What more do you want? Want me to come over to your house and do it in person?"

"No!" I hissed. "I want you to pull your head out of your Stanford-clad ass and maybe realize that just because you don't see people doesn't mean they're not there!"

There was a pause. "What are you talking about?"

"Nothing. Look, I'm sure you've got a busy afternoon of highlighting college catalogues and doing Spanish vocab flash cards, so we can cancel the tutoring. In fact, cancel the rest of the sessions. Forget you know me. I'm sure it won't be hard."

Hell no, not her.

"So what, then?" Henry fumed. "I call you to apologize for the fact that you drank too much vodka, and your response is to just . . . disappear?"

"Sometimes it feels that way," I muttered.

"Well, if you want to disappear so bad, maybe you should." He was pissed, way more pissed than when I had spilled beer on his *National Geographics*. (Oops, forgot about that one. Well, he deserved it.)

I couldn't help but laugh. "Henry, I think you've finally found the one thing we can agree on." And then I pressed "end" and watched my arm vanish as it hurled the phone into the corner of my room.

Henry was right. Why didn't I just disappear? After all, I was *invisible*. I could get on a plane for Fiji, and no one would know. I could move into the Ritz Carlton and charge room service to other people's credit cards. I could fly to Paris and eat at cafés and go to museums and crash in homes that were too big for the people inside them.

I could go to Houston and see my dad.

I lay in bed for the rest of the morning, never once bothering to reappear.

chapter 18

"The inmates were running the asylum."

I've never been so happy to get to Monday in my life.

It was drizzling a little bit outside, so I put in some extra Frizz-Ease and hoped for the best before getting in April's car that morning. May was curled up in the backseat, her hoodie pulled low over her eyes and her iPod set to LOUD. She hadn't said anything to me since the party on Friday, but I didn't care because I wasn't saying anything to her.

April had tried a couple of times on Sunday, but I flat-out ignored her, slamming my door or going downstairs or even showering. I think I washed my hair three times over the weekend, letting the water drown out how betrayed I felt. I had tried to stop reading my sisters' minds just to be respectful, you know? But now, I didn't even care what they thought. May disappears and follows me like a spy? Super-creepy. April dates some guy to keep him away from me? Jealous much? She was always trying to scare me, always saying what could maybe happen, what we shouldn't do. For all I knew, her "visions" of me and Julian and the red lights were totally made up in her own mind.

If you needed a serving of repressed crazy, you could definitely swing by our house and pick up a slice, is what I'm saying. It's like, my sisters think I can't take care of myself, when really, *they're* the ones who don't have it together. Barfing at a party? Dating a weirdo as part of some big master plan? The inmates were running the asylum. But I was this close to getting invited to Cabo with Mariah, and I wasn't about to let my sisters ruin *this* for me, too.

The ride to school on Monday was long, thanks to April's driving. I knew May was pissed because she didn't even comment on it, just stayed huddled in the backseat, and when I finally turned on the radio to a song I liked, a thought escaped her and made its way to me.

Outta here.

I didn't even acknowledge her, just tried to smooth my hair down and make sure that steam wasn't coming out of my ears. I can't even ditch without April having a conniption, and now May was gonna bail on school? Nuh-uh. No way. *Let April save the world on her own,* I thought. *There's a beach house in Cabo waiting for me.*

Mariah and I had texted a little about it on Sunday. *Cabo still snds amayzing!!* I wrote to her, and by the time she wrote back two hours later, I was a nervous wreck thinking that she had forgotten, that she had been drunk and never meant to invite me.

But then the little words splashed across my phone. *u have no idea its awsome*, it said, and I did a little dance right there in the middle of the kitchen, right where my sisters could see how happy I was.

Not like in this Car of Doom and Ever-Present Gloom.

As soon as April parked, I got out and started to walk away, slamming my door super hard because I know it annoys April. "Wait, June!" she called after me, but I ignored her and went up the front steps.

I really hoped she saw it coming, too.

As soon as I got inside, people from the party said hi to me. Derek, of course, waved and smiled with his buck teeth, and I said hi to a couple of girls that I knew wanted desperately to be Mariah's friend.

The word "Cabo" was bouncing around their brains, too, and I just smiled benevolently and said, "What's up?" as I glided to my locker before finding Mariah.

She was sitting outside near the auditorium, looking as hungover as May had been on Saturday. Huge sunglasses obscured her face, and I realized that I needed a pair just like those. "Hey," she croaked when she saw me. "I'm wrecked."

She wasn't lying. Her thoughts were moving at half-speed. "Did you just wake up?" I asked, sitting down next to her.

"Twenty minutes ago," she grinned. "Blake drove me here."

"He's up this early?"

She grinned wickedly. "He never went to bed."

I knew what she was implying, but it wasn't true. Blake had been up getting high and playing PS3 all night while Mariah slept in her bed at home. I could see her texting back and forth with him, trying to get him to sneak over, but eventually he stopped writing back.

"Wow, that's awesome," was all I said, though, filing the information away for later use. "So what's up for today?"

Mariah sighed and flipped her cell phone around and around. "I'm already over today. I'm ready for tonight."

"Oh, yeah? What's tonight?"

She caught her tongue between her teeth and smiled at me. "There's another party."

"You're having another party?" I gasped. I was so jealous that it made my eyeballs almost turn green. With a mom who felt guilty about leaving the house, a sister who could see the future, and another sister who was a freakazoid ghost, I'd have never been able to have a party in our house. Some people were just luckier than me. "Did your mom and stepdad not come home?"

"No, they came home. I'm not the hostess this time; I'm just an attendee. It's over at one of Blake's friends' apartments. They just moved in; it's gonna be awesome."

Going to a party at someone's apartment sounded so grown-up that I could barely stand it. "I'm in," I said. "When?"

"Tonight. Duh, I just told you." She patted my cheek a little too hard. "Keep up."

"I'm up," I said, shifting away a bit. "But when like time? And how do I get there?"

Mariah shrugged. "I dunno. Tell your mom you're going to the movies. Isn't that what freshmen do on school nights?"

"I don't know," I told her. "I don't hang out with freshmen."

Mariah moved her sunglasses and looked down her nose at me before pushing them back up and grinning. "You don't anymore," she said. "Blake and I will pick you up at seven thirty. Sucks to be you if you're late."

"I'll be there," I said. And I would, no matter what crazy scheme April cooked up this time.

chapter 19

"The red lights attacked every part of me."

april

Julian was waiting by my locker when I got to school on Monday. "So," he said, "call me crazy, but I think you're ignoring me."

"You're crazy," I said automatically. I had seen this little exchange coming since the first text message he sent on Saturday morning. He sent four more over the course of the weekend, but I only responded to the one that said, "Can we do it again soon?" I said yes because I already knew that we'd be doing *something* soon enough. It was an easy question to answer.

"No, I'm not crazy," he insisted. "Why'd you clam up over the weekend? That's not cool. I thought *guys* were supposed to be all weird and aloof."

"You think I'm weird and aloof?" I asked, putting my hands on my hips.

"Well, yeah, kind of." He squared off with me. "Look, you called me on my shit, remember? Fair's fair."

I sighed and spun my locker open, not even caring if I had the right books or not. It was barely October, and I was already over this school year. "I'm sorry. I'm just fighting with my sisters. Things are really weird right now."

"Wanna talk about it?"

I wanted to so badly that I could almost taste the words on my tongue. "No."

"Wanna . . . get coffee again? Go to a bookstore? Throw rocks at senior citizens?"

"Do I wanna *what*?"

"Just checking." He smiled down at me, and I suddenly felt small. I wondered if this was how May felt whenever she disappeared, like she could be crushed by people who were looking straight through her, but then I remembered that I didn't care how she felt anymore, not after she had been so stupid on Friday night.

"I've got a ton of homework," I protested. "I have to think about my grades for college."

"You sound like that kid who wears all the Stanford gear," Julian snickered. "And I have homework, too."

"Okay, so . . .?"

Red lights, sirens, Julian's face, June's face, someone crying . . .

"April?"

"Yeah?" The flashing red lights were all I could see, and they burned.

"Where'd you go?"

"I'm right here." I slammed my locker without exchanging any books and looked at him. "I had fun," I told him. "I had a lot of fun, but things are just crazy right now." Crazy like the more time I spent with him, the more intense the visions were. I was starting to feel them in my stomach, like someone was grabbing and squeezing.

Julian just looked at me for a long minute before saying, "Is this because I was honest with you and actually told you how I felt, and now it's all weird between us?"

I looked everywhere but at him.

"Because if that's the case, then you need to get over it." He leaned a bit closer and made eye contact. "You had fun. I had fun. I want to go out with you again. If you're not into it, that's cool. But I'm not a liar, and I don't think you are, either."

I couldn't even begin to tell Julian all the ways I had lied to him. "I had fun, too," I admitted, which was the truth. "It was probably the most fun I've had since we moved here."

"So what's the problem?"

"Me?" I offered. "I'm kind of crazy?"

Julian raised an eyebrow. "If this is crazy, I think I can handle it."

I didn't say anything because I *couldn't* say anything, and then Julian said, "Look, if you want, we can do homework at the bookstore over at the Commons tonight. The coffee's shit, but I promise the company will be better."

I flashed forward and saw us sitting together, two huge textbooks that went ignored for most of the time. "Okay," I said. "That'd be good." And it would be.

And, a tiny voice inside my brain reminded me, it would once again keep Julian and June apart.

* * *

Getting ready for my second date was a lot quieter than getting ready for my first date. My sisters weren't squealing and teasing me, and my mom was working late and not getting all teary-eyed at the idea of us growing up. At the time, it had been annoying, but it was lonelier now.

I hadn't seen it coming.

I had made sure that June wasn't doing anything stupid that night, but all I saw was my mom coming home from work, honking twice in our driveway, and then June running out and being dropped off at the movies. My mom was having her second date with Chad, as well, though I knew she wasn't as excited about it as the first one.

I brushed my hair, put on the bra that June had loaned me, and went downstairs to wait for Julian. May was hovering around somewhere, but where, I didn't know. She had gone invisible more and more lately, especially when my mom wasn't home. She might as well have been living in another country for all I saw her now.

I met Julian at the door. "Well, for a crazy person, you look really nice," he greeted me.

I fought back against the sirens and lights again, willing it to go away. "Thanks," I said. "I wore my best studying clothes."

The café at the bookstore was half-empty. Usually in the afternoon, it's packed with kids from our school, but now it was quiet, save for the espresso machine that rumbled and hissed every so often. I caught Julian glancing at me a few times over his calculus homework, but I only knew that because I was glancing at him, too.

"I'm sure enjoying this romantic tension," he finally said without looking up from his notes. "It's almost as relaxing as the espresso machine and that guy who keeps clearing his throat."

I laughed. I couldn't help it. "I find a little romantic tension can boost your GPA by at least two-tenths of a point."

"Valedictorian, here I come." He pushed his books away and leaned back in his chair, stretching. "Do you study like this all the time?"

"Like what?"

"Like you're performing brain surgery."

I guess I was gripping my pen a bit too tight. "Oh, um . . ."

"Your sisters?" he guessed.

Well, that and trying to ward off visions of you and June in a traumatic accident, I thought to myself. It was nice to be able to think things without June butting in. But then Julian took my hand under the table, and I stopped thinking about my sisters. Or homework. Or how to breathe.

"ATTENTION CUSTOMERS! OUR STORE WILL BE CLOSING IN FIVE MINUTES! IF YOU HAVE ITEMS YOU HAVE NOT YET PURCHASED, PLEASE MAKE YOUR WAY TO A REGISTER AT THIS TIME!"

The loudspeaker was just that, very loud, and we jolted apart. My fingers felt sort of lonely once Julian's hand had moved away, which was never how I imagined describing my fingers until just then.

"They have a way with subtlety here," Julian said.

"And shitty coffee," I agreed. "They have it all."

Julian laughed. "Hey, I warned you about the coffee."

"Next time, we bring our own."

He nodded and then slammed his book shut. "Wanna get out of here before they make us buy a kitten calendar or something?"

"Lovely," I said.

Which was how I ended up sitting in his car in an empty parking lot. With Julian. The orange streetlights were only enhancing the red lights in my mind, and I willed them to stay away. How could Julian be so nice and involved in something so bad? Was I not seeing something? Why couldn't I see past that scene? Why couldn't I figure out who he really was?

"April," he said, and my brain cleared as I looked at him. "What is it?"

"English quiz tomorrow," I said automatically. "I'm a little stressed."

"You probably already have an A in the class, I'll bet."

I did, and tomorrow's quiz would only confirm it. "Yeah," I said, but we were still looking at each other. And then he leaned forward, and the sirens got louder and louder until our lips were nearly touching and I could hardly feel myself breathing.

I only halfway realized that I was about to get my first kiss, and I know I'm not Little Miss Experience. But I could tell it was going to be good. *Waaaaaay* better than good. Julian smelled nice. And when he put his hand on my shoulder, the red lights dimmed for a second, and all I could see was him, his hands on my face, and the way his jacket felt under my fingers.

"April?" he whispered against my mouth, and I swear it took me a few seconds to realize that he was talking to me.

"Hmmm?" *Shut up and start kissing*, I thought hazily. *Why was he talking right now?*

"April, your phone."

I blinked and glanced down at my phone, which was vibrating in my bag. "Oh," I said. "That's . . . yeah."

"Wanna answer it?"

No.

"Okay, yeah, hang on, just don't . . ." I tightened my hand in his shirt, like he was about to run away or something, and grabbed my phone. There were three missed calls from May, all of them a minute apart.

And then the visions slammed into my brain, the red lights attacking every part of me, shining everywhere and blinking as fast as my heart could go.

chapter 20

" We've gotta go right now."

Bliss. Sweet sweet bliss. Everyone else in our house went out to have a life, and I got to stay home by myself.

Except that I was annoyed.

I mean, what the hell? I finally decided to jet on our family and go somewhere else and what did my sisters do? Nothing. June the nosy mindreader didn't even try to get more information. April the pushy future-teller didn't even try to be all snide and tell me about weather patterns in Texas. I knew they could see something, anything, but I guess it didn't matter. Maybe I had stayed invisible too long. Maybe they weren't even interested anymore.

Whatever. I had plans now.

I dragged a duffle bag out of the back of my closet and tossed it on the bed, then started to pack for Houston. My dad was just gonna have to deal, and I'd learn to live with cowboys and humidity and people who say "y'all" with no irony whatsoever. Maybe I'd actually stick around there; maybe I'd stop disappearing all the time.

At least it wouldn't suck as much as this place.

I worked my way through a bag of Cheese Puffs as I packed, getting orange powder on all my clothes and not even caring. The more I packed, the angrier I felt, though, and I threw some socks into the bag with such force that they practically bounced back out. "Whoa, Turbo," I said to myself, then realized that June would have said the same thing.

I was imitating June now. Definitely time to leave.

I planned to leave the next morning, maybe pretend I had left something behind at home and go back after everyone else had already left for school or work. I had cash saved because—let's be honest here—it was not like I was going to the movies with friends and spending it. I could take a cab to get to the airport, board a plane, and be in Houston by the time April and June got home from school. I had my dad's address and a cell phone. And, oh yeah, *I could become invisible*. What more did I need?

As an added bonus, I'd also be missing the European history quiz at ten a.m. the next morning, but thinking about that made me think of Henry, which made me think of barfing, which made me want to stay away from the Cheese Puffs, and I loved Cheese Puffs too much to give them up.

I was dragging them and my duffle bag towards the laundry room when the doorbell rang. Eight thirty at night. I had seen enough movies to know that it was probably the monster from *Scream* coming to hack me to bits, but all *he* had was a stupid Halloween mask. I had invisibility on my side. Let him try to kill me. Who doesn't like a plot twist, after all?

But when I opened the door, it was worse than the *Scream* dude. It was Henry.

"Oh," I said, quickly shoving the duffle bag out of his line of sight. "I thought you were a murderer."

"Um, no," he said. "I know you hate me, but I'm not a murderer."

I leaned against the door. "So? Did you stop by to sell me Girl Scout cookies? Are you raising funds for the homeless?"

"There's a quiz tomorrow. I thought you might need help."

The Cheese Puffs churned in my stomach. "I don't need help," I said.

"Are those Cheese Puffs?"

I glanced down at the bag. "Maybe."

"May."

"Henry."

"You're being weird," he said.

"As opposed to my normal cheerlead-y self, you mean?"

"You're, like, *flushed*."

He was right. It was warm, way too warm, like being under an interrogator's spotlight. "Look, Henry," I said. "You came here to see me and—"

"Is that a duffle bag?"

I glanced down at it, then back at him. "Maybe."

Henry narrowed his eyes at me. "Are you going somewhere?"

"Lacrosse field trip," I said. "I enjoy whacking the hell out of people with mallets."

Henry took a deep breath and ran his hand through his hair. It was way shorter than it needed to be, which annoyed me in ways I cannot even describe. I could see the tips of his ears, that's how short it was. "You don't play lacrosse," he said. "And can I please just come in?"

I stepped back from the doorway and waved him in. "Mi casa es su casa."

The last time we had talked, I had been hungover, but now the hangover was gone, replaced by something angry and fiery, something worse than ever before. "One hour," I said. "And that's it. I hope this is enough volunteer credit for you, so you can graduate sooner than me and I never have to see you again."

"Well, if it makes you feel better—" Henry started to say, but I cut him off.

"I feel *great*, Henry," I snapped at him. "Really."

I didn't have to look at him to know that he was gazing oddly at me. I could feel it on my skin, making me feel more visible than ever before. I wanted the whole world to feel how I felt just then, frustrated and stupid and tilted, like the world was off its axis but I was the only one flying out into the unknown.

"Seriously," I said with a sigh. "Can we just study?"

Henry looked at me, and I levelled my gaze at him, staring back. "What?" I said. "Did you want me to ask permission first?" If I was going to get him to leave, I had to do it fast. Otherwise I'd never get to finish packing. And then my sisters would come home and figure everything out, and I'd be stuck here. That idea felt like someone was sitting on my chest, trapping me here with no place to go.

So I decided to find out how far I could push Henry.

At first, he pretended that nothing was wrong. He pointed out alliances and treaties like they still mattered. He talked about Prussia and kings and violent coups and beheadings. I pushed my pencil around, "accidentally" spilled my water on my notes (which were illegible to start with), yawned twice, and said yes to everything that Henry asked me, even if it wasn't a yes-or-no question.

It took me until nine before I was pretty sure that I was starting to hit Henry's limit. I wanted him to spin out of control. I wanted someone to know how it felt to be me. But all he did was just sigh or push his fingers through his badly cut hair with increasing speed, until he finally put his highlighter down and turned to look at me.

"Why are you packing?" he asked quietly. "I mean, the truth. Why?"

I startled. "What does that have to do with European history?"

"Nothing."

"Then maybe you shouldn't worry about it."

"Are you gonna miss the quiz tomorrow?"

I started to laugh. "You're serious?" I said. "That's all you care about, whether or not I'm gonna miss the precious quiz? Don't you get it? None of this matters. None of it. In five years, no one's gonna give a shit about some stupid surprise quiz, and yet you act like it's the most important thing ever! But there's more than just this, Henry!"

I picked up the highlighter and tossed it across the table, where it bounced angrily onto the floor. "You act like you know everything and you're so smart. But you don't know anything."

"I know that you're running away," he challenged.

"I'm going to see my dad in Houston," I scoffed. "Not exactly the same thing."

"Are you gonna move there, though? Like, permanently?" Henry bent down and picked up the highlighter, setting it back on the table.

"Why? Would that just make your day?"

He stared at me, his eyes like a wounded puppy's, deep and hurt. "No," he said quietly. "Not really."

"Yeah, right," I huffed, starting to slam my books shut. "Yeah, I'm sure you'd love it if I stayed. I'm sure tutoring me makes you feel smarter than ever."

"No, that's not it!" he said, and I was almost relieved to hear Henry finally yell back. "That's not it at all! You never listen to me. You never—"

I spun in my chair to look at him. "I've heard everything you've ever said!" I shouted back. "I know what you think about me!" Just thinking about that night at the party made me wince. Getting drunk wasn't even the worst part of it, not after hearing Henry say, "Not her," not after hearing everyone else laugh at the idea of me.

I grabbed the highlighter again and hurled it across the room once more, then snapped my eyes to meet his. "Look," I told him. "You're a jerk. You're a complete asshole, and if you think I'm sticking around just so you can keep making fun of me behind my back, you're crazier than I am. I don't know where I'm supposed to be, Henry, but it's definitely not here with you!"

Henry looked like I'd slapped him, which I sort of wanted to do. "Why," he finally asked, "are you so *mad* at me just because I want you to *stay*?"

I sat back in my chair like a collapsed balloon, the words hitting my brain and my heart at the same time. I had wanted him to be angry, just like me, but all I had done was make him feel hurt.

Just like me.

"I-I'm gonna get some fresh air," I said, scrambling out of my seat before the disappearing started, and I stood up and yanked the sliding glass door open, stumbling into the backyard. It was overgrown and weedy because my dad had always been the one doing all the lawnmower stuff.

I took some deep breaths and tried to stay in the shadow of the trees, just in case Henry was watching. I could feel my feet tingling, and I pressed through the soles of my shoes and down into the earth, trying to root myself. I had a vague memory suddenly, standing in our old backyard with April and June, hopping around on hot bricks. Me and my sisters. Happy.

Tears hit my eyes, and I couldn't make them disappear, no matter how hard I tried.

After a few minutes, the back door slid open, and I heard someone come outside. "Go away," I said, not even looking over my shoulder.

Henry took another step outside. "Are you okay? Do you want me to go call April? Or June? I can, if you want." He sounded nervous and unsure, and I couldn't blame him.

I shook my head and hastily wiped my eyes. "No."

My right pinky finger tingled, and I shoved it back into my pocket while pulling my hoodie up over my hair, trying to hide as much as possible. It was getting darker earlier now, and colder, too. "I'm really fine." Now my toes were sending out warning signals.

"Are you sure?" I heard Henry shut the door behind him. "Because I know you're not, like, the friendliest person, but you . . ." He trailed off.

I took a deep breath and turned around to look at him. He looked sort of small and cautious, like I was a hurricane about to pick up and drop him far away from familiar things.

I knew how that felt, too.

"Everything is just so fucking confusing all the time," I blurted out. "And it's not getting easier, either. I mean, my parents got divorced, and we had to move here. And now I'm fighting with my sisters, and I don't even recognize my family anymore. I don't even recognize *me* anymore. And," I added, taking a deep breath, "you really hurt my feelings."

"What? When?"

"At the party!" I cried, and now it felt like I really was crying. "Mariah asked you if you wanted to sleep with me and you said, 'Hell no, not *her*.' Like I was this . . . this thing on the bottom of your shoe."

Henry looked stricken. "You heard that?"

"Obviously!" I said.

"But I didn't even see you—"

"Does that even matter? It's okay to say that when I'm not there?"

Henry took a cautious step forward, and I took one back, trying to stay away lest my entire head disappear from the stress. "May," he said carefully. "Did you really think I was gonna tell Mariah that I liked you? I mean, c'mon. *Mariah*?"

"You could have pleaded the Fifth," I said, sniffling. "Just like all those tobacco executives do whenever they're on trial."

"Okay, yeah," he admitted. "I could have done a lot of things. But Mariah, she totally caught me off guard. And all those stupid friends of hers were there, and I just didn't want her to . . ."

"Didn't want her to what?"

"I didn't want her to know how much I liked you."

Well, knock me over with a Cheese Puff.

"What?" I noticed tears were streaking my face, and I tried ungracefully to smear them away with my hoodie sleeve.

Henry took a deep breath. "You're funny and you don't care and you're always doing your own thing. You're kind of everything that Mariah wants to be, only she just does it all wrong."

"Wait, wait, wait," I said. "Back the truck up. You *like* me?"

"Um, yeah. Is that okay?"

I didn't know *what* it was. To the best of my knowledge, no one had ever liked me before, aside from the people who were biologically obligated.

It was sort of better than being in Houston, not gonna lie.

"Yeah, it's okay," I said. "Sure, yeah."

Henry shoved his hands into his pockets and glanced towards the house. "Your dad's not gonna fly out here and beat me up or anything, is he?"

I shook my head. "Nope. My mom might, but she's on a date tonight. She's seeing this guy named Chad. *Chad*."

"Oh." Henry shoved his hands in his own pockets. "So when did they get divorced?"

"Four months ago. We moved here in August."

"Yeah," he said. "I get it. My parents divorced when I was ten and Mariah was nine. It's rough."

I opened my mouth to tell him that he didn't know how rough it was, not really, but I started telling him other things instead. I told him about our last day of school, about how my parents had sat us down that night and looked back and forth at each other for a full minute before June finally blurted out, "Are you getting a divorce?"

I told him how April had cried and how June had been both sad and excited since most of her friends' parents were divorced and now she could "totally relate" to them. Henry laughed when I said that, and I laughed, too, even though it hurt my throat.

I even told him about how I had gotten wasted at my friend's house, how everyone was so worried that they didn't know *what* to do, how my parents looked at me like they were scared of who I was becoming when I didn't even know who I *was*. The details were so sharp that they were cutting right through me. They would never be dull.

They would never disappear.

"But June, June didn't even *cry* until she found out we had to move here," I told Henry. We were sitting in the grass now, side by side as the dew soaked through our jeans. "She liked her friends. She didn't want to leave."

"Yeah," Henry agreed. "You know Mariah? She got all messed up when my parents split, too. It doesn't help that my dad's a douchebag. He doesn't even call that much, not since he got remarried. Mariah keeps thinking that she's gonna go down to his beach house in Cabo. She's always inviting her friends down there, but we haven't gone there in years. I don't even know if he has it anymore."

"June's not messed up," I told him, shaking my head. "Not like me."

He smiled. "You're not that messed up."

"Henry," I told him. "You have no idea."

"What about you?" he said. "Did you cry when you had to move?"

I shook my head. "I never cry. Well, except for right now." I gave a shaky laugh and wiped my eyes again. "God, I'm such a girl right now, I'm sorry. This is totally not part of your tutoring responsibilities, I know."

Henry just wrapped his arms around his knees. "Do you get to see your dad a lot in Houston?"

"Not really," I said. "I was supposed to go there next month, but he got busy with work. I know he misses us, though." I swallowed hard and tried not to think about that day, having to pick between two parents and break one of their hearts three times over. That was the sharpest blade of all.

"May." Henry scooted closer to me. "It's okay."

"Oh, yeah, it's *fantastic*," I sniffled. "It's *great*. Seriously, this has been the best twenty-four hours of my life."

"No, I mean . . . no, it's *not* okay. But it's okay to not be okay."

I just looked at him. He was peeking down at me through his hair, which had curled up in the evening air.

"Everyone's messed up," he continued. "My sister's failing Spanish, and she's hanging out with Blake. But she's not a bad person, you know?" Henry sounded like he was trying to convince himself, not me. "It's just how it is sometimes. Things hurt, and they hurt for a long time. You have to fight back, or it wins. Mariah doesn't fight back. But you do. That's why I like you."

I watched Henry as his hand methodically pulled clumps of long grass out of the ground and let them fall back into the soil. "I kinda understand how your sister feels," I said. "Much to my surprise."

Henry grinned. "Yeah, maybe you do."

"Like, what's that saying? 'Desperate times call for desperate measures.' People do desperate things all the time."

"Yeah," Henry said softly. "I guess she's desperate."

"I'm really sorry," I said, wiping my eyes with the cuff of my sweatshirt. "I don't usually unload on people like this."

"S'okay," he said, just as quietly. "It's nice. You're always so sarcastic. It's like you're always lying about how you really feel." He looked up from the grass and met my eyes. "I like it when you're honest. It's like I can really see you."

"Sometimes it feels like I'm invisible," I mumbled without thinking, and then it hit me.

"Oh my God!" I gasped, immediately looking down, wondering which parts of me were missing. But I was there, all fingers, all toes, and Henry was watching me with an odd expression on his face.

"What?" he asked.

"N-Nothing," I stammered, feeling my heart start to speed. "I just, I though I saw a bug."

Henry just smiled. "Mariah hates bugs, too."

"I don't hate bugs," I immediately said. "I just don't like anything with more than eight legs."

"So you're anti-centipede?"

"Yes. And God help the millipede that crosses my path."

Henry's grin widened across his face. His front teeth were a little crooked, but it was charming and didn't scream for an orthodontist. "I know what you mean," he said after awhile. "About wanting to disappear somewhere."

"Stanford?" I whispered.

"Yeah," he admitted. And then he began to tell me about his parents, how his mom doesn't know what to do with Mariah. "They're always fighting," he said. "And Mariah just keeps hanging out with Blake."

"Yeah," I agreed. "You know, sometimes having a sister is worse than some stupid boyfriend or girlfriend or whatever because at least you can break up with him or her. With your *sister*, though?"

"It's a life sentence." Henry finished my thought with a sigh, and I laughed. "But at least Mariah's hanging out with your sister tonight."

I stopped laughing. "What?"

Henry shrugged. "I dunno, some party. I heard Mariah yelling on the phone to Blake that they have to pick up June at the movie theater."

I had never felt more present in my body than I did right that second. "June's going to a party with your sister?"

"I guess so."

"Oh," I said, but I was starting to get a strange creepy-crawly feeling in my bones. Mariah and June were out with Blake, and no one was watching. I was 99.9 percent sure that April didn't know about June being at this party, seeing as how she hadn't organized another spy mission, and I also knew about her accident visions, the red lights and sirens that kept her up at night.

But I also knew that June was a mindreader! She was always telling us how no one could lie to her, that she was—

And I suddenly realized the one thing that June didn't know.

Anyone could lie to June. All she hears is what people *think*. She doesn't know if it's the truth.

If Mariah and I were—and I couldn't believe I was even admitting this—anything alike, she had to have a lot of denial packed into that brain of hers. (I mean, anyone who thinks Blake's a great guy is probably not skilled at seeing the big picture.) But could June see through that? She hadn't even realized what *I* had been up to, packing for Houston and wanting to leave. What was she missing with Mariah?

I stood up and started looking for my phone. "Shit," I muttered. "Shit shit shit."

"Wait, what's—?" Henry tried to ask.

But I was too busy digging my phone out of my pocket to answer. "Stupid skinny jeans," I muttered. My heart was starting to wallop my ribs again, and I felt kind of sick, just like when I almost hit Avery with the car.

"Are you all right?" Henry asked me. "Is June supposed to be grounded or something?"

I shook my head at him and turned away. "Pick up," I said to the phone. "Pick up now, April!"

But it just rang four times and went to voicemail, and I hung up before leaving a message. "Dammit!" I said. "April always puts her fricking phone on 'vibrate' when she studies!" I whirled around to look at Henry. "Do you know where Mariah and June are?"

"Probably Blake's apartment," Henry frowned. "That's where she hangs out with him."

"Okay, but do you know where that is?" I could hear my voice getting higher, more panicked.

"Yeah, I've gone to get Mariah a few times. Wait, May, why, what's—?"

But I was already grabbing his hand and dragging him into the house. "C'mon," I said. "We've gotta go, Henry. We've gotta go right now."

chapter 21

"This was a very, very bad idea."

We had been at this party for two hours already, and I was ready to go.

First of all, it smelled weird, like old beer and someone's bong and I don't know what else, maybe bad food in the refrigerator. There wasn't even any art on the walls, and I was pretty sure the couch had been brought up from the dumpster outside. The carpet didn't look any better, so I was leaning against the wall, trying to make sure that I never actually touched it.

I was going to douse myself in hand sanitizer when I got home, that was for sure.

I guess it would have been better if I could have hung out with Mariah, but she and Blake had been fighting nonstop since we got to the party and Blake started answering a bunch of texts from someone. At first, Mariah teased him, saying, "Ooh, do you have a new love interest?" But then they each had a couple of beers, and, well, it sort of devolved. "Who are you talking to?" Mariah started yelling at him, and no matter who he said it was, Mariah thought he was lying.

I could hear them screaming down the hall even while I pretended to be interested in the episode of *Project Runway* that was on the TV screen. Someone's iPod speakers were playing loud, so loud that it distorted the bass and kind of hurt in that not-good way, but I could still hear Mariah. I have to say, I was sort of impressed at her yelling abilities. That's just a God-given talent; you can't teach that sort of skill.

"It's a girl, isn't it?!" she was screaming. "You're talking to some skank, some fucking bitch who probably—!"

"I'm talking to *Mike*!" Blake yelled back. "God!"

They were just about to bring the models out for final judging when Blake and Mariah argued their way into the living room. Mariah was all teary-eyed and furious, her empty beer bottle danging at her side, her brain still kind of sober but completely hurt. She was flipping through girls in her mind like a stack of cards, trying to figure out who it was that now had Blake's attention.

Blake's mind, on the other hand, was only thinking of one girl, and it wasn't Mariah.

It was Avery, the girl May had almost hit with the car. I could see him thinking about her, kissing her upstairs at Mariah's party before someone walked in on them. It was sort of gross to see the way he thought about her, like she consisted of body parts and nothing else.

"Let me see your phone then!" Mariah said, holding out her hand to Blake. "If it's just Mike, let me see it!"

"Would you leave me the fuck alone?!" Blake shouted back.

"It's final judging, shut up!" some guy from the couch yelled, his bong balanced on his knees. "Show a little respect!"

I turned to Mariah. "Um, Mariah, maybe we should—"

She didn't even look at me. "Let me see your phone!" she said again. "I mean it! You're lying to me. I know you're lying to me! June!" She suddenly whirled, glaring at me. "Don't you think he's lying?"

"Uh," I said, trying to stall. "I don't *think* he's lying, per se—" It wasn't technically a lie; I *knew* Blake was lying. I didn't have to think it.

Blake's phone suddenly beeped again, and he flipped it open while finishing the last of his beer. Big mistake.

Mariah flew into a rage, going after him with her fists. "Let me see it!" she screamed as she started to pummel him, and a few guys and I tried to pull her off of him. Well, I halfheartedly tugged at her shoulder, since I personally wouldn't have minded seeing Blake get a stray punch or two.

"What is your problem?!" Blake yelled, throwing the phone onto the table, where it landed next to a potted (and very dead) African violet. "Here, God, look at it! I don't care!" And then he turned to me. "Control your *friend*!"

"Control your *dick*!" I shouted back. I don't know who was more surprised by that, Mariah or Blake or me, but I didn't care anymore. This whole situation was ridiculous, and I wished I had stayed at the movies, where I could have at least had some popcorn with my drama.

Blake glared at me and then stormed outside, leaving Mariah a crying mess in the living room. "I thought he loved me," she said. "We were gonna go to Cabo for winter break!"

The idea of Blake being able to cross the border was dubious at best, but I didn't say anything because Mariah was already hysterical enough. I looked around, waiting to see if anyone else was gonna try to take care of her, but apparently final judging on *Project Runway* was way more riveting than the real-life craziness happening in their living room. "Oh, geez," I said under my breath, then put my arm around Mariah's shaking shoulders and leaned against the table with her. She crumpled into me, still crying, and I saw Blake flashing in her brain, along with images of her dad.

I did not *even* want to know what the connection was there.

"Look," I said to Mariah, rubbing her shoulder the way April would always rub mine whenever I was upset. "Think of it this way, why would you want to date someone who lies to you?"

"But he said he *loved* me!"

I tried not to roll my eyes. "Blake probably says a lot of things," I told her.

"He probably says them to that ho," Mariah sniffled.

"Exactly," I started to say, but just then I heard an engine start outside, a low guttural sound that I recognized.

So did Mariah.

"Is Blake leaving?" she screeched, hopping off the table and rushing to the front door, where Blake's taillights were rapidly disappearing out of the parking lot. "That asshole!" she screamed.

I watched just over her shoulder. Not that I was the president of Blake's fan club or anything, but I didn't want to be left without a ride home from the party. And I couldn't obviously call my mom or my sisters, since no one knew I was here. And if we called Henry, then he would probably call May.

A tiny panicked spiral started to spin in my stomach.

Mariah, however, was too upset to think about anything other than Blake. "Fine!" she snapped, slamming the door so hard that it shook the windows. "Fine, you bastard! You forgot your stupid phone!" She had a sort of triumphant look on her face, like a villain in a Disney movie, the kind that used to give me nightmares when I was a little kid. "Where is it?" she muttered to herself.

We both went for the phone at the same time, but she reached it first and snapped it open, scrolling through Blake's phone like she had done it a million times before. And judging from her thoughts, she had. "Mariah, c'mon, let's just call a cab," I said. I had seven dollars and a pack of delicious gummy worms on me, and I wasn't sure if that would get us very far. But we could worry about that later. The guy in the corner was already trying to figure out if either Mariah or I was going to sleep with him, and my panic spiral got a bit more intense.

The music was still blasting, but I didn't need to hear to know that Mariah had found her proof. It was written all over her face.

"He's meeting up with her," she finally said, sounding kind of angry and kind of broken. "They're meeting at the park on Mulholland and Old Topanga. Who the hell meets at the *park*? What is it, a *playdate*?"

"Who is it?" I asked her, trying to peek at the phone.

"Some Avery chick," Mariah said. "Do you know her? Is she ugly?"

I just shook my head in a vague sort of way. "She doesn't exactly look great in khakis," I said. "C'mon, let's just get a cab. We can go back to my place or your place, hang out, watch a movie."

"What, and play board games like you did with your old friends? This isn't kindergarten, June!" Mariah glared, ripping herself away from me and cradling the phone in her hand. "Hey, Nick!"

A guy on the couch looked up. "What?"

Mariah held out her hand. "Keys," she said. "You're out of beer."

Nick's thoughts were so smoked that I could barely see them, but when he just handed over his car keys, I knew it didn't matter. No matter what anyone else thought, I knew the truth: This was a very, very bad idea.

"Mariah!" I hissed behind her. "This is crazy! You don't even have a license! And you're only fifteen! You can't buy beer!"

"I have a permit!" she said. "And whatever, we're just going to the park! And it's not like Nick even gives a shit about where we're going." She narrowed her eyes at me. "So are you coming or not?"

I hesitated in the doorway, stalling for time. The party had spilled out into the parking lot by this point, people smoking and drinking and crowding all around the tiny doorway. Someone's car was playing rap music, which clashed with the music coming from inside the house. No one seemed to think it was strange that Mariah was leaving in someone else's car. Maybe this was just an average Monday for them, I had no idea.

One thought was strong above all others. It was mine.

I wish my sisters were here.

"Well?" Mariah demanded, her hand on the door to Nick's car, a beat-up Corolla. "If you're coming with me, do it now!"

"Where are we going?" I asked.

"The park!" she said. "Duh, where else? We're gonna confront them! If he thinks he can just *lie* to me . . ."

Her brain was working, that was for sure. She wasn't trashed, wasn't high, and she *did* at least have a permit.

"Fine," I said. "But then you're taking me home."

"Whatever," she said. "Just get in the car."

"The back window's down," I said as I climbed into the front seat. "That's not really safe, anyone could just—"

"Just get in," Mariah interrupted me.

She was just starting the engine when another car came careening into the parking lot. "Mariah!" someone yelled as a car door slammed, and I turned around and saw Henry starting to run after us. "Hey, Mariah, wait!"

"Don't you wanna wait?" I said, my hand already on the door handle.

"For Henry?" Mariah scoffed as she shifted the car into "drive" and started to accelerate. "Please."

I looked over my shoulder again. Henry was close enough that I could see how upset he looked. If the car hadn't already been moving, I probably would've gotten out and asked him to take me home. Maybe he could be bribed into not telling May with seven dollars and some gummy worms.

Mariah hit the gas harder and the car sped forward, cold wind breezing in through the car's busted-out window. "Look out, Blake," she sneered. "Shit's about to go down." I winced and reached for my seatbelt, finally remembering my sisters' warnings for the first time in my life.

But when I looked down, I saw that it was already fastened safely around me.

chapter 22

"There's been an accident."

april

The vision hit me so hard that I almost doubled over in the front seat of Julian's car. *June following Mariah out of an apartment. Red and blue lights, sirens, June's face scared in the front seat of a car.* It came again and again, relentless.

"Oh, God. Oh, God. Oh, God." The words didn't even sound like mine, but I kept saying them.

I saw Julian turn towards me, looking like he was ready to start picking up the pieces. "April?" he said, his voice a little unsure. "What—?"

I could see the street signs in my head, *Mulholland and Old Topanga. The dark corners, the dim streetlights. Red lights, bright white lights almost blinding me . . .*

"It's my sister," I told Julian, and I barely recognized my own voice. "We have to go. Right now. It's June, it's . . ." *Other cars, lights, Avery—*

Avery?

"It's *everyone*!" I told Julian tearfully, not knowing how else to explain it. "We have to go!"

"April, you're shaking!"

"Come *on*!" I cried, trying to grab and turn his keys, which had been sitting idle in the ignition. The vision was slamming into my brain again and again, and I put my hands to my temples and covered my eyes, trying to find space to think.

"April, what—?" Julian reached out to take my hand, but I skittered away and started putting my seatbelt on. "C'mon!" I told him. "Drive, drive, let's go!"

"Okay, fine, where are we—hey!" He grabbed me by the shoulder first and made me look at him. He was scared of me, I could tell. "April, talk to me, what—?"

I looked up at him. "It's my sister," I said, and I could hear everything in my voice that I hadn't said before. "She's with Mariah! It's not . . . it's not okay! She's supposed to be at the movies!"

"But how do you know this?"

I unbuckled my seatbelt and started to get out of the car. The park was probably a half-mile away. I could run there, but Julian yanked me back before I could open the door. "Okay, okay, just tell me where we're going," he said, starting the ignition.

"The park on Old Topanga by school," I said as the vision came again. It didn't hurt, not the tiniest headache or pain, but my body felt like it was being ripped apart. "I didn't see it," I whimpered.

"What didn't you see?" Julian demanded. He was driving with one hand and had his other hand back on my shoulder. I couldn't even feel his touch.

"I—I'm supposed to watch her," I said against my hands. "I didn't see her coming here. I didn't know she was . . . I was . . . I was with you."

"Don't tell me this is all because we almost kissed."

I could tell Julian was trying to make me laugh, relax, do something other than scare the crap out of him, but I just stayed rigid in my seat, feeling the seatbelt cut into my skin. It was too tight. Everything felt too tight. "I didn't see her because I almost kissed you," I whispered. "I wasn't thinking."

"April, what the hell are you talking about?"

"Turn right," I replied as my heart moved into my throat. But I knew we wouldn't get there in time. The sirens, the lights, the noise, they were in my head and they weren't leaving now. They weren't going anywhere until it was over. "Oh my God," I said again. "*I missed her*."

"You didn't," Julian said, and he let go of my shoulder as he steered and grabbed my hand instead, pulling it away from my face. "We'll get there; we'll find her."

"No, we won't," I said. "We won't." I fumbled for my phone, flipping it open and seeing three missed calls from May. She hadn't left a message. But just seeing the number three made my stomach lurch, and I had to fight to not throw up. I tried to call her back, but it rang and rang, the most frustrating sound in the world.

Julian and I rode in silence for the next minute. His jaw was tight as he clutched the steering wheel, and I put my head in my free hand and tried to see past everything, tried to get something new, something that would tell me that June was all right. We sat at a red light for so long that I thought it was part of my vision at first, but when Julian made an impatient sound and drummed his fingers against the steering wheel, I realized that I was still in real life.

And there was no more time to wait.

Before Julian could do anything, I threw off my seatbelt and bolted out of the car, leaving the passenger door open as I ran up the dark street, past our high school, past the dry cleaner's on the corner.

"April, wait!" I heard Julian yell, but he was still stuck at the light, and two oncoming cars were keeping him there.

I still had my phone in my hand, and I dialled 911 as I ran.

"911, what is your emergency?"

"Old Topanga and Mulholland," I said, my breath coming so hard that I could barely understand myself. "There's been an accident."

I ran harder, the cold eucalyptus air filling my lungs and shoving me forward, crickets somewhere chanting a rhythm to match my furious pace. *Go go go*, I chanted in my head, trying to see straight ahead even as the visions covered my eyes. *Get there, get there, get there. June, June, June.*

I was so winded by the time I arrived that my ribcage felt like a broken accordion. The park was nearly pitch-black, and I stopped right at the entrance, gasping for breath and trying to figure out what was happening. There was nothing, no sound other than crickets and pond frogs and the very distant sounds of traffic.

"Where is it?" I cried out loud. "What's happening?" Was this all there was? Had I gotten it wrong? Maybe June had left here and was going to the party, and my brain had flipped the vision. I didn't realize I was crying until I tasted the salt on my lips, and I whirled in a frantic circle, trying to figure out what had gone wrong.

That's when I saw Blake and Avery.

They were standing by the fence, not even a hundred feet away from me. They were kissing a little, Avery's little voice murmuring above everything else. Her hair was the color of the night. In the distance, I could hear sirens heading our way, the ones I had summoned.

"No!" I yelled at Blake and Avery. "No, you can't!"

They looked up in confusion, their faces suddenly illuminated by white light, and when I glanced over my shoulder, I saw the car coming towards us, its headlights burning into my eyes. I could see the red lights, too, the brake lights of other cars as they got out of the car's way, all the lights as perfect as I had seen them in my visions, and I suddenly understood.

I was the accident. Not June. It was me.

I stood and watched as the lights came closer, too paralyzed to move.

I guess even when you can see everything, some things will always be a surprise.

chapter 23
"Suddenly I was invisible and running."

may

If June and I didn't die during this whole escapade, then I was going to kill her.

A lot.

I didn't even know why I got in the backseat of the car. All I knew is that Henry pulled up to the apartment, and I saw June getting into the car. Suddenly I was invisible and running, sliding into Mariah's car through the open window before Henry even noticed I was gone. He was probably worried now, wondering where I had gone. Great, another problem to add to the list. (And also, I was super-bummed that I was invisible while slipping into the car because I'm sure that was some epic *Dukes of Hazzard*-style shit right there.)

At least I had gotten June's seatbelt around her, clicking it into place while Mariah wailed about something. June looked as nervous as a squirrel, big eyes and twitchy, and I knew that it was bad.

"He swore he wasn't cheating!" Mariah sobbed as she drove. "He promised me!"

"If Blake's gonna lie to you, then he's not worth it," June said, trying to calm her down. "You don't need him."

All this was over *Blake*? Oh my God, you have to be joking.

But Mariah was too upset to even listen, and she took a deep, shaky breath and continued to cry. "He p-promised, though!"

Was Mariah slurring now? Had she been drinking? My God, could this possibly get any worse?

June looked stricken. "Mariah," she gasped, "you're not pregnant, are you?"

So yes, it *could* possibly get worse.

"No!" Mariah shouted, and both June and I fell back against our seats in relief. "Are you crazy? No, I'm not pregnant! I just . . . he said he wouldn't leave! I can't—I just can't. Why do guys keep *leaving*?"

The girl was doing the full-on ugly cry, and despite my cold, cold heart and the fact that she was possibly driving me and my little sister straight to our deaths, I couldn't help but feel a bit lightheaded, hearing her panic, hearing her voice these feelings that were so close to what I had gone through, too.

In fact, the more I thought about it, the more I was sure that this wasn't about Blake at all.

June was starting to realize the same thing, I could tell. She always looks like she's watching a movie when she's reading people's thoughts, and now as she gazed at Mariah, her profile just looked sad. "There's no Cabo house, is there?" June said quietly.

Mariah sniffled and made a gross snotty sound, but didn't reply.

The car picked up speed, sailing through a yellow light, and I prayed that there was a cop around who would pull us over and stop the whole crazy train.

"Hey," June said. "You know, Mariah, it's okay. You still have your mom, right? And Henry, he's still around. He showed up at the party tonight; that's gotta mean he cares about you."

"Screw them."

"Oooookay," June said slowly. "Maybe that doesn't count. But a lot of people like you, Mariah. They do, they really really do, and I just know this, okay?" When Mariah shot her a disbelieving look, June added, "I just *do*, and please don't ask me why or how."

The words didn't work, and Mariah zoomed the car up towards Mulholland, still crying. She had *so* been drinking, I could tell. I hung on to the back of the seat, feeling the wind from the open window that I had leapt through tangle my invisible hair, and I started to laugh from sheer nerves. Only I could hear it, though. It sounded sort of crazed and sort of hysterical, and that's when I knew that I was scared, too.

"Okay," June said, and now she was babbling. If I laugh when I get nervous, June goes into motormouth mode. "Here's the thing. You know my sister May? The skinnier one who always looks angry?"

Mariah didn't answer.

"Well, when our parents first announced they were divorcing, she took it really hard. She got totally trashed on tequila, our parents were all worried, and then my dad moved to Houston and broke a promise to her, and it really hurt her a lot. And sometimes she gets mean because it's easier for her to keep people out than let them in. Does that make sense?"

Mariah gulped and nodded. So did I.

"And now . . ." June's mouth was trembling a little, and I could tell she was so scared and trying to be brave. "Well, I mean, even though she's rude and drives me insane and has no fashion sense whatsoever and makes fun of me for every little thing, I still love her. She's my sister. And I know that she feels the same way about me.

"Some people leave, yeah," June continued. "And it sucks. But some people *don't* leave, and they never will. And sometimes people are there, but you just can't see them. But they're still there."

I couldn't believe how sincere and strong June sounded. Could. Not. Believe. She was right, too, she was so right. And I suddenly felt terrible for even thinking about running away, for leaving my mom and my sisters. The pain was so fierce that it burned, and I swallowed hard and decided that I wasn't going to kill June after all.

In fact, I was probably going to hug the crap out of her.

And that's when I saw that June and Mariah had turned around in their seats and were staring at me.

June's eyes were huge, absolutely huge in her face, and I glanced down and saw my body. "Oh," I said. "Hi."

"Hi," June said. "How . . . how did—?"

"What the?" Mariah gasped.

"Is April here, too?" June said, looking confused.

I glanced around. "Does it look like she's here?"

June cocked her head to the side, frowning. "But I can *hear* her." And then her eyes snapped forward, looking out the windshield. "No!" she screamed, and I followed her gaze and saw April standing in the headlights of our oncoming car, her body frozen, Avery and Blake a few feet away, all of us staring at each other in horror. Mariah screamed, trying to slam on the brakes, but it was too late.

"No," June whispered. "*April.*"

"Not this girl!" April had shouted the day I almost hit Avery with the car. I could hear her words in my brain, like she was still saying them.

Not this girl.

It probably took less than a second for me to throw myself into the driver's seat and grab the steering wheel, but it felt like hours, even days. All I could hear was Mariah yelling in my ear, and I hit the brake hard, slamming her foot down along with it. I jerked the wheel to the right, and then there was screeching and screaming and I heard both April and June scream, "May!" just before everything stopped.

chapter 24

"I couldn't imagine ever letting them go."

For a minute, I thought we were dead. All of us.

And then my head started to hurt, and I realized that if I were dead, I probably wouldn't have the mother of all headaches.

The air smelled like brakes, the sound of skidding still so sharp in my ears that it made them hurt, too. When I opened my eyes, I saw the dashboard and my sister May leaning over me, her breath hot on my face. She had looked like a freaking *warrior* when she grabbed the steering wheel, the headlights illuminating her face as she steered the car away from April and Blake and Avery. May still looked that way, wild-eyed and determined.

"Junie?" she was asking. "June? Are you all right?"

"Yeah," I said slowly, because I was. My head hurt a little, but I hadn't banged it. My legs were still moving, and whatever we had hit, we hadn't hit it that hard.

I was okay.

"Where's April?" I asked suddenly. "Are *you* okay? Where is she? Where's Mariah?"

But Mariah had already staggered out of the car in shock, looking at the accident scene, at the crumpled right headlight that resulted when May steered the car into the gravel parking lot and skidded into the wooden fence. Mariah looked fine, too, just shocked.

"April's okay," May said to me. "I'm okay, too. Look, she's over there. She's fine. She looks as goofy as ever. C'mon, June, it's okay now, don't cry."

"I'm not crying," I said automatically, but I was. I just hadn't realized it until May pointed it out.

I climbed gingerly out of the passenger seat, opening the car door and holding it while May crawled out behind me. The minute she was out, I launched myself at her, flinging my arms around her neck, hanging on so tight that I was afraid I would break her ribs. I thought she would pull away or make some sarcastic comment involving my choice of nightlife excursions, but instead all she did was hug me back, and that's when I realized that May was crying, too.

I could hear footsteps pounding towards us, crunching through gravel, and I stepped back long enough so that we could grab April and pull her to us. She was sobbing, her tears ragged and panicked as she clutched at us. I hugged my sisters, and they fit against my sides like two jigsaw pieces that would never fit anywhere else. I couldn't imagine ever letting them go again, like releasing them would be to surrender the best parts of myself.

We stood there for a few minutes, crying over each other as the sirens grew louder in the distance, and I finally looked up long enough to say, "Is anyone . . . ?"

"No," April said, hiccuping a little. "No, everyone's fine. You didn't hit them. Even the car is okay. It was just a headlight."

"May grabbed the wheel," I told her as May nodded. "She wasn't there and then she *was*." I was sobbing again, huge terrible messy tears that were probably creating Dior mascara rivers on my cheeks. "I'm sorry!" I cried. "I should never have gone out with Mariah! I—I didn't know; I thought it would be *okay*!"

"No, no," April said, and even May was shaking her head. We looked at each other, all of us starting to realize what had happened, what had been happening all this time.

"Junie Bee," May finally said, "I wouldn't have been in the car if you hadn't been in it."

I sniffled and realized what May was saying. "So Mariah would have hit . . ."

May nodded and wiped her face with her shirt sleeve.

"If I had stopped you from going out tonight," April said, her voice shaking with the idea, "Blake and Avery and Mariah, they would . . ."

I nodded through my tears, getting a little overwhelmed by everything that had happened. "And if May hadn't sucked so much at European history, then she wouldn't have met Henry and he wouldn't have driven her to the party and . . . and . . ."

May laughed a little through her tears. "Thanks, June," she said. "But I'm passing history now. One more reason to like Henry."

I looked over April's shoulder and saw Blake and Mariah standing around each other, not talking but not moving away, either. Mariah was still crying.

But whatever, they were *alive*.

I reached down and used April's sleeve to wipe my eyes. She let me. "I thought you would have seen me go to the party," I sniffled. "I mean, I didn't *want* you to, but I thought—"

"I kissed Julian," April said, and both May and June looked up at me. "I missed seeing you because I was kissing him. Well, I *almost* kissed him. It was close."

I sniffled a little. "How close?"

April gave me a wobbly, teary smile. "Let's just say everything happened exactly as it was supposed to."

The sirens were only a few blocks away now. April had called 911, I could tell. "I swear," I said to my sisters, "from now on, I'm not gonna pretend like I know everything just because I can read minds. Those days are over."

"And I'm not gonna be so crazy protective," April added, still shuddering a little.

"Yeah, seriously," May said to her. "That didn't really work out so well."

"And *you*," I told May. "You don't get to leave."

She nodded, but I wasn't done. "I mean it," I said. "You have to stay with us." Just the idea of May not being around made me queasy, and I clung to her elbow. "Like, seriously. We need you."

"Okay," she said quietly. "I know. I understand."

"You were gonna leave?" April asked, looking from me to May. "Are you kidding?"

"I'm not leaving," May sighed. "It was a stupid idea. The only leaving I'm doing is the superfreaky supernatural kind of leaving. But you know what?" she said. "No one ever gets to say anything bad about my driving *ever again*."

"Done," I said, then watched as the red lights came over the hill, just like April had said they would.

chapter 25

"You drove like a bat out of hell."

april

It took three police officers and two paramedics to determine that the fence around the park had taken the brunt of the accident. May had offroaded the Corolla so neatly that if it hadn't been for the busted headlight, you would think she had meant to park the car like that. The impact was so low that the airbags hadn't even deployed on the car. ("Does that tin can even *have* airbags?" May muttered to me, and I had to admit that I didn't know.)

Blake looked pretty nervous being questioned by the police, but the truth of the matter was, he had just been standing by a fence when a car almost hit him. Being a jerk and cheating on your girlfriend weren't illegal.

Unfortunately.

Mariah was still a mess, shaking and crying as one of the officers tried to talk to her. He didn't look too happy with her and I was pretty sure that had something to do with the fact that she was semi-drunk and fifteen years old. "Oh, geez," June said under her breath. "I should probably . . . is she gonna be okay?"

I nodded. As far as I could tell, Mariah would be in school next week, looking tired and subdued but still there. There'd be a hearing and fines and I certainly didn't see a driver's license any time soon in Mariah's future. "I think she's gonna be fine," I told June. "Not right away, but she will be."

June walked over to Mariah, put an arm around her shoulders, and started to talk to her. Mariah listened and nodded, and I could sort of hear the conversation. "Trust me," June said at one point, "the truth is the best way to go. Don't get me started on this tonight."

May was standing near the car, talking to another officer. "I don't know," she was saying. "I mean, I saw *The Fast and the Furious* a couple of years ago. That probably helped a little."

"April!" someone suddenly yelled, and when I looked over, I saw Julian running towards me, his car parked haphazardly down the road. He looked scared and confused as the red lights bounced off his face, just like I had seen. The lights were on June, too, the red glow highlighting her as she looked worriedly towards Mariah.

It was my vision, only now I understood it. Julian was here because of me, not because he wanted to hurt June, but because he cared about me. He was trying to protect me. I walked over to him on legs that felt like Jell-O, and when I got close enough, he reached out and grabbed my arms. "You okay?" he gasped. "Is everyone all right?"

I nodded and then hung onto his forearms, steadying myself. "You drove like a bat out of hell," I told him. "Thanks."

"You *ran* like a bat out of hell. What happened?"

I gave him a quick rundown, skipping the parts where May had been invisible in the backseat of a car, June had used her mindreading abilities to calm Mariah down, and I had predicted (at least somewhat) the whole thing. I figured what he didn't know wouldn't hurt him.

"So everyone's okay?" he asked.

"The right headlight didn't make it," I said. "But other than that, yeah. We're fine."

"I hope you know that you scared the shit out of me."

"You and me both," I replied, and then I wrapped my arms around his waist and held on. "I'm really glad you're here," I said into his shirt. "Even if I'm strangling you like a boa constrictor."

"Strangle away," he said, patting my back. "I'm not going anywhere."

After a minute or so, a cop came over to us. I had already talked to another officer, but the story wasn't that complicated. All I had really done was just stand there. May and June had done the heavy lifting.

I separated myself from Julian and leaned against his side, my knees still a little shaky as the cop spoke. "You okay, young lady?" His nametag said Sgt. Beauford. It sounded French. I was sure May liked him already.

"I'm fine," I said. "I was just standing there. Did anyone get hurt?" I already knew that my sisters were fine, but I sort of hoped that maybe a piece of headlight had hit Blake and given him a *Phantom of the Opera*-esque scar.

"No, it doesn't seem like it. The other witnesses"—he pointed at May and June and Mariah and Blake"—said that the driver swerved to avoid the young man and a girl."

"Yeah, Avery," I said.

"Can you describe her for me?"

"Yeah, she's right . . ." I glanced around but didn't see her. "I swear, Officer, I didn't hit my head. She was here. I saw her. She has this black hair and her eyes are sort of—" I widened my eyes, trying to imitate what Avery looked like when she was in the path of an oncoming car, a look that I knew *waaaay* too well.

He just made a note and nodded. "She may have run off. Don't worry, we'll contact the school, get some information on her."

"Is everyone else all right?" But the truth was, I was only asking to be polite. I already knew it would be okay. There would be no emergency rooms because no one had so much as bumped their heads. People were just shaken up, and Mariah would get busted for a DUI and have to do alcohol counseling and volunteer work. (No disfiguring scar for Blake, either, which was a bummer.) The legal jargon was too tangled up to sort through, and honestly, I didn't care anymore. My sisters were safe. That's all that mattered.

After the cop walked away, I turned back to Julian. "Hey," I said.

"Hey," he replied, shoving my hair behind my ears.

"We got interrupted earlier tonight."

Julian might have been blushing, but it was hard to tell under all the flashing red lights. "Oh, really? Which part? Remind me."

I stood up a little straighter and put my arms around his neck, bringing my face towards his. "This part," I said. "Ringing any bells?"

"Mmm, almost," he teased. "Maybe a little closer?"

I smiled against him, our lips finally touching. I'm not Little Miss Experience, but it was good. *Waaaaaay* better than good. Julian smelled nice, and when he put his hand on my shoulder, he filled my vision as the red lights finally faded away.

chapter 26

"Promise you won't freak out."

may

We didn't get home until almost midnight, and by the time we did, all I wanted to do was crawl into bed and fall asleep and wake up sometime around Christmas.

My mom hadn't stopped hugging us since the minute she showed up at the almost-accident scene. Even now as we walked into the house from the garage, she was hugging April and holding June to her, her face puffy from crying. "Mom, we're fine," I said, but all she did was grab me back towards her. It was sort of hard to get through the door like that, but the four of us managed to squeeze through.

I knew June was getting the worst of my mom's fears, and I finally had to tug June away from her and say, "Go wash your face, that Dior stuff makes you look like a spider," and she gave me a grateful glance as she disentangled herself and went upstairs.

"Mom, we're really okay," April was saying for the millionth time. "Really. We're fine."

"I want to throttle that Blake," my mom muttered. I was starting to think that Blake might be safer in jail than on the street where my mom could get him. "When I think about how he just left June at that party—"

"If it makes you feel better," I told her, "I can kick him in the nuts for you."

My mom paused and looked at me. I waited for the inevitable "violence is never the answer" lecture, but all she said was, "How hard?"

I grinned. "*So* hard. I can even go for—"

"What matters now," April said, cutting me off before I could tell my mom exactly what I had wanted to do to Blake, "is that we're fine. June's fine, everyone's okay, and we should probably all go to sleep."

My mom hugged April extra-tight before kissing the top of her head and letting her go upstairs. I started to follow her, but my mom pulled me back and gripped the top of my arms, holding me out at arm's length. "May," she said as her eyes welled up, "why is there a half-packed duffle bag by the front door?"

It seemed like a hundred years ago, but when I looked over, the bag was still there, its trip to Houston suddenly cancelled. "I just . . ." I started to say. But then my own eyes were getting wet, too, and it kind of hurt to talk. "It was just a bad idea," I managed to tell my mom. "I just wanted to be somewhere, but now I want to be here. I'm gonna be okay, Mom. It's getting better. *I'm* getting better."

She was still squeezing my arms, almost hurting me, but I didn't care. It felt real. It reminded me that I was there. "You are very, very important to me," my mom finally said. "And you are very, very important to your dad and your sisters, too. I know that a lot has happened lately—"

"To put it mildly."

"—but it doesn't change how much we care about you and love

you. Nothing will ever change that." She squeezed harder and held my gaze. "Is that clear?"

My throat ached. "I know that," I said. "I just kind of forgot for a little while."

She hugged me then, kissing my hair over and over again. "Okay," she said. "Don't do it again."

"I won't."

We stood there for a few minutes, hanging on to one another. All this crying was starting to make me feel waterlogged, and if the doorbell hadn't rung, I probably would have had to wring myself out like a wet towel.

"Who's ringing the bell at this hour?" my mom asked, letting me go long enough to wipe her eyes.

"It's Henry!" April and June both chorused from upstairs. Of *course* they knew who it was.

"I should probably get it," I said. "He drove me to the party tonight. I should see if he's doing okay."

My mom nodded, and I went to answer the front door, pulling it open to see Henry standing on the front porch. "Hi," he said, when he saw me. "I know it's late. I just wanted to make sure you were all right."

"Yeah, we're fine," I said, as June came downstairs, her face clean of probably one hundred dollars' worth of mascara. "My mom's pretty shaken up, though."

"Yeah, I know what you mean," he said. "I think Mariah's gonna be locked in her room until she's thirty. Hi, June."

"What's up, dude?" she said. "Thanks for driving my sister to the party tonight. You're like a superhero by proxy."

Henry smiled and blushed. "I don't know," he said. "I'd probably look terrible in a leotard. How are you?"

June shrugged and leaned into my shoulder. "I'm fine," she said. "But I'm grounded for at least two months for sneaking out to the party."

"What?" I said. "Mom never said—"

"Trust me," June interrupted me. "I'm grounded. April confirmed."

"Got it."

"And don't worry too much about Mariah," June said to Henry. "She's kinda over Blake now."

"Really?"

"She'd rather drink pond scum than see him again," June clarified, and I knew she wasn't making any part of that up. "If I'm ever allowed to use the phone or computer again, tell her I'll talk to her later. Oh, and—"

But she suddenly stopped herself from talking, which was pretty much the equivalent of witnessing a miracle, and she just smiled and waved goodbye. "See you later, Henry," she said. "Thanks for being cool."

I just sighed as she went back upstairs. "Normally I would want to strangle her," I told Henry, stepping outside onto the porch with him. "But she gets a free pass tonight."

"Just for tonight?"

"Well, probably for the rest of her life," I admitted, then glanced down at my feet. "Uh, I haven't said thank you yet, you know, for driving me to the party and—"

"Are you kidding?" Henry said, laughing a little. "May, I came over here to say thanks to you. Mariah told me what happened."

"Um, yeah, about that. What exactly did she tell you?"

"That you had been in the backseat the whole time. She must have been pretty drunk because she didn't even see you, but June said that you were there. May, you got in that car so fast that I never even saw you *move*, and if you hadn't been there . . ." Henry trailed off, but I understood. Now that the adrenaline had faded and real life took over, it was hard to think about what could have happened.

"I know," I said to him, and he looked up at me and held my gaze for a long minute. His hair didn't look so stupid anymore, not when he was so close to me. And his lips were nice, too. I mean, not that I was looking at his mouth or anything, but they were nice, in a lips sort of way.

At first I thought the fluttery butterfly feeling was because I was disappearing again, but when I glanced down to check, I was still all there. Not even a toe was missing. And then I looked back at Henry and realized that the butterflies were from something else entirely.

Henry's mouth got closer and closer to mine, and just before he was about to kiss me, I whispered, "Henry, if something weird happens, promise me you won't freak out."

"May," he whispered back, "if I haven't freaked out yet tonight, I'm probably not going to."

"Good point," I said, and then his mouth was on mine, and I felt like I was disappearing all over again, becoming someone else entirely, and at the same time staying right where I belonged.

When he pulled back, I smiled like a dork. "Sorry," I said. "That was just . . . um . . . yeah."

"Was it okay?" Henry asked, a faint blush forming underneath his freckles. I was surprised to discover that maybe he was nervous, too.

"Way better than okay," I admitted. "Don't worry, tutoring

European history and promoting Stanford are, like, the least of your skills."

"Really?"

"Oh, yeah."

Henry grinned and then kissed me again before pulling away. I reached up and touched my mouth quickly, just to make sure my lips were still there, and then he was jingling his car keys in his hand. "I should probably get back home," he admitted. "I just had to do that first."

"Good idea," I agreed. "Both parts."

"Okay. I'll see you tomorrow?"

"Sure, yeah." I wasn't really capable of saying big words at that point, but I hoped the stupid grin on my face told him how happy I was. Judging from the stupid grin on *his* face, it did.

My mom was in her bathroom, brushing her teeth and getting ready for bed as I went back upstairs. April was in her room, tapping out something on her computer, and she looked up when I peeked in. "Did you know . . . ? That Henry was, uh . . . ?" I asked her.

"Only for the past thirty minutes or so."

"Oh." But I was still smiling, and from her room next door, I could hear June giggling happily to herself.

chapter 27
"Then I defy you stars!"

june

By Tuesday, word had gotten around that we had been in a pretty exciting situation. I don't know how people found out, but they did, and I spent most of Tuesday morning reassuring people that yes, it was scary, and no, no one had died, and yes, Blake had totally cheated on Mariah, and no, I couldn't go for coffee and give them all the gory details because I was grounded and pretty much going to be locked in a tower for the rest of my teenage years.

"Two months," my mom had said. "No phone, no computer unless it's for school, no e-mail, no chat, no iPod, no shopping . . ." My mom thought for a minute. "What else is there? Did I get all the technology? Oh, wait! No texting, either. I think that's it."

Parents are so cute sometimes.

Another thing that was new: I could really hear April and May now, even across hallways or classrooms. It was like we were all set to the same frequency, and I could turn it on and off whenever I wanted. (I know I'm not supposed to, and it's, like, all shades of unethical. But I kept going into their thoughts all day Tuesday. I guess I just wanted to be sure that they were there.) I could hear everyone else, too, of course, but I could crank down the volume until it was just quiet noise. And then it was sort of pleasant. I realized controlling my power was actually sort of easy—I just had to focus on my *own* thoughts, and everyone else's just dropped down about ten decibels, like background music when you're at the dentist.

Avery didn't come back to school that day, either. Rumors flew about where she was, and it got ridiculous around fourth period when someone floated the idea that she had been kidnapped by aliens. I mean, really. Original much? She didn't come back on Wednesday, either, and by Friday, I was pretty sure she had either ditched permanently or been shipped off to boarding school. I tried a couple times to find her thoughts, but she was gone for good. I couldn't hear a single thing.

I talked to my sisters about it one night. We've been talking a lot more, mostly because I'm on lockdown and I don't have anyone else to talk to. They're still weirdos, I can't lie, but it's sort of nice. May even let me paint her fingernails, and when she managed to pick the ugliest color ever (a matte black called "Spider Webs", ew) I didn't say anything. Good thing she's not the mindreader.

"So," I said to April one night when May was sprawled out on her bed reading "The Invisible Man" and April was bent over some math project at her desk. "You know what's weird?"

"The past two weeks?" she offered.

"No," I said. "Well, yeah, I mean. It's been nuts. But you know what I was thinking about yesterday when Mom was driving me to my orthodontist appointment? What if May never almost hit Avery with her car?"

May lowered her book just long enough to glare at me. "Did we not agree that no one could ever make fun of my driving skills again?"

"I'm not making fun," I told her. "But what if we never even saw her? Do you think we would've gone all kerplooey?"

April laughed. "Probably."

"But we don't know," I said. "What if we hadn't seen her and everything would have been normal? I can't even really remember what she looked like."

"That's your mind being kind," May said without putting her book down this time. "She was a psycho hose beast. Let it go."

"I think I already am," I murmured, but no one heard me.

By the time I got to English class on the following Tuesday afternoon, I was wiped out. I was also sort of sad that Mariah wasn't there, since she had been my friend. And now I felt like a lonely little island sitting by myself in the middle of the classroom. April had sworn up and down that Mariah would be back next week, but that wasn't much comfort on a Tuesday.

"Okay, bodies," Mrs. Ames said. (She always calls us "bodies," which I think is weird and probably shows that she has some issues she needs to work out in therapy.) "You all have your copies of *Romeo and Juliet*, I assume?" She waved her paperback copy. "And you've done the reading assignment?"

I had, actually. Now that I was practically locked into my room except to go to school, I had a lot of time to do homework. *A lot of time*. *Romeo and Juliet*'s pretty cool, but it helps that I've seen the movie, the cool one where Mercutio's a cross-dresser. In fact, I think Juliet should have hooked up with him because Romeo was an absolute idiot for not checking to see if she was alive before he off'd himself. *My* ideal boyfriend would at least look for a pulse. ("Put a mirror under her nose!" I had screamed at that part in the book.)

I was just getting out my spiral notebook with the glittery purple cover (don't even be jealous) when Caitlin, the girl sitting next to me, whispered across the aisle. "Psst!" she said. "Hey! You're June, right?"

I raised an eyebrow, hoping to look like one of those mysterious silent-film stars in those boring flicks my dad used to watch on cable. "Yeah," I said. "I am."

I didn't even have a chance to read her mind before Caitlin continued talking. "Okay, hi," she said. "Listen, can I ask you a question?"

I was fully prepared to tell her where I got my notebook from, or my shoes, or my bag, when she held up her copy of *Romeo and Juliet* and asked, "Did you understand of this?"

I flipped through her mind quickly, just to make sure she wasn't acting dumb on purpose. But no, she was completely confused. *I* almost got confused looking at her thoughts. "Um, yeah," I said. "I liked it. It's good. Especially the part where Mercutio dies because—"

"He *dies*?" Caitlin flipped through the book. "I didn't even understand the part where he dies!"

I hesitated for a brief second, then said, "Well, if you ever want to get together and study or hang out or something . . ."

"June!" Mrs. Ames called from the front of the class. "Maybe you can answer my question!"

Crap-ola.

"Um, could you repeat the question, please?" I asked.

Mrs. Ames sighed heavily. "I *said*, what does Romeo say when he hears that Juliet has died?"

June wants to study with me!

Caitlin's thoughts were so happy that it was like being bombarded with glitter, but it didn't matter because my thoughts were pretty peachy keen, too. She thought I was *smart*! She wanted to *study*!

With *me*! April was totally going to die when I told her about this, and I wondered if she had already seen it happening.

"June?" Mrs. Ames prompted. "We're waiting. What did Romeo say?"

I grinned to myself and sat up straight in my chair. "He said, 'Then I defy you, stars!'"

Indeed.

chapter 28

"I'm just really gonna miss you."

One month later . . .

"Does anyone know where I put my purse?" My mom hustled through the kitchen and into the dining room, looking over every available surface. "I had it this morning and now . . ." She rifled through a stack of laundry on the stairs, then circled back. "June, honey, have you seen it?"

"Mom, it's not like I can read the purse's mind or something." June sounded amused and just stuck her tongue out at me when I shot her a warning look. She had a blast coming up with all these little double entrendres about her mindreading abilities. I guess it was more interesting than doing algebra homework at the kitchen table. That was pretty much the only place she had been allowed to go for the last month. Sometimes Henry brought Mariah over, and she and May did homework together. I guess Mariah had really gotten back on track and dumped Blake the night of the accident. She still wasn't my favorite person, but June just said, "She has her flaws like the rest of us." And it was a hard point to argue.

Besides, I already knew that Mariah was gonna graduate from

high school in three years and end up attending UCLA, so really, I couldn't hate her too much.

"No, I know you can't read the mind of a purse, sweetie," my mom was saying to June, "but I swear it was just . . . Where's May? Maybe she's seen it? May!"

"I'm upstairs, Mom!" I heard May yell from her room. She was really good about not moving through the house invisibly and giving everyone heart attacks, but sometimes she slipped up. The last time was when the three of us were having movie night. June and I were all settled on the couch, and all of a sudden, May was there, too.

We're still finding popcorn kernels in the cushions from when June screamed in surprise and flipped the popcorn into the air. But May's getting better at not disappearing on everyone, literally and metaphorically speaking. She's also trying to start a lacrosse team, which, okay, sure. Whatever works for her. I don't ask too many questions because she seems a lot happier now.

While the Great Purse Search continued, I ran upstairs to my room, getting ready to go out with Julian. I already knew he would be eight minutes late, so I had a few minutes to spare. It's weird dating someone who puts the "punk" in punctual, but I was getting better at dealing with it.

"Don't worry, Mom!" I yelled down the staircase. "You'll probably find it later tonight! You always do."

Her face suddenly appeared at the bottom of the stairs. "Have you seen it?

"No, but you've never really lost it before." She and Chad had their third date coming up, and I had already snuck some stain-remover wipes into the purse's side pocket before it went missing. (Let's just say there would be an incident with some hot and sour soup.)

"So where are you and Loverboy going?" May asked me from her bedroom, where she was busy adding photos to her Paris scrapbook. She must have had hundreds by now, which made the vision I had had that morning that much more difficult.

"Just to the movies and dinner," I said. "Or we might go to Vegas and get married. I don't know—the visions are fuzzy."

"Ha ha," May said, glancing up at me over her laptop. "Make sure Elvis marries you if that's the case. Go big or go home. That's what they say in Texas."

May had lots of knowledge about Texas, now that she had spent a long weekend with our dad going to Austin and eating barbecue. "Hey, when in Texas," I agreed, then sank down on the bed next to her, watching as she copied and pasted for a few minutes.

"What's with the sisterly closeness?" she finally asked.

"Nothing," I said with a sigh. "I'm just really gonna miss you."

May rolled her eyes. "Earth to you, I just got back. And you'll be gone for five hours with your boytoy. I'm pretty sure you'll make it through."

"Not *today*. I mean later. When we're older."

She frowned. "What do you mean?"

"I mean when you're living in Paris."

May looked at me and then smiled the biggest smile I've ever seen from her. "Really?" she said. "For serious really?"

I nodded, and my throat tightened as I reached over to hug her. "It's really far away," I whispered.

"It's just an ocean," she whispered back. "It's just saltwater. We've got blood on our side, right?"

"Of course." I hugged her tighter, though.

"AAAAAAAAPRIL!" June screamed up the stairs. "JUUUUUUUULIAN'S—"

"I know!" I yelled back, letting go of May so I didn't deafen her. "I don't know why June doesn't get that I know when he's gonna be here before *she* does."

"I think that's just June's annoying side, not her mindreading side."

"Lucky us."

"MAAAAAAAY! HEEEENRY'S HEEEEEERE TOOOOOOOO!"

"June, you're not an intercom system," I heard my mom say. "Put a lid on it."

I went downstairs just as my mom was yanking her purse out from behind a sofa cushion (right again!) and June was opening the door for everyone. "Hey, you," I heard Julian say.

"What up, homes?" she said back, and they did their typical fist bump. "Clear a path, dude. You're not the only boyfriend visiting today."

"Oh, hey," Henry said as he came up the path, Mariah close behind him. She looked better than she ever had, even though she still wore tons of eyeliner. (I had mentioned to June that maybe Mariah could invest in some eye-makeup remover, and she had just rolled her eyes and said, "Whatever, April, this isn't *The Breakfast Club.*" I still have no idea what she was talking about.)

"You're late," I said to Julian, even though I couldn't stop myself from smiling at him.

"I'm always late," he shrugged. "That's why you like me."

"Oh, really?" I looked towards Henry and Mariah. "Hey, guys," I said. "How nice of you to be *on time*."

Julian sighed and just hugged me to him. "You're difficult."

"I know," I said. We had plans to go to a used bookstore over in Burbank and then the movies. I like used books because they're full of stories that have already been read. Sometimes I can even find a book that has an inscription inside. Like "To Jo, love Alex," that sort of thing. As much as I can see the future, I like discovering the past, too.

"You're grossing me out," June said, pretending to gag as Julian bent down to give a quick kiss. "C'mon, Mariah, let's go do exciting things like solve for X. Let them all be jealous!"

May bounced downstairs, smiling when she saw Henry. "Hey, nerd," she said.

"Hiya, dork," he replied.

They really are perfect for each other.

"Wanna go study about incestuous royal families and bloody murders?" she asked him. "Or do you wanna study European history instead?"

Henry laughed and followed her into the kitchen just as my mom came out. "Oh, hi, Henry," she said. "There's a Sprite in the fridge for you. Hi, Julian."

"Hi, Mrs. Stephenson," they both said. (Okay, so we were still working on the last name thing.)

"April, honey, I'm probably not gonna be here when you get back so . . ." She came over and hugged me goodbye. "Have fun, be safe, all the Mom stuff."

"No worries," I said.

"Have fun, you two."

Julian walked me out to the car. He always washes it on Saturdays, and it was shining in the autumn sun. He held the door open for me, and I slid in. The little pine-tree air freshener I had hung on the rearview was swinging back and forth, and I made a mental note to replace it the next time he picked me up.

"So," he said as he got in and started the car. "I assumed you looked at traffic reports online, just like always."

"Don't take the 101," I replied. Julian thought I was addicted to traffic Web sites. He had no idea how much time I've saved him over the past month.

"Ha. Tell me something I *don't* know." He began to drive down the street, and I put my hand in his, twining our fingers together.

"Okay," I said. "Here's something you don't know. I knew I was gonna kiss you the first time I saw you. Well, the first time I recognized you."

He just laughed. "Yeah, okay. Sure."

"I did!" I protested. "Fine, don't believe me!"

"You know what *I* know?" Julian said. "You're extraordinary."

"I already knew *that*." I grinned, and I held his hand tight in mine and smiled to myself, excited to see what would happen next.